A History of Saints

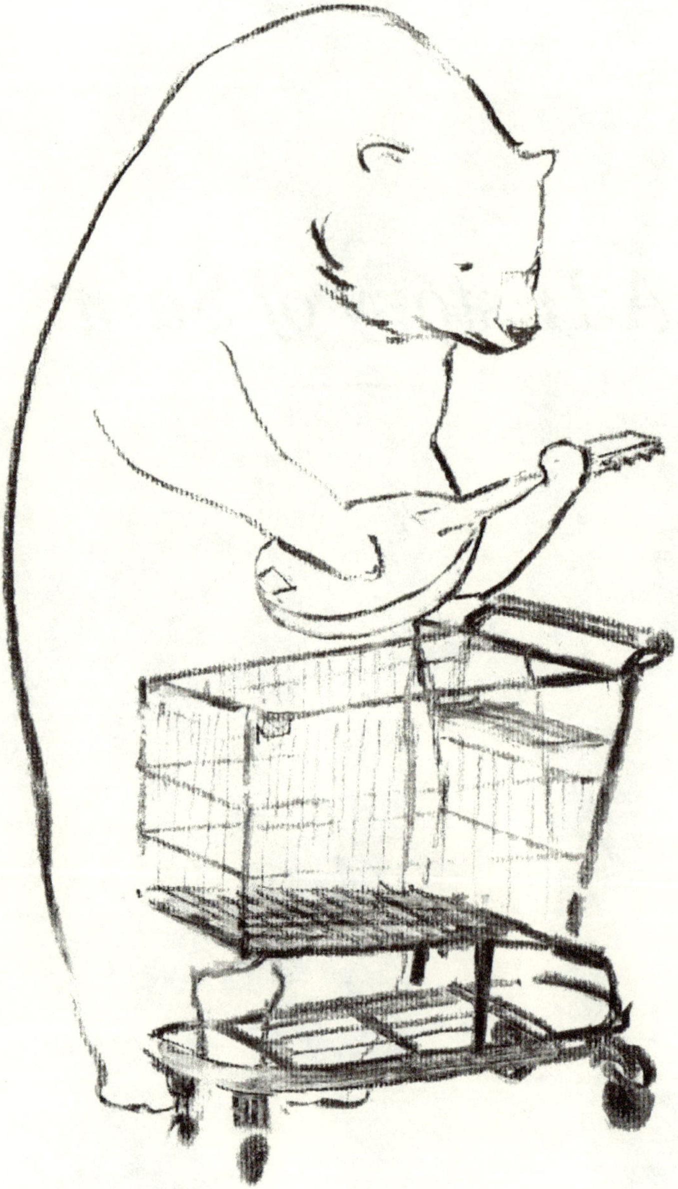

A History of Saints

*A Novel of
Identity and the Dangers of Indecision (or Haste)
During an Economic Downturn,
Including
Dog Handling, Courtly Love, Gardening and Cooking,
Sexual Fluidity, Belly Dancing, Poetry, Loss, and Addiction*

WRITTEN AND ILLUSTRATED BY

Julyan Davis

Shadelandhouse
MODERN PRESS

Lexington, Kentucky

A Shadelandhouse Modern Press book
A History of Saints:
*A Novel of Identity and the Dangers of Indecision (or Haste)
During an Economic Downturn, Including Dog Handling, Courtly Love, Gardening and Cooking, Sexual Fluidity, Belly Dancing, Poetry, Loss, and Addiction*

Copyright © 2021 Julyan Davis

All rights reserved. Printed and manufactured in the United States of America.

For information about permission to reproduce selections from this book, please direct written inquiries to Permissions, Shadelandhouse Modern Press, LLC, P.O. Box 910913, Lexington, KY 40591, or email permissions@smpbooks.com.

A History of Saints is a work of fiction. Characters, incidents, names, and places are used fictitiously or are products of the author's imagination. Any resemblance to actual events, locales, organizations, or persons, living or dead, is entirely coincidental. Any references to real places are used fictitiously. To the extent any trademarks, service marks, product names, or named features are used in this work of fiction, all are assumed to be the property of their respective owners and are used only for reference. Use of these terms does not imply endorsement.

Published in the United States of America by:

Shadelandhouse Modern Press, LLC
Lexington, Kentucky
smpbooks.com

First edition 2021

Shadelandhouse, Shadelandhouse Modern Press, and the colophon are trademarks of Shadelandhouse Modern Press, LLC.

Library of Congress Control Number: 2021946018
ISBN: 978-1-945049-19-4 (HC)
ISBN: 978-1-945049-30-9 (PB)

Cover art, frontispiece art, and illustrations: Julyan Davis

For Finn

The history of saints is mainly the history of insane people.
—Benito Mussolini

Dramatis Personae

In order of appearance:

FRANK REED, *cat fancier, hoarder, asylum owner*

ANGUS SAXE-PARDEE, *flea marketeer, philanthropist, sleuth, and socialite*

NUMEROUS CATS

TWO FERAL CHIHUAHUAS: LAKEISHA AKA 'KEISHA *formerly Angelica*, GEEZER AKA GEYSER *formerly Rover*

COREY SULLIVAN, *student of Wellnosity, amateur poetaster*

MALCOLM DZIEDZIC, *aspiring country star, former reptile keeper*

ANDROMEDA ANDY MEGAN BELL, *journal keeper, unintending cow person*

ELAINE HULSEBUS, *secretary with benefits, voice of reason*

J.J. ANTIETAM, *rolfer, golfer, real estate guru*

TREY SHEEK, *mottled benefactor, outdoorsman*

EMILY NAZARIO, *lover, martyr*

LEAF PRINGLE, *therapist, not rhinoplastician*

MAYBELLE JOLENE DZIEDZIC, *sugar addict, sibyl, sponge*

JUAN PEREZ, *observer, illegal*

LIDA BARFIELD, *out-of-state trauma nurse, survivor*

TWO GODDESSES: *Tansie and Gina*

TWO STREET WALKERS: *Kelsey and Jasmeena*

THREE MOUNTAIN TYPES: *Harley and Hessy Hicks, Old Minyard*

JOHN LEONARD LENNY BEASLEY AKA ROGER BEASLEY, *Bahamian, ornamental hermit*

Contents

Prologue xv
    A barely palpable hit – The blue-collar genealogist

Chapter One 1
    A gift from an admirer – The Not-So-Great Recession –
High Cotton – The gentle hand – Breed standards in the Chihuahua

Chapter Two 11
    Pest control and identification – The halfway household –
Least favorite foods

Chapter Three 17
    Codebreaking – Gigantism in the rural South – The Grand Tour
– A dog without worries

Chapter Four 27
    Malcolm and Angus discuss the muse – After careful consideration
– A minimalist moves in – Volleys fired at Antietam –
Last words (continued?)

Chapter Five 39
    Sculpting materials of the world – Destiny and like, coincidence –
The bond of felinophobia – Chasing wide cads

Chapter Six 49
    Downstrifing your life – Foliate borders and drollery –
Little sponge or sibyl? – A change of solar system

Chapter Seven 59
    Nomenclature for pets – Democracy in action –
A lengthy departure – Angus springs into action

Chapter Eight 69
Fort Asheville – Bright bungee cords regifted – command vehicle surveillance technique – Morning cocktails – A plea to an awesome poetess

Chapter Nine 79
Accolades for all – A nurse of heroes – Longevity through carpentry – Corey finds his Cyrano

Chapter Ten 91
Goddess interrogation – An end to Frank's worries? – Asheville's varied groceries – Covert quatrains

Chapter Eleven 103
Repurposing your dog corral – Costume design and paint effects for winterwear – Risks of leaf burning – Lion cuts postponed

Chapter Twelve 113
Delayed poetry appreciation – Prey meets predator – yourtrophybride.com – Masculine belly dance

Chapter Thirteen 121
Frank meets Lida again – A plea to exercise ghosts – Iguana disposal – 'Final words of a freind'

Chapter Fourteen 131
Life without an epidermis – A sizeable, shuffling adversary – Death's fingerprints – The comfort of sausages

Chapter Fifteen 141
Humanoid compassion – A mottled benefactor – Antelope in the headlights – All for Juan – Ursus americananus

Chapter Sixteen 153
The worst kind of potato – A new phone for Tansie – The truth about Baladi – A one-pipe problem

Chapter Seventeen 165
*Disgruntled hoarders – A folly for the yard –
Hardly a huge, ripped genius – The eardy bird*

Chapter Eighteen 179
*The leathery connoisseur – Fair strollers of our streets –
Varied vernacular of the Appalachians – Sirtaki prompts Baladi*

Chapter Nineteen 195
*Samurai reprisals – The chances of cheese theft –
Scurvy in the home – Moussaka/musaka*

Chapter Twenty 209
*A new medievalist – The flat-backed canine –
Chivalric fatigue explained – Misguided sugar babies*

Chapter Twenty-One 221
*Stretchy, but unripped – The path of the cow person –
Pizza delivery – The "worse" Munchausen's*

Chapter Twenty-Two 235
*Challenge to a duel (first draft) – The confused unicorn –
A sentry of Pomerania – Police escort*

Chapter Twenty-Three 247
*Learning while cantering – An "ed to rachel discord" –
The kindly spider – dancetrain*

Chapter Twenty-Four 263
*A hero of firefighters – The penitent Bahamian –
A total value-add – The perfect food*

Epilogue 275
*A town transformed – News from the grotto -
il y a tout un monde de jardins à cultiver*

About the Author 285

Prologue

One of the best and most effective combinations of whistle and red light with which Nature ever danger-signaled recreant and unthinking humans is fatigue.
 —Herman H. Rubin MD, *Eugenics and Sex Harmony*

At the next light Frank struck an individual dressed as a mattress. A marshmallow glimpse of a great, pale blue rectangle came flailing into the path of his truck, there was a muffled thump, and then the poor devil was hurled away, thrown back onto the grassy curb.

Across the busy intersection every single vehicle stopped. Drivers stared. One outraged witness blew a horn.

Jolted from sleepy reverie, Frank tumbled out of his truck and hurried to the stunned bedding. The cartoon face might have been ecstatic, but the gloved hands were ominously still, folded across the object's chest in rapt expectation.

"Oh man," said Frank. "I'm so sorry…" This, he told himself, is what happens. You have killed a man because you were thinking about donuts.

As he knelt over his quilted victim, though, Frank was relieved to hear a sigh and then see a crease delineate a waistline. The mattress struggled to rise. Frank heard shouts and looked up to see advancing mattress store employees, dressed as people. "Fine," he heard a muffled voice. "I'm fine! Jesus, this thing can take a hit."

Frank recognized the Caledonian timbre. "Angus?"

"I was trying to get your attention, Frankie," Angus managed to get to his knees but then angled off sharply, folding down toward the tarmac, losing a Disney shoe in the plunge. A woman shouted from her car, "Oh for God's sake, help him!"

Another Samaritan chimed in, "Will someone please help that man?"

"It could be a woman," said a tiny feminist in an SUV.

"Are you alright, Mr. Sex Party?" asked the store manager as he reached them. He turned to Frank, assuring him with menace, "I saw the whole thing, okay? I saw what happened."

"It's Saxe-Pardee," Angus corrected him. "Angus Saxe-Pardee. This man is a good friend of mine. He's only partially to blame."

"I'm his landlord," said Frank.

They helped Angus to his feet.

"You could have internal bleeding," the manager told him. "Concussion. Worse." He was still scowling at Frank.

Angus shook them off. "I'm fine, I tell you! This thing's like bloody armor."

"He came out of nowhere," Frank said.

"Not if you were looking," said the manager.

"For what? Mattresses?"

"Extraordinary," said Angus. He patted himself down, then examined his forearms. "Not a scratch. I'm fine. Pay me enough, you could run me over with a truck. Right here! Film the whole thing for your customers. I think it speaks volumes to the sheer resilience of your product."

"That's not one of our products, Mr. Sex Pardee. That's just a foam suit." The manager circled Angus, now looking for damage to the costume. "Where's your sign?"

They looked around, and Frank pointed to the large red *MATTRESS SALE* sign lying in the road beside his truck. A police car pulled up and parked a wheel on top of it.

A History of Saints

"I've got this, Frankie. Nae worries," said Angus.

The policeman got out and waved at the cars to make their way around him.

"Hit and run," a driver suggested, pointing at Frank. "That guy over there."

Angus heard this and cursed the woman, raising a fist as she drove off.

The officer strolled up. "Y'all okay here?" he wanted to know. "Ain't nobody hurt?" He asked a few questions, then suggested they relocate the discussion to the mattress store parking lot. The bright placard was left, forgotten, at the scene of the crime.

The officer took Frank's and Angus's details and wrote them down. Angus spelled his name out. "Saxe?" asked the policeman. "As in Saxe-Coburg and Gotha?"

"Indeed." Within his suit, Angus sounded impressed. Placing his hands on his approximate hip area, he tilted slightly, this way and that, to now address the gathered employees and curious shoppers. In turn, they watched the mattress closely, as though such study might clarify Angus's muffled accent. "This town!" he began in wonderment. "A local cop, no more than that, and yet familiar with the great houses, the Ernestine duchies of Thuringia? America, aye, it never ceases to surprise. So easy to dismiss as a nation of philistines and yet, and yet…"

The officer turned to Frank. "You say you know this guy?"

"He's one of my tenants," said Frank. "But I didn't know he was working out here. As…this."

"Times are hard, Frankie."

The officer turned back to Angus. "Age?"

"Sixty-seven years young, sir."

"Have you thought about maybe like, an easier job?"

"I'm not dead, laddie," Angus said, his indignation diminished by the mattress's huge, grinning face. "Watch this!" He danced a few steps, and the circle of onlookers widened to give him room.

xvii

"Aren't you burning up in there?" asked Frank.

Angus shouted something. He spun around a few times, then stopped to cough violently.

The fact that Angus had clearly not been injured by Frank and that, anyway, Frank was Angus's landlord, seemed to satisfy the crowd, and they now began to drift away.

It was decided that Angus should take the day off—perhaps even the rest of the week.

Frank waited for Angus to change clothes and then drove him home. A number of questions crossed his mind, but he said nothing. Beside him, the old man squinted at the passing scenery, then suddenly voiced an answer to a question Frank hadn't considered.

"Those jobs won't last forever," he told Frank. His white hair was plastered to his skull with perspiration. "I have a gift for gestural theatre—dance, of course—but the future for this kind of thing is forced air inflatables."

"I never thought of it as a thing," said Frank. "You know, a professional field."

"It's not for everyone," Angus admitted. He looked at Frank. "Are those wee crumbs around your mouth?"

Frank wiped his mouth. "I was just at the donut shop."

"Shouldn't you be at work?"

"I was on my way when you jumped…," Frank sighed. "What will you do now? Will they take you back?"

"Not likely. Anyway, that little shit was trying to sue you."

Frank nodded.

"Don't worry," said Angus. "I have my finger in multiple pies."

"Right."

"Including yours. Don't forget, amigo, your problems are my problems. Your monkeys are my monkeys."

Frank started to say something about everyone minding their own monkeys.

"Make a left here," said Angus.

One

Of the two great families of pets—or pests, depending upon the viewpoint—which enliven mankind, the canine is infinitely less to be feared than is the feline.
   —Herman H. Rubin MD, *Eugenics and Sex Harmony*

FRANK SKIMMED THE classifieds. There were a handful of jobs on offer and dozens of places for sale. One ad in particular caught his attention.

> ROOMS AVAILABLE. WALK TO DOWNTOWN FROM THIS HISTORIC PROPERTY. LIVE **GONE WITH THE WIND** FOR ONLY $400 A MONTH. PETS NEGOTIABLE. CALL (828) 555-0165.

Frank read this again. As he did so, a trilling, insistent note sounded from above. More followed. There was a pause, and then the tune began again. Frank waited. The notes tinkled down the stairs, jangled across the hall, tumbled into the kitchen. With the melody arrived his tenant. Angus disengaged his tin whistle with a wet click and sang loudly, "*And it's there that Annie Laurie gied me her promise true.*" He gave Frank a yellow grin.

"Did you write this?" Frank held up the paper.

"Good morning, Frankie."

"Is this one of your monkeys? That's your number, isn't it?"

"It was nothing," Angus raised a hand in regal dismissal. "Think of it as a gift from an admirer." He tucked the instrument into the belt of his robe and crossed the kitchen to pour himself a cup of coffee. A cat was curled in the sink. Angus muttered something at it.

"Well, thanks," said Frank, "but this is, you know, *my* house."

"I thought you'd be pleased."

"I don't like surprises. Anyway, there's only the one room available."

"What about the slave quarters? They're ready, no?"

"I guess." Frank looked reluctant.

Angus was referring to the annex behind the kitchen. Although Frank had assured him the house was built in 1866, a fact that seemed to make it emphatically postbellum, Angus disagreed. He was determined to envision slaves in the quaint apartment with its wide floorboards and beamed ceiling. "A house of this size?" he'd insisted. "No, I think not. The old ways died hard. Think of them in there, Frankie! Christ! The laughter, the banjos…"

The growing possibility that a Black man might be president had fueled in Angus a wild, if often tactless, cultural enthusiasm. From the balcony off his bedroom (in fact an expanse of rooftop for the porch below—unsafe, fragile, yet now decorated with his tomato plants) Angus had taken to hailing any person of color on the street—waving at them with loud, incomprehensible Celtic salutations.

With a grunt, Angus sat down heavily across from Frank. "Mark my words," he began, then stopped. Another of Frank's cats lay stretched across the kitchen table between them. The tail twitched. Angus set his arm against the length of its belly and swept the animal away in a swift arc that gave him room for his coffee cup.

"Easy on the cats," said Frank.

"Mark my words, Frankie, this too will pass. You're going to weather this storm and make back every penny you put into this place. I'll continue to help you. See there!" He snapped his fingers and simultaneously pointed in one fluid, disconcerting gesture, indicating a blackened piece of wood taking up a chair. Frank looked at the piece of wood.

Angus had reworked a plank into a rustic sign to hang above the door to the annex. *High Cotton* was spelled out with some care, a homely touch to welcome the renter he sought for his landlord. He'd tooled the words with a poker, using the fireplace in the kitchen for his handiwork until Frank had pointed out it was August and directed him outside to the barbecue.

Angus reached for the sign. He ran an appreciative hand over the lettering. "What are you doing today?" he asked.

"I have the termite guy coming by," said Frank. "You?"

"I'm still recovering."

"You said you were okay."

"I may have another job prospect. Also, that was yesterday. I'm an old man, Frankie. At my time of life a man can't just get run over every day. By his friends."

Frank watched him add creamer to his coffee and then use a sooty, downturned thumb to stir the two together.

"Ever seen that before?" Angus asked.

"Never."

"It's a lumberjack thing. Sign of a real man."

"Is that coffee still hot?"

"*For no one but a logger stirs his coffee with his thumb,*" Angus sang, his white eyelashes interlocked, his blood-filled face forlorn.

"What song is that?"

"Some old thing." Angus looked into his cup.

Frank picked up the sign and put it back on the chair, taking more care than Angus to avoid smudging his hands.

Once Angus's sign was in place above the door to the annex, Frank would have no more excuses. For the past week, in the fierce August heat, he had followed Angus's directions as they cleaned and redecorated the tiny apartment. The place had to be emptied first. Old fireplaces and antique sinks, rows of leaded church windows, splintered barn lumber and floorboards—all were stacked in the courtyard under the stairs, except for a large concrete rabbit, which they dragged across the flagstones and set by the fishpond next to a little statue of Saint Francis.

They furnished the room with a queen bed and a rustic chair of woven branches to match. Frank put the big, working TV on a delicate table and hung a mirror on the wall. He even found clean sheets for the bed, but he had done no more. It was hard to envision a customer for Angus's notion—a room to be let out by the night to tourists looking for something less genteel than the surrounding bed and breakfasts, an option for the more frugal visitor, hobbled by this new recession, someone who wanted a taste of what Angus called "the real Asheville."

"Maybe," Frank had said.

"You know what I mean," Angus told him. "The tourists come here to gawk at the hippies. Give them a night in a place like this where they can pretend they're back in the sixties, contemplating their bloody navels. They're here for all this New Age nonsense, man! Hang a dream catcher or two, scatter a few rocks about the place."

Angus had read Frank's look of dismay that his home might pass for a commune as doubt in the venture. "Don't worry," he took Frank by the shoulder. "The rest of us can hide away!"

———

Frank bought the house back in the late '80s, when downtown Asheville still had more storefronts boarded up than not and the once-elegant Victorian homes of his neighborhood stood in disrepair along the wide streets, long-divided into low-rent housing. Carolina Court, the oldest of them all, then lay invisible from the sidewalk—its graceful porches all buried under a great, gray nest of winter kudzu. The house had stood empty for ten years before he bought it. Vines had crept into the house through the buckled siding, branches lanced through missing windowpanes. There were mouse nests in every drawer and bird nests in the chandeliers. Even so, it was still more than Frank could sensibly afford at the time.

His dream was always to restore the place and, in doing so, to add the necessary bathrooms and fire exits to make it a profitable inn. Slowly, he had salvaged each gray and peeling room from the elements—replacing windows, scraping paint, patching the woodwork.

Around him the city prospered and, over the next two decades, downtown grew crowded—condos appeared above each new store, restaurants opened on every corner. Tired and empty buildings were suddenly precious with potential. Along Frank's street, one after another of his neighbors sold up their homes to wealthy retirees from around the country. The streets that people had once been afraid to walk at night were returned to quaint avenues of Arts and Craft cottages, busy with Yankees walking their dogs, while the largest homes found fresh life as inns, celebrated for their gardens and blinding displays of festivity at Halloween and Christmas. Among all this change, Frank's own plans remained just that. Success dodged his unhurried pursuit until the inevitable, quite unexpected, Great Recession changed everything.

Now Frank watched Angus, uneasy with anticipation. What would he say next? What disconnected observation, what vehement fact was welling up inside that sodden head?

Like his two other tenants, Frank found himself subject to this strange old man. He was reminded of a movie or a book he had read once—a story where the captain was just a timid ghost beside his staff sergeant. Or was it his lieutenant? And all the men thought the captain was such a loser until he saved them all. Or maybe just got himself shot. He couldn't remember the details. It might not be a bad idea, he told himself again, to get a background check on his tenant. When Frank brought up Angus's Scottish roots, Angus had only shaken his head and grimaced, "It's complicated."

Angus looked up suddenly. From his crooked smile it was clear that any self-pity or empathy for his conjured lumberjack had been fleeting.

"Hey," said Frank.

"I know what you're thinking."

"You do?"

"Of course! But you're wrong."

"I am?"

"Yin and yang, Frankie. Nothing remains the same. All will be well." Angus searched the pockets of his robe, then offered Frank a plastic locket—a grubby, pink thing in the shape of a fortune cookie. Frank sighed at the familiar offering.

"Take one."

"I'm okay. Thanks."

Angus opened the cookie and unfurled one of the little papers inside. Peering at his own tiny handwriting he read slowly, *Interea insomnes nocte ego duco, diesque.—Donne* [1]

He rolled up the observation and put it back. "That one was in Latin," he added.

"Yup."

Initially Frank had found Angus's enthusiasm for the written word a pleasing quality. Since his arrival, Angus had passed

---

[1] "I sleep not day nor night." John Donne, *Meditations Upon Emergent Occasions*

out tattered books as gifts, and reading was a daily comfort to Frank. He read promiscuously, picking up anything he came across, finding a comfy chair to settle into, the luxurious act entwined with memories of shady summer afternoons and snug winter nights, with humming ceiling fans and blankets and snacks. At first, Angus's little ritual with the fortune cookie had been pleasing, too.

"Oh," said Angus. "That's Donne. John Donne."

"Any idea what it means?"

"It's in Latin."

"Right."

"In the future I might add a translation," mused Angus the scribe, "on the reverso. Strange that he would write in Latin, eh? What was he thinking?"

"You sure it's not some Roman guy?"

"The attribution was very clear, Frankie."

Frank thought of his youngest tenant. "Have you tried those things on Corey?"

Angus rattled the silent cookie for Frank to admire. "Of course. The epigram, the maxim, the apothegm, ha! These are your gateway drugs to the untended mind…"

"And you're the dealer?"

"You can laugh, but I'll tell you, if I died, I'd probably come back as one of those mobile libraries. That would be my wish, anyway. Either that or a Samurai warlord."

Angus's phone rang in his pocket. His struggle for it exposed his belly—a swirling Charybdis of white hair, wild against a pair of ancient briefs. "Hello?" His eyes lit up. "No, no, this is it. Carolina Court. You have the right place. Let me pass you to the man." He handed the phone to Frank. "It's a wee lassie!" he mouthed theatrically.

As the Great Recession took hold Frank had decided to sell his home. Nothing happened. After a while he took the place off the market, with the new idea of renting out every room he could. Friends advised him to take his time finding tenants, but in his panic for cash he ignored them. There followed some difficult moments. He was forced to ask one tenant to leave. Property was stolen and Desmond, Frank's oldest and very first cat refugee, vanished for some time and was at last found dead—paws folded, Egyptian-severe in a closet. This chaos had finally settled. For months life had been calm. Frank took Angus's phone with foreboding.

"Well?" said Angus, when Frank handed the phone back.

"She seems nice."

"What's her name?"

"Andromeda."

"That's a mouthful," said Angus.

"I was hoping to leave that room empty for a while."

"You can't afford it, man! And you need to rent High Cotton, too, now that we've got rid of David…"

"I liked David," said Frank. He missed the recently departed lodger—another lost soul but one who was never late with the rent. "And we didn't get rid of him. He just left."

Angus waived this defense aside. "Now he's gone, you have six bedrooms and four of us. You need the money. You need women. You need the gentle hand…"

"The what?"

"Anyway, if you don't rent it, you'll have it full of your junk before the end of the week."

Frank thought about Angus's choked room but said nothing.

"What does she do, this girl?" Angus asked.

"She waits tables. She's a dancer."

"Belly dancer?"

"She didn't say."

"A name like that? I'll put money on her being…those aren't cats." Angus pointed. Two tiny dogs were visible beyond the screen door. Frank and Angus watched them. So did the cats.

"No," said Frank. "They're eating the cat food, though."

A History of Saints

"Chihuahuas. Now there's a clannish breed. Looks like you've got an apple head and a deer head right there."

"What are you talking about?"

"I used to breed dogs, back in Florida." Angus shook his head, "No toys for me, though. Working dog man, myself."

"They're hungry," said Frank.

"Good morning, lads!" Angus shouted. The dogs scattered.

Two

How much can these whitish workers consume? One study suggests a colony of 60,000 termites might devour six inches of a 4"x4" piece of wood in less than six months! In reality, appetites vary according to temperature and preference.
—"Wood-Destroying Pests of the South,"
Annual Report, 2006

EACH EVENING FRANK'S tenants gathered in the brightly lit kitchen, with its red walls and high cabinets. An old fridge, covered in postcards and expired announcements, held their varied groceries. They all ate at about the same time, navigating one another and the cats as they heated leftovers and searched for plates and silverware.

For a while now the house had been filled with only men. It gave these nightly meetings a strange camaraderie, something vaguely penal—dinner at the halfway house or perhaps a gang preparing for a heist. In the movies, Frank recalled, the Mob was always around a kitchen table, one guy making a big fuss about the right way to make spaghetti sauce. There was that same kind of generational hierarchy here, too, he thought. Angus could be the bitter patriarch; Frank and Malcolm, his two prodigal sons; and Corey, the young gangster in training.

Frank looked around him and was glad this crowd had nothing planned. Between the three older men slumped around the table, watching the boy cook, there must have been a dozen failed careers, not including Angus's recent stunt work for the mattress store.

Back in the '70s, before the house was left to vanish behind its kudzu veil, it had suffered a period as a boarding house. The story went that it evolved into a haven for local men escaping domestic troubles. Rooms were rented for nights or months by husbands in disgrace, in divorce proceedings, or seeking respite from a dominant spouse. Carolina Court was renamed Divorce Court by the neighbors. The old house must feel disappointed, thought Frank. Not much had changed.

Still, he felt comfortable in the current company. Efficient men alarmed him. He was still feeling challenged by the pest control man from that afternoon. Of course, it had been Angus who was responsible. It was Angus who found the insect nest, Angus who somehow retrieved a stained report on termites from his room, Angus who insisted it was best to call a professional when it came to such matters.

Frank had waited an hour for the exterminator, but he didn't mind. Any time spent in his yard was a pleasure. Recovering the lost lawns and flower beds, the pathways and tumbled urns from an acre of kudzu had made a gardener of Frank. It was too early to water, so he did a little judicious weeding. He was moving a few pots into the shade when the big, taciturn man at last arrived, with no apology for being late. Frank led him to the evidence. Watching him spray the woodpile, Frank asked, "There's some pressure-treated wood out back. Would termites eat that?"

The bug man had looked Frank up and down. "What's your least favorite food?"

"Sorry?"

"Your least favorite food. What is it?" The bug man stopped spraying and stared at Frank, waiting for an answer to this impossible question.

"A termite will eat pressure-treated," the man said. "Eat what he has to to stay alive. Anyway, these is jest flying ants."

An acre of kudzu

"Do you guys want any of this?" Corey asked.
"What is it?" asked Malcolm.
"Curry."
"The hell it is," said Angus. "My father used to spend a day making a curry. The real thing. Made your gums bleed it was so hot."
"Maybe later," Frank told Corey. "Thanks."

Corey was a tall, good-natured kid, and Frank felt a paternal concern for his future. He was studying something at the university—Health and Wellnosity, as far as Frank could recall. Everything Corey wore fit him snugly and was emblazoned with a tick, a flourish, or a letter across it—markings to indicate his flawless judgment in athletic fashion.

When he wasn't in school, he was out scaling nature in some way—riding over it, kayaking across it, climbing up it. Retelling these adventures was the entirety of his conversation. Watching Corey strap some new conveyance to his vehicle, Frank empathized with Mother Earth. The mountains around Asheville were full of this Lilliputian activity. Nature just lay there and took it. "You only love me for my body," she must be sighing.

"I ate a pepper one time, little bitty thing," said Malcolm. "I don't know, man, that thing was hot. No bigger than this." He pinched his fingers and shook his head in disbelief. "Crazy. A little pepper like that."

Malcolm was a musician when he wasn't doing odd jobs around town. Over the years he and Frank had found themselves working side by side, and Frank was glad to welcome him as a tenant when he first started renting rooms. Malcolm had a tentative moustache and wore his thinning hair pulled back into a ponytail. He seemed to live entirely on popcorn, cigarettes, and energy drinks. A couple of weekends a month he had custody of his little girl, Maybelle Jolene—an obligation that did not lessen a daily concern that he should have chosen Nashville over Asheville for his music career. This worry, along with an unending, half-hearted quest for a stage name, kept Malcolm Dziedzic comfortably taxed.

"I like spicy," said Corey. "Spicy is awesome."

Frank tried the termite man's riddle out on his tenants. "What's your least favorite food?" he asked them.

Corey turned from his cooking and looked at Frank. The student in him dutifully took on the challenge. "Least favorite food?" he whispered. "Least favorite food?"

"I'll eat anything," said Angus. "Bona fide starvation will teach you that."

Frank wanted another beer, but he stayed in place. He looked around at the men, at the black cat complicating one black diamond of the linoleum floor, at the strange hooflike rubber shoes Corey was wearing. Another passage was coming to a close. David had gone. The elfin visits of the tiny Maybelle Jolene had not been enough feminine energy for Angus. He had triumphed again. A young woman called Andromeda was set to collide with Carolina Court. From their lively conversation on the phone, Frank already knew she was likely to take the room. Andromeda. Was that a star or a galaxy? And who was she in the pantheon of Greek mythology? A painting of a beauty in great peril came to Frank's mind, undressed and artfully chained to a rock.

The subject of women was easy communion in the house, particularly for Frank and Malcolm. It was a subject that connected them all, a mystery that would now have to be considered covertly. With some girl in this kitchen, wafting about in a leotard, offering them tasty fancies, everything would change. There would be less slumping, more shaving—a dress code of sorts. Angus's pleasant distraction felt like work to Frank. "Oh," he said. "Those weren't termites by the way, Angus. The guy said they were flying ants."

"Aye, well, it was always fifty-fifty."

"Huh. You seemed so sure."

Corey brought his plate over to the table. As they cleared a place for him, Frank decided to tell them about the girl.

"We have a new renter," announced Angus. "A belly dancer. A woman."

The others looked to Frank.

"Frankie rented her David's room," Angus went on.

"But he hasn't left," said Corey.

"It's empty," said Frank.

"But there's a book in the corner."

"That's a sock," said Frank. And how had David been stolen away, he asked himself. A woman. A friend and reliable tenant lost to some siren, as even now they discussed bringing another on board.

Corey looked dismayed. "He's gone? But how do you know? Are you sure? He lives out of a suitcase." He added reverentially, "That's his entire philosophy in a nutshell."

"Regular fucking Aristotle," said Angus.

"He went to Texas," Malcolm told them, "with some girl."

"Is she pretty?" Corey asked Frank. "The belly dancer?"

Frank pressed his face with his palms. "I don't know what she looks like," he said. "I just spoke to her on the phone. She's coming by tomorrow to see the place. I don't know what kind of dancer she is either, Corey. And sure, I'll take some of that curry, thanks."

Angus poured himself a noisy glass of wine as Corey found Frank a plate.

"My least favorite food is probably sweet potatoes," Corey told them as he sat back down. He blinked in astonishment, a look of baroque wonder slowly widening his eyes. "But I totally love sweet potato fries! That is so crazy."

Through a cat-sized hole in the screen door, the ring of netting matted with years of accumulated feline hair, flew a hissing cat. Every man watched the animal land and make a sharp right into the hallway. Another cat followed.

"It's the raccoon," Frank guessed.

Corey walked over to the door. "Dogs," he said. "Super cool. There're little dogs out here. You got some dogs, Frank?"

"Apparently."

Three

At the Laughter Clinic, Moira came to grasp that 'joy' needs to be 'here,' not 'there.' She had that 'greener grass fixation.' Happiness is not about changing your address.
—Alex Havelock, Instant Joy!

> Seriously u r leaving?
> I cant believe it fwiw
> I love u, k? Jesus
> Andy u r making way
> 2 much about nothing
> relationships r
> hard sometimes! Wycm
> please? O and yes u r a
> lesbian btw whatever
> Dale says
>
> Received:
> Aug 14 8:46 am

In fact, David had left a book. He'd placed it on Frank's desk where, despite its bright orange cover, it was at once invisible among the other paperbacks, newspapers, and unopened bills. Frank noticed it while watching the alpinist progress of a spider across this serrate world.

The title *Instant Joy!* sounded like cleaning product, but it promised far more—a three-hundred-page guarantee of happiness. From the praise on the back cover, it was clear that the author, Alex Havelock, was not going to give up on a dour world easily. He had already hammered away his point with *Wake up Smiling!*, *Laughter: The Good Hysteria*, and *What's so Bad? (About Living?)*.

Frank took the book to the kitchen. He opened the worn paperback to find almost everything underlined in pencil—titles, subtitles, whole paragraphs, and, laboriously, separate words for line after line. Words like *harmony* and *upbeat* sat on little pencil rafts, each waiting its turn on the tide of Havelock's good news.

Had David been this diligent reader? Perhaps not. Inside the cover was scrawled an inscription in a fat, cherubic hand. *From Mallory to Mallory!!!* Maybe one of these Mallorys had felt compelled to underscore Havelock's words. It was a mystery. Like a codebreaker, Frank found himself reading only the rare lines unworthy of graphite emphasis: "That was in 1987." "Perhaps you've heard the old joke?" "CEO Tom Wurhling comes to mind." "My first wife disagreed." "Naturally, she blamed Eddie."

There was a knock at the screen door. A towering, lifelike statue of a girl stood in the courtyard. The pixelated figure spoke through the dusty screen. "Hi."

"Oh hey," said Frank, rising from his chair. "Come on in. Come in."

The girl pushed the screen door and stepped in lightly. Frank shook her long hand. From its high vantage point, her freckled face looked about the room. "This is awesome," she said.

"Well, thanks," said Frank. "Glad you like it." The girl's height impressed him—6'1", 6'2", he guessed.

"I'm Andy," she smiled. "Andromeda."

"Andy? Right," Frank raised a hand. "Frank."

"Are those all your cats?"

"Pretty much."

"Cool. I like that one with the stubby tail."

"Thanks."

"Is that good?" she pointed. Frank was holding the paperback to his chest.

"Oh, this?" Frank held up the book. "No. Not really. Someone just left it for me. I don't need it. I'm…already joyful."

"There's like, a super long history of depression in my family," she told him.

"Really?" A faded group portrait of melancholy giants crossed Frank's mind, slumped in overalls and gingham, straining the planks of some sepia porch. "I'm sorry," he said.

"That's okay," Andy smiled brightly.

"So you want the tour?"

A faded group portrait of melancholy giants

Frank loved to show people his house. When he put it on the market, he broke with preferred tradition, choosing not to absent himself when realtors brought potential buyers around. Instead, in his stained T-shirt and torn pants, he led an effusive tour of the property. Who could he trust to point out every charming eccentricity, every restored detail? This pride was his reward for the years he had spent crouched at baseboards or stretched over ladders. It occurred to him that there was, in fact, no inch of the great, rambling house, inside or out, that had escaped his caring hands. From the masonry warm against the dirt of the flower beds to the bricks that capped the chimneys, he had rebuilt Carolina Court. There was something miraculous to Frank in this labor of love. Skills he had learned in restoring the house he had promptly forgotten upon the completion of each project. This lost knowledge amazed him. A bathroom might have been tiled by Frank, but the proof he was involved was now only one of many stained DIY manuals on the bookshelves. He had remembered, however, how to hang drywall and how to prep and paint a room, and these talents—together with a pressure-washing service—now helped pay the mortgage.

"Well," he told Andy, "this is obviously the kitchen. Everyone kind of uses it, but it works out fine. I guess I should tell you there's four of us, four guys, right now."

"That's fine," said Andy. "I come from a big family."

"Well, good. Y'all just have to squeeze yourself a little room in the fridge and in the pantry." He pointed at the floor. "Now those boards there are original heart of pine."

Frank led her into the entrance hall, dominated by a staircase of dark oak. Its ornate ascent was reflected variously in a dozen assorted mirrors. A long window seat filled an intermediate landing. This sunny spot had been abused by the cats. The fabric of the foam cushion that was not shredded was heavy with their combined hair. "The staircase was added later," he told her, "probably in the twenties. The original staircase would have been a straight shot. Malcolm's in there," Frank continued, indicating what was once the dining room. "He's a good guy. He's a musician."

"Cool."

"What kind of dancer did you say you were?"

"It's like, mainly interpretive. Contemporary."

"Okay."

"I work a lot with other media."

"Uh-huh," Frank nodded. He pointed to the torn seat as they went upstairs. "I try not to let the cats get everyplace."

"This place is huge," said Andy. "It reminds me of my grandma's."

"Where are your family from?"

"Augusta. Well, Graniteville, really."

"How long have you been in Asheville?"

"Just a couple of months. I'm staying with a friend, but I need to find my own place. It's kind of a bad situation. Oh!" she cried. "This place is amazing!"

The upstairs landing held several tired rubber plants in Chinese pots—all drooping arms and yellow fingers in alien lamentation. Angus's door was ajar. Frank steered the girl away from any glimpse of what was within. "You'll be in here," he said, opening another door onto a large, empty bedroom.

Andy put her hands together, "Awesome."

"Now, this is a working fireplace," said Frank, crossing the room and dealing with the lone sock. "But I'd rather just use the furnace, come winter." This was a new rule he had recently had to reinforce, far ahead of cold weather, having found Angus not just lighting fires in the kitchen but also busy cooking Middle Eastern dishes in his room.

"Oh, I'll be fine. This is awesome! I feel home already."

The wood floor shone between them. Andy's head brushed the low, sloping ceiling. She's a pretty girl, Frank thought. New Age Barbie, wedged into a doll's house attic by the childish hand of fate. "Now the bathroom," with David's sock he indicated a doorway. "It's shared with Corey's room, but you just lock the two doors."

They crowded into the little space. "Sorry, that's not full-sized," said Frank, referring to an old claw-foot tub.

"I love it!"

"This was originally a closet, of course. That tub's all that could fit. You're okay with this shelf for your things?" He moved Corey's shaving foam and pocketed a length of dental floss.

Back in the bedroom, Andy twirled her arms. "This floor makes me want to dance."

"Well, okay," Frank smiled back. "You can move in when you want, pretty much."

"Do you need references and stuff? I can get a letter from my boss."

"If it's no trouble," said Frank. "Whenever."

They met Angus in the courtyard. A number of coats were slung over his shoulder, and he carried an armful of books. He strode up to Frank and the girl and took a bow that somehow suited the old clothing draped over him. "Is this the fair Andromeda, then?"

"This is Angus," Frank told Andy.

Angus searched through his stack of books and found a slim volume, "This is for you, Frankie."

Frank took the gift and read aloud, *Little Body, Big Spirit: Living with the Chihuahua.*

"Also this," he handed Frank a crumbling tome. The title was almost worn away. Frank could make out the words *Eugenics* and *Sex*. "It's a little dated," Angus agreed, "and the fellow may have been a Nazi of some sort, but he has some salient points to make, particularly about dieting. A lot of your problems, actually."

"Thanks."

"I will shower you with presents in due time, Andromeda."

Andy laughed, "It's Andy. Everyone calls me Andy."

"Andy?" said Angus. "Not me, lassie! What do you think about the place? Does the Court suit you?"

"Carolina Court," Frank explained. "It's the name of the house."

"It's amazing."

"I hear you're an artiste?" Angus fluttered his eyebrows.

Andy blushed. With a practiced line, she dismissed all her worldly hopes. "Oh, I'm just a waitress, really."

Turning his attention to Frank, Angus reached into his pocket and took out a small harness. "The woman said it was for a cat, but it'll do for one of them." He gave it to his landlord.

"I haven't seen them this morning, Angus." Frank added to Andy, "There's been a couple of dogs around the place."

"They'll be back," Angus assured them. "When they return, they need to be caught and tagged."

"Well now...," began Frank.

"If you don't want them, I'll take them," said Angus.

"Right."

"Is that one of my socks?" Angus asked.

"No."

As Andy left Carolina Court, she stopped to open her phone. More desperate texts had arrived. She looked to the heavens, turning her palms upward in pretty supplication, trying to focus on the guilt she so surely deserved. What had she just done? How could she end a relationship so easily? What kind of person was Andromeda Megan Bell? What kind of brightly colored bird was that?

She started to text a reply and then stopped, giving her head a fierce little shake. She was acting too quickly. Emily deserved more than a text. She should turn around at once and tell the nice fat men that she had changed her mind. Andy did turn around, but she stopped at a new decision. Before she made even one more choice, she should consult her journal again and the notes she'd made during her last session with her therapist, Dr. Pringle.

A small white dog was looking at her now. It had a high forehead and a slightly pointed skull. Andy waved at the dog. It looked like a dog without worries, enjoying this quiet sunny street—a dog that did not have a double shift tomorrow or a phone filled with cries from a broken heart. The dog closed its eyes and opened them again. The thin line of its mouth was lifted by a slight smile.

Andy envied the wise dog, but right now she needed to focus. Dr. Leaf Pringle was always telling her that. Being a horrible person would have to wait until later. She had told Emily she was leaving, so she needed to leave.

Perhaps here, in this quaint old house, she could at last find peace. Perhaps here she could begin again. Andy's phone rang suddenly, and this time she decided to answer it. She got into her car, opened the phone, and pulled away—the inevitable tirade beginning on the other end of the line.

As the car moved off, a black dog joined the white one. Rover was not as long as Angelica, but he was taller. His dark face was as troubled as hers was at peace.

The dogs had met a week before, scavenging for scraps behind a grocery store. Angelica had lost her owners at an early summer picnic. Curiosity overcame fidelity, and she kept beyond their lengthy search by following the railroad tracks toward Asheville.

Rover's flight was intentional. He had seized his first chance to escape, fleeing from an obese woman who sold feists and ferrets from a trailer in Sodom.

On their fourth day together, Rover had tried to mount Angelica. His enthusiasm offended her, and she had bitten the smaller dog. They were, however, at least in agreement that Carolina Court, dotted as it was with bowls of water and ever-replenished cat food, was an important discovery.

"Crikey!" said Angus. "Did you see the rack on that girl?" He lit a cigarette. "Well? Did you?"

"Yes, Angus," sighed Frank. "They were at eye level, after all."

Angus considered this. "Aye," he said. "She's no wee."

Behind Angus's purple face Frank caught sight of the Chihuahuas turning into his driveway, but he said nothing. Angus's lust made him feel old, and helping his tenant chase small feral dogs around the yard had no appeal.

Angus sorted through his haul of coats. "Look at this beauty," he held up a polished suede jacket. "This reeks of past triumphs. Collegiate conquests."

For someone who never stopped talking about himself, Angus remained a mystery to Frank. His conflicting stories cloaked him until he was impenetrable and unlikely, as though he had decided to wear all at once his collected wardrobe. What past triumphs was he referring to? What collegiate conquests? As far as Frank knew, Angus had arrived from Florida by bus, having supposedly cashed in a fortune in real estate. While still inside the bus station, he was accosted by a drunk. Angus's long military career and training in several martial arts allowed the older man to put his assailant in hospital, where the two patients had become fast friends. Upon their discharge, the men had stumbled upon Frank's flyer for an available room and turned up at his door. Frank had turned away one drunk and let the other in.

"Stay very still," whispered Angus. He was suddenly coiled, a rusty spring.

"What?" said Frank, knowing full well.

"They're in the herbaceous border directly behind you. Don't move! Pass me that harness, very slowly now, Frankie."

"What about the other one?" Frank whispered back.

"One at a time, laddie. One…at…a…time."

"Do you have a leash?"

"String. String will do."

"I've got string," said Frank.

"Me, too. In my room."

"What are they doing?"

"Blackie's taking a piss. The white one's watching us."

"I'll get some string," Frank offered.

"Don't move!" Angus seized his arm, then let go. "No, you're right! Walk slowly toward the kitchen. Bring me a length of string—no, two! Six feet will do. Don't look back, you hear?"

"I won't."

"Alright, Frankie boy, now softly, softly."

Frank padded off to the kitchen, able to resist even one glance back at hunter and prey. He paused at the table, then sat down, picking up *Instant Joy!* to resume his reading. "Naturally, she blamed Eddie."

Four

Your new Chi will resist a collar or harness. In the chapter "Tiny Houdini," I used the phrase "have head, will follow." The opposite applies here—your precious will try every trick to back out of his, or her, constraints.

—USAF Colonel Rex Marigold, *Little Body, Big Spirit: Living with the Chihuahua*

MALCOLM TAPPED ON Angus's door. "Hey, man," he said. "You got a minute?"

"Sir Malcolm," Angus's voice welcomed him from the dark. "Laird of Elderslie and Auchinbothie. All the time in the world for a fellow minstrel. What can I do for you?"

"You met this girl, right?" asked Malcolm.

"Come in, come in," Angus beckoned. "Find a chair." If his landlord was a hoarder, a trait that had metastasized when Frank became the owner of a large, empty house, Angus's bedroom revealed him an amateur. In the few months since he'd arrived, he had filled the room, each day returning with booty found at flea markets, yard sales, and thrift stores. Clothing racks obscured the windows, and his bed was heavy with further garments—an undulating sea of fabric studded with worthless flotsam. Angus dragged some coats off the bed, and Malcolm took the seat created by this action.

"I don't know, man," said Malcolm. "I mean, is she going to be trouble, you think?"

"Andromeda? Trouble?"

"Yeah, you know, like, make stuff complicated?"

"How?"

Malcolm groaned. "I don't need this crap anymore."

Angus was amused. "Do you need a drink?"

"I thought this place was like, all guys now. A place for like, just guys, y'know?"

"Go fetch your jigger," said Angus. "Your shot glass."

Some weeks before, Angus had given Malcolm a guitar pick and a shot glass celebrating Key West. From the rewards of his foraging, Angus often found gifts for the others. Aside from dated manuals on dogs and mental health, Frank had received something plastic from China that could attach a pair of sunglasses to a windshield and also polish them. In fact, the two revolving pads did not touch the glasses, but the sharp spindles did, boring a white dot into the center of each lens. Frank decided to live with the scratches, even if the effect gave him a look of psychedelic surprise.

Angus's kindness extended into the broader community. One evening Frank had found him on the front porch with a couple of streetwalkers. They discussed this visit after the ladies had left with their selection of frocks and pumps. "A singular event," Angus assured Frank. "One time only. Christ would have done the same."

"I told you I don't drink anymore," said Malcolm. "'Sides, it's like, ten a.m."

"You live dangerously, Malcolm. Alcohol is your only defense against the old slings and arrows."

"Didn't work for me," said Malcolm. "What's she like, then?"

"Gorgeous. A stunner."

"Aw, man. I knew it. That doesn't help any."

"Supersized, mind you."

"Fat?"

"Tall. Taller than you, boyo," Angus was enjoying himself. "Your reaction to having this goddess crashing about the place is revealing. Are you worried she'll fall for you and you won't be able to resist? She'll pick you up, carry you off into the sunset?"

"Nah," said Malcolm. "It's just…"

"*C'est dur de mourir au printemps, tu sais,*" Angus sang. "Now that spring is in the air, pretty girls are everywhere…"

"What you want women around for anyway?" Malcolm asked. "It's not like stuff worked out so great for you, either."

Angus had told Malcolm of his several marriages and somehow made this sound like an achievement. To the alarm of his American audience, he enjoyed condensing his marital experience into an old history class study device. "Divorced, beheaded, died, divorced, beheaded, survived," he would shrug.

Now he considered Malcolm's question for a moment. He stroked his bare thighs gently. He was wearing boxer briefs and his favorite fishing vest.

"Without beauty in this house," said Angus, "we will be reduced to utilitarianism."

"I don't know about religion and stuff," said Malcolm. "Women, man, they stir stuff up."

"How so?"

"Well, they just sit there, don't they? Waiting for us to say something stupid."

"I would have thought you'd want the muse close by," said Angus. "Your songs are all about women, right?"

"I work from memory," said Malcolm with a thousand-yard stare. He toyed with a pattern of sequins on an afghan coat.

"Do you want that?" asked Angus. "It would go with your ponytail."

"What happened to your hand?"

"Nothing. A dog bite."

"A dog bit you?"

"The price of kindness, Malcolm," Angus examined the makeshift bandage. "A small dog is safer today, whatever the little fucker thinks."

"One of those Chihuahuas? I saw them over by the grocery store." Malcolm sometimes performed in the parking lot there.

"They may roam," Angus said. "I sanction that, but they will not roam nameless."

"What are their names?"

"It's interesting you ask."

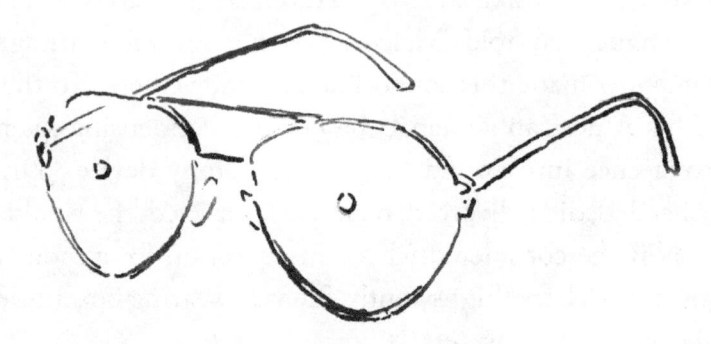

A look of psychedelic surprise

On his way to buy cat food and, to his irritation, some kind of dog food as bait for cat-sized dogs, Frank dropped in on a rational friend. He had known Elaine for years and periodically did some work for her. Elaine wanted his advice on her building a small addition to the house—a prospective apartment for her mother.

Like Frank, Elaine had meandered through her youth, following rock bands and testing communal lifestyles. For a while she became a midwife for some Mennonites in Oklahoma but at last had settled as the content secretary of an Asheville accountant, enjoying excellent benefits and a tiny mortgage. Frank considered her steadied life a triumph.

Elaine was in her garden. Just say hello, Frank told himself as his rusted truck rattled up alongside her picket fence, don't say anything about Andy moving in. Elaine had been the first to express concern about Frank renting rooms in haste. Frank often sought his friend's reassurance that he was making good choices. At the same time, however, she had a way of narrowing her eyes and giving these choices long, silent, extremely careful consideration that unnerved Frank.

"Hey, stranger," she said, walking up to his window. "What you been up to?" She smiled at Frank.

Under the sun's interrogation, Elaine's face was etched with fine lines. She rarely wore make up and kept her hair pulled back in a neat bun. Frank saw in her at the same moment the flower child she had been and the delicate spinster ahead. "Off to the pet store," he said. He climbed out of his truck and followed her into the garden.

"How are you managing over there?" Elaine asked.

"All good."

"I don't believe it for a second," she raised her eyebrows. "How's that Angus?"

"He's got me looking after dogs."

"Oh me. He has dogs?"

"Kind of. Chihuahuas. They came by the house. He thinks he can catch them."

"You know he's bipolar, right, baby?"

"He's something."

"Well, you just be careful."

"I got another tenant," Frank confessed.

"Six of you now?"

"Five. David left. Angus found a replacement. She's a girl."

"Well," said Elaine, "she would be."

"She'll do fine," said Frank. "She can handle herself. She's…," Frank stopped.

Elaine's eyes were narrowing. Frank's choices were being considered. He shifted his weight back and forth, examining first his sneakers and then his fingernails as he waited for her verdict.

"David's gone?" she said at last. "Why did he leave?"

"I don't know," said Frank. "No point leaving a room empty, that's what Angus said."

"Angus should mind his own business, is what I think."

"Yeah. He's got too much time on his hands."

"And what are you doing the rest of the day? 'Part from buying cat food?"

"Buying dog food."

"I'm going to stop by one of these days and check on your menagerie," said Elaine. "The animals, too."

When Frank returned from the pet store Angus voiced his frustration. "Next time you're going out there would you let me know? I need to get temporary tags made for the doggies and find a harness for the white one."

"You've got names for them?"

"Potentially," said Angus. "If my system is accurate. You're getting ahead of yourself, Frankie. They need to be captured before we can make any attempt at that."

Frank moved on from Angus's "system." "Did that cat harness fit?"

"Well enough. He'll grow into it. I could have done with a little help." Angus eyed Frank suspiciously as he recalled his disappearance. "I've received three further calls, by the way."

"About what?"

"The available rooms."

"But we—I just gave the room to Andy."

"What about Corey? Do you think he's really happy here?"

"He's fine, Angus," Frank said. "Leave him alone."

"And High Cotton?"

"Just tell them I'm full up right now, okay?"

"One's a rich girl, Frankie. I told her about the slave quarters. Sounded like she could afford it. Rich girl."

"Really?" Frank asked, then changed his mind. "No, no. One at a time, Angus." He thought for a moment. "Anyway, you said the whole purpose of the slave—of High Cotton—was to rent it by the night. Remember? Kind of a casual B&B?"

"That would never work, Frankie!" Angus laughed as though Frank had made a tremendous joke.

Andy arrived one evening with all her possessions. She brought her suitcases and a little glass table in her car, while a futon, a chair, and a blue desk were brought over in the bed of a friend's truck. She refused all help from Corey and Malcolm, who were left to watch as she and her friend carried the furniture upstairs.

"She seems nice," said Corey, when they were out of earshot. "D'you think that's her boyfriend?"

"Maybe."

"And she's a belly dancer?"

"Frank says she's just a regular dancer," Malcolm explained.

"Cool."

"You think she's cute?"

"I guess. Yeah, kind of."

From the way Corey watched the new tenant go back and forth past them, Malcolm could tell he was curious. Young love, he thought, what could be more tragic? Malcolm had not written a song in months, but he now felt the stirrings of inspiration. Perhaps Angus was right after all about him needing a muse? *Poor boy thinks…Poor boy believes this world's his oyster…* What the hell rhymed with *oyster*?

"I wish you could have let us help," Corey said, when Andy and her friend returned.

"That's okay," she said. "Travis owes me." Andy gave Travis a big sideways hug, bending his shaved head into her armpit.

"Yeah," said Travis. The piercings on his face made it look like there was a glitch in the kitchen lighting.

"You didn't have much at all," said Corey. He had shown up with bikes and snowboards and camping gear.

"I know," said Andy, "but I kind of like it—just having a few things to move."

"I really liked it," joked Travis.

"He's so funny," Andy praised Travis. "But I was glad to get out of there fast. I was in a totally negative relationship."

"Is there any other kind?" said Malcolm.

The dogs navigated the neighborhood. Angelica had to keep stopping for Rover. The pale blue harness and its little bell incensed him, and he threw himself periodically on the ground, writhing to free himself of its constraints. The cats, lazily stationed at intervals around Carolina Court, watched the dogs come and go, opening an eye at the tinkling sound of their approach, ignoring the jingle of their departure.

From his balcony, Angus studied the Chihuahuas through a pair of damaged binoculars. He admired their purposeful ventures through the surrounding yards. "You have no plan in mind," he said aloud, "yet you are dogged." Rover's occasional fits were noted with equanimity. When the dogs stopped to stare up into an oak close to the house, Angus's binoculars found the squirrel fussing in the branches above them. He scrawled something in a notebook, one of several he carried on him in the pockets of his fishing vest, then went back to a more general surveillance of the street.

Angus cursed. Into his view had bobbed the narrow head and Mongolian beard of Frank's neighbor, J.J. Antietam. From their first meeting, Angus had singled him out as an enemy. For J.J., the recession was an opportunity, providing him the necessary leverage to buy up local property at a discount. Angus had been present when he had turned up at Frank's door with an offer to buy Carolina Court.

J.J. was the owner of The Self Center, a gingerbread Victorian just down the street. Under his direction the old house had been cruelly renovated into offices, and each of these rented out to what Angus referred to as a "nest of therapists." The center's considerable success providing counseling and alternative medicine now tempted its owner to expand his business. Frank's rambling home would perfectly answer this need.

Angus cursed again and looked around his balcony for a projectile. Nothing injurious was at hand, so Angus resorted to a fistful of cherry tomatoes, which he hurled with insufficient force at the approaching figure. "Antietam!" he yelled. "Heads up, you bloody charlatan!"

His target looked around, then saw Angus's profile against the sky. Taking the Scotsman's shout as a friendly one, and unaware of the silent barrage that had just taken place, the neighbor brought his hands together as if in prayer, then bowed his head. "Peace, my brother," he called out. "Beautiful morning, Angus."

"Don't 'brother' me, Antietam! And it's still not for sale!" Angus bellowed.

"What?"

"You heard me."

"Are those your dogs?" J.J. asked.

"Yes," Angus was peremptory. "Keep moving, Antietam. Nothing to see here."

"Is Frank at home?"

"Out."

"Terriers?" J.J.'s good humor remained impenetrable as he failed to decipher—or chose to ignore—the fierce tone camouflaged within Angus's accent.

"Don't even try it, Anteater." Angus raised his binoculars. "Antelope head, Anteloper, interloper!"

"My ex had a Jack Russell. Love me some little dogs. Cute little—"

"Small dogs cute, eh? In ancient China, the Peke protected the goddamn court! Thought you'd know that with all your acupuncture la-di-da. Tucked in the emperor's sleeve, aye, a weapon to be unleashed…"

"The Peak?"

"Don't judge a book by its cover, needle head." Angus pointed to the jingling Rover. "That one's a real biter."

O u left ur uggs
here too amazn how
you can just run away
from evrything u said
matterd so much
u r just makn the same
mistakes ovr and ovr
again as u have always
done like w ur dad
and blake and even
ur sistr wen u
think about it
U r a heartbreakr
but this heart is 1
u r not going to
shattr into tiny pieces
and cast into the dark
waters rushn into the
past or whatver i will
set ur boots on the frnt
porch so long amigo
a survivor surviving

Received:
Aug 18, 10:43 am

Andy read this parting text and tapped out a reply that felt too short. *Thx Emily im sorry.* It saddened her that her ex remained so upset, but Emily's constant messages were having a numbing effect. A relationship, Andy decided, was nature's way of distracting you from a difficult world, but if you wanted to enjoy the world, a relationship often got in the way. For now she just wanted to go to concerts and festivals and treat herself to the awesome veggie dogs at Eco Eatery. She planned to get back to dancing and take guitar lessons. She had also decided she was straight—not even bi—although Leaf Pringle said she didn't have to make that decision right away.

Andy took some hope in the last words of Emily's text. Had she perhaps reached the final stage of grief? Emily was an amazing person, Andy told herself, although maybe sometimes hyper-controlling but in a loving way, and she would totally find someone else—someone better and kinder than her. She whispered goodbye, but as she touched the phone to her lips it trembled as another text came in.

Five

Amor est passio quaedam innata procedens ex visione et immoderata cogitatione formae alterius sexus.

(Love is an inborn suffering which results from the sight of, and uncontrolled thinking about, the beauty of the other sex.)
—Andreas Capellanus, *On Love*

THE MIDDAY SUN fell in a few orange slashes across Frank's antiques and oriental rugs. Frank sat in his entrance hall—the one place he fought to keep as formal as he originally meant his whole house to be. He pressed an old Bakelite telephone to his ear.

"Uh-huh," he said. "Yup." His aunt's lengthy explanation at the other end of the line was brittle and hard to hear, as though the phone, restored to work once again, allowed Frank to converse across time with the distant voices of its heyday.

An ornate mahogany coat stand nearby had a white scratch, he noticed. In fact, all three coat stands needed dusting and polishing, as did the grandfather clocks and the console tables and the banded oak barrel by the door that held the umbrellas and walking sticks. "Uh-huh," said Frank. "Well, okay then." Frank set the vintage phone down among its companions. He heard footsteps above, then saw Angus's hunched form descend the stairs.

"Trouble?" asked Angus.

"My uncle fell," said Frank. "Broke a hip."

"Age?"

"I don't know. Eighty? Late seventies? They want me to build a ramp for a wheelchair."

"At that age you'd be better taking a shovel," said Angus. "If I break a hip, shoot me, will you?"

"Of course. What the hell is that, by the way?"

Angus was holding a large, gray ball. "Guess," he said. "It's a ball of cat hair, Frankie." He set the thing among the phones where they could contemplate it. "Strangely beautiful, eh?"

"Why are you doing this, Angus?"

"Cleaning house for you? D'you know how long it took me to garner this?"

"Days?" Frank guessed. "Have you got nothing better to do?"

"Hours, Frankie. A matter of hours. A circling motion of the hand across your fabrics and pillows, and voilà! I could gather three or more just like this."

"Please do. Just throw them out, okay?"

"In Africa, they would fashion this into a sculpture of a cat. Sell it in the market. Not in this country. People would recoil, call it unsanitary."

"Probably."

"Your felines are polluters, Frankie, shedders—most of them matted with wee twigs and leaves."

"So?"

"Have you read *Little Body, Big Heart*?"

"*Big Spirit*."

"The Chihuahua is basically hairless, y'see." Angus stood with his arms crossed, his hands tucked tightly under his armpits as if he could barely contain his delight at this claim. An alert white hair, lit by the sun, stood sentry on the tip of his nose.

"What are you saying? Are you suggesting I get rid of the cats? Replace them with Chihuahuas?"

"God no, man! Of course not. They're decorative, elegant creatures in their own parasitic way." Angus took the ball. "Still, would it be so bad?"

Corey lay in the darkness and listened to Andy in the bathroom between their two rooms. An electric toothbrush demanded its two-minute contract and gave its humane pause to say the task was halfway over. Corey heard a jar being opened and closed. There was a rustle, a silence, another rustle, then her hand upon the key to his adjoining door. The bathroom light went off. He heard the turn of her own key as she went to bed. Could this woman be more fascinating?

Corey considered destiny, then coincidence, then destiny again. How was it possible that two people, one from Tennessee, one from Georgia, could end up sharing the same bathroom? Yet it had happened. He could have stayed in Knoxville to study Health and Wellness, but he preferred Asheville. In his brief conversations with Andy so far, he learned that she chose Asheville only after driving through Asheville on her way to Knoxville.

Nothing Corey had learned in science class could answer this accident of fate. Right now she could be going to bed in his hometown. At the exact same moment in time he would just be lying here, probably already asleep, next to David's empty room. As he saw it, Andy could be anywhere on the planet instead of next door. He spelled out the extraordinary facts: he was now housemate to a humanoid who could not only dance and sing but was about to start guitar lessons. On top of this, Andy had clearly mastered David's philosophy of the simple life. She practically had no stuff. Each morning Corey witnessed Andy leave her austere retreat to enter the world, armed only with a journal and water.

In comparison to such a person, Corey felt slight and unformed. He wanted to be different. He imagined telling Andy that he was changing to be like her, evolving each night to exactly copy her, like the faceless pod people in that old sci-fi movie. That might sound weird, though. He pressed his head back into his pillow and blinked at the dark ceiling, awed by the turning, tilting heavens beyond.

Angus's guest drank his beer—a ravenous infant at its milk, the bottle raised high in one hand, plugged to his red face. He eyed the porch beyond this urgent task, while his free hand drifted, dusting the surface of the wall behind him, searching for some purchase to steady his balance. Only when the bottle was entirely drained did he dislodge it, examining its vacuum with disappointment.

"You liked that, Troy?" said Angus.

"Trey."

Angus had met Trey at a junk shop where they both wanted the same cat carrier. A scuffle was avoided when a shared dislike for cats emerged, and soon they were laughing at the folly of their dispute. Trey insisted Angus have the carrier. Angus suggested a drink. As they wandered the rainy streets, they discovered a further tie: Trey knew Angus's attacker from the bus station.

Buying beer at a convenience store, the two felinophobes were delighted to find that the cans fit neatly into the carrier and, thus equipped, they set off in search of their old drinking companion. They found him, slumped but affable, in a nearby park. During the reunion, Angus had an idea. After his injury he had received no support from Frank or the others in harnessing Angelica and re-harnessing Rover. In exchange for the pet carrier and further beers, would Trey help him with a small favor?

Now the hunter studied his assistant with satisfaction. Apart from his name, which vexed Angus, Trey was the man he needed on a night like this. Age might have thickened Trey around the middle, but he had kept the strong legs and shapely ankles of a runner. "You're a fierce-looking bugger, Troy," Angus told him. Trey's nose was broken, his skull dented like an old prizefighter's, and this stern aspect was strangely enhanced by the fluttering lashes and cupid lips of a DeMille ingénue.

Against the porch rail were set the tools they might need: a large fishing net, a garbage can, tennis rackets, blankets, Trey's cat carrier. At the far end of the rail were two new harnesses, a pair of scissors, and a pile of dog treats.

"It's getting on," said Angus. "We should start."

"Another beer for you?" asked Trey, reaching for the cooler.

"You should leave those for later," advised Angus, opening a map. He laid it out on the table between them. "These are their preferred routes. They generally approach the courtyard from the east, across the front lawn here. It's close to their grazing time now."

"What are these things again?"

"Dogs, remember?"

Trey's head was very close to the map. "They go all over," he said. "Did you buy this?"

"I made it," said Angus, pulling the map away. "It doesn't matter. How are your eyes?"

"I lost my glasses, but I don't need them."

"Alright, then." Angus pointed across the lawn. "They'll follow the path from the street, most likely."

"And we put them in the bucket?"

"We lie the garbage can on the ground. Over in the corner. We might run one in there."

"Do we hit them with the swatters first?"

"The tennis rackets? No, we don't hit the dogs, okay? They're too small."

"Like Chihuahuas?"

"Christ. I told you, they are Chihuahuas."

"Are these those biting kind?"

"No." Angus explained his strategy again and gave his guest a tennis racket, a blanket, a harness, and a handful of treats. "You go for the white one, right? The female. The racket is to guide her—just that. You throw the blanket over her, give her time to get calm, stroke her, talk her down, then put on the harness."

"Is this your phone number?" Trey asked, looking at some details written by Angus along the harness strap.

Angus ignored him. "Go over there, in those bushes, and just wait. Try not to run the dog toward the back of the house, you understand? They can get out that way. Corner her."

"You're like that guy on the TV, the one who can talk to dogs."

Angus nodded, "I'll deal with the rogue male."

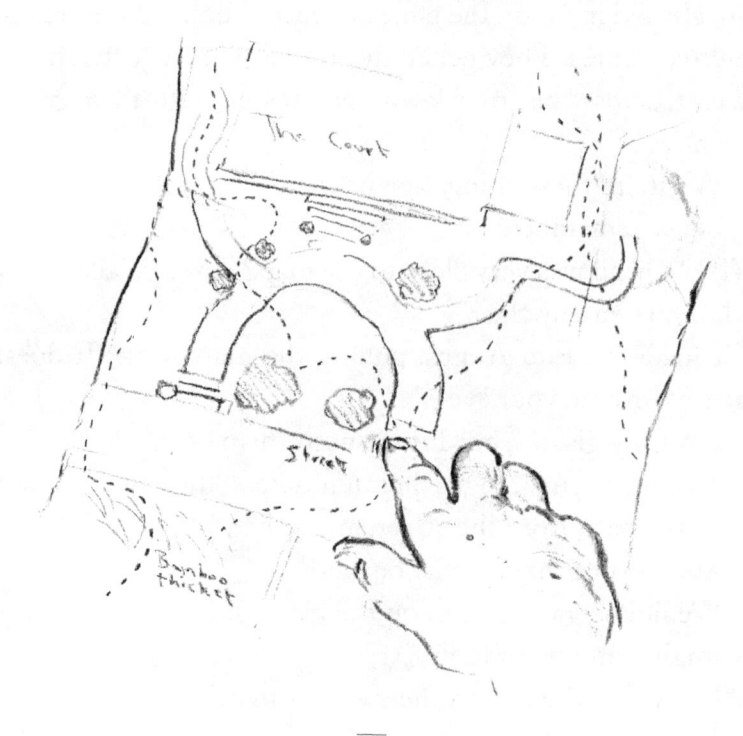

The two men stationed themselves in opposing bushes. Angus lit a cigarette, enjoying how the tobacco smoke blended with the perfume of the garden. The lawn turned violet, and the sky darkened from rose to a nebulous blue. As the birds fell silent, the sound of the cicadas swelled. Somewhere a guitar was being played. Mosquitoes began to swarm around Angus's head as he watched the stillness of his fellow trapper. "Troy?" he whispered. "Troy?" Angus ran over to find the man asleep.

"Wasshapen?" asked Trey.

"You fell asleep, you useless…," said Angus. "Here, let me get you a beer. Wake you up."

"Thanks, man."

Angus ran back with a bottle and crouched beside Trey. "Wait!" he said. "They're coming! They're coming up the street." He wrestled the beer away from Trey's eager grasp, "Get ready, Damn you!"

The dogs trotted up the path. Trey stumbled to his feet and set off in the opposite direction, wielding his swatter.

"That's a cat!" shouted Angus. "That's a cat, you idiot!" He hurled the pet carrier aside as useless and went after Rover, who had braced himself for flight. Behind Angus, in the soft light, the homeless man tripped, recovered, and set off after another cat.

Rover bunched at Angus's approach, then scuttled through some hostas, turning sharply to run back between Angus's feet. Angus gave chase. Rover's bell rang wildly. Angus kept close behind, already breathing heavily. As they crossed the lawn, Angus glimpsed Trey abandoning one hunt for yet another. A white shape flitted along the fence line. "That's another fucking cat!" Angus yelled, simultaneously trying to direct Rover back toward the corner of the yard and the garbage can.

Rover feinted. Angus feinted in return. The black dog flattened, almost invisible against the mulch of the flower beds. This then was "pancaking," Angus realized, the evasive action so vividly described by Colonel Rex Marigold in his guide to the breed. Rover scuttled on, pancaking as and when he saw fit. Angus threw the blanket several times in vain, imagining the effective nets of the gladiators, wishing now he carried their trident.

Trey had finally spotted Angelica. Beyond a low-hanging tree, she was watching the pantomime, her head slightly cocked, her eyes bright. "Doggie," Trey cajoled. "Little doggie!" From a crouched start, he ran full tilt at the dog with a phantom's disregard for the heavy limb between them. The tremendous blow shook leaves from the branches. Trey's blanket fell beside his body, and his racket spun away into the undergrowth.

Angus had captured Rover. They sat together in a flower bed, the Chihuahua wrapped in his arms. The dog struggled intermittently, the bell and the growling muffled, one exposed foot stabbing the air. Angus remained still, taking a moment to recover his breath and enjoy his victory. He took hold of the tiny paw and whispered calming words to his captive.

"I bik my tug." Trey called out.

"What are you saying, Troy?"

"Id's Twey. I bik my tug, Anguth."

Angus staggered over. Angelica was sitting beside the wounded man. "You've bitten your tongue," said Angus. A black sheet of blood shone down the front of Trey's shirt. "Stick it out. I'll take a look." Angus examined the injury. "It's all there," he said, using his stiffened handkerchief as a field dressing, "You'll be alright."

Trey patted Angelica's domed head. Her eyes closed with satisfaction at each stroke.

"Can you put the harness on her?" Angus asked him.

Trey unwrapped his tongue, "You cod the udder wun?"

"He's in here," Angus pulled the scissors from his pocket. The dog's distant protests grew louder.

"He thounds angry."

"He is angry." Angus pulled away the blanket to reveal a furious black face.

"He's cude," said Trey, reaching toward Rover.

"Careful, man!" warned Angus.

"Hey," said Trey. "He'th already got a hardess!"

"I told you that on the porch." Angus passed him the scissors, "Can you cut that thing off him?" Angus let Trey take over, and he lit another cigarette as he watched the man put the new harness on Rover and adjust it to fit. "A successful mission," he said. "The casualty rate is acceptable."

"Yeth," Trey now had both Chihuahuas in his lap. "Theeth are neat dogths."

In a humanitarian gesture, Angus climbed to his feet and went to find Trey's beer. It was still upright beside the pet carrier. "A beautiful night," he said as he returned.

"Lod of wide cads," said Trey, before fastening the bottle to his face.

"White cats?" said Angus. "Too many." He struck his assistant a smart blow between the eyes. Trey looked at him in astonishment over his beer.

"A mosquito, Trey."

Andy waited until she knew Emily would be at work before she drove over to collect the boots. They were sitting on the step beside a selection of bungee cords that were still in their unopened packaging. A note was attached. It read: *I bought these for our trip to the beach. Use them to hold stuff together in your new life. What a shame you had no time for the true ties that bind. Goodbye, galaxy girl, my universe.*

Andy was startled to hear Emily's truck roar up behind her. Her erstwhile lover jumped from the vehicle and strode up the gravel drive. She wore her cap backwards, and it made her fast, boyish movements look even more purposeful. "What are you doing here?" she demanded.

"I came to get my UGGs," Andy said softly. "Thanks for these," she added after a silence, holding up the bungee cords.

Emily folded her arms and shook her head.

"I'm sorry, Emily."

Andy started to leave. Emily made a gesture that suggested disbelief and cranial agony all at once. "Walk away then," she told Andy.

"I'm sorry."

"You came here for your UGGs, that's all. You came back for a pair of boots." They stood in the bright driveway, Emily shielding her eyes with her arm, as though Andromeda was the sun.

Six

Admittedly, many dreams are senseless, meaningless jumbles, inspired by too much potato salad and knockwurst before going to bed.
  —Herman H. Rubin MD, *Eugenics and Sex Harmony*

Elaine said, "Andy seems a nice girl, and Angus seems calmer."

"He's between projects," said Frank. "Now he's got those dogs contained, he's decided he wants to cook for us all."

"I hope those two aren't related."

Frank laughed. "He's been threatening to cook since he got here—'global cuisine.'" He nudged a heavily smoking citronella bucket away from them with his foot. "My guess is he's trying to impress Andy." They sat in the courtyard, sharing a bottle of wine, taking in the stealth of cats around them and the bedlam of birds above.

"Those glasses are still freaking me out," said Elaine.

Frank took off his sunglasses and looked at the two white dots, rubbing a thumb over the scratches without hope. "I don't notice them anymore."

Elaine returned to Frank's concern. "I think you can leave without too much worry," she said.

"Yeah," said Frank, "It'll be fine. It's just a few days. I'll take Juan with me."

Would Angus go back to cooking meals in his fireplace while he was away? Frank tried not to think about it. He would drive to the coast, build the ramp for his uncle, then head home before his tenant did any more damage to his garden.

"Do you want me to come by while you're gone?"

"That's okay," said Frank. After a while he said, "I was nuts buying this place, but it's even crazier trying to keep hold of it."

"You can't sell it in this market," Elaine told him.

"All it's good for is cat storage. A cathouse."

"Doghouse now, too."

"Insane asylum." Frank went on, "I've been reading this terrible book. Anyway, it said all this stuff about how to be happy, like simplifying your life, downsizing. 'Downstrife your life.'"

"'Downstrife'?"

"It's an invented word. I guess only the author uses it."

"I hope so," said Elaine.

"Look how simple Corey's life is. Malcolm's, too. Andy has her neat little space. They're all living comfortably out of just one room."

"You too, Frank."

"Well, you're right," Frank raised his glass to this truth, "Cheers to my simple life."

Andy was happy at Carolina Court. It was a place to recover and to hide from Emily, but the rambling house was much more than that to the fugitive. She imagined herself a guest at a once-fine hotel or the heroine of some dusty, haunted estate. She kept her room immaculate and purchased a little, handheld vacuum cleaner to clean every corner. Her furniture was arranged around the room in a way that pleased her—the blue desk at the window, the little glass table beside the futon. A few clothes were arranged in the narrow closet, and her shoes laid out in a tidy row beside the door. As a gift to "welcome her aboard," Angus had given her a cribbage game in the shape of a Viking boat. She set this on the windowsill. Although the mast was crooked and many of the pegs that doubled for its Nordic crew were missing, Andy liked the model ship.

Each morning Andy sat at the desk to write, only to find herself gazing out of the window at the activity in the garden below. To start with, there was always the spotting of the cats. How many would be visible today? And where? They gathered in groups of two or three—at a distance from each other, but groups nonetheless—sitting formally like Egyptian deities or lounging like odalisques. Were they engaged in some silent discourse or just deathly bored?

Andy's room was directly above the path that connected the front and the rear of the house. Beneath the window, her housemates came and went. Corey would leave for class on his bike, wobbling over the uneven bricks that led down to the street. Toward lunchtime, Malcolm would head into town with his guitar, wearing the battered straw Stetson he would set on the ground for coins.

For days Angus had been working with the little dogs in the front yard. If Andy leaned forward, their class was just visible—the Chihuahuas sniffing the ground at the end of long lengths of string, Angus shouting names from a list on a clipboard. "Alec? Bill? Bill? Brian? Chuck? Dan? Dennis? Dennis? Eric?" Every now and then he made a hurried notation. It was intriguing, but she had already learned there was no need to seek information from Angus. He would let her know his progress when she saw him next. The dogs seemed oblivious to the Scotsman tethered to them. "Antonia? Amelia? Amelia? Ariel? Bethany? Brittany? Claudia? Duchess?"

Andy opened her journal. When she arrived from Graniteville her first friend in town had suggested Andy start one. Tansie lived in West Asheville at The Goddess Temple, formerly Tantric Karma. Everyone there kept journals, Tansie explained, except Amber who was majorly dyslexic.

She was grateful for Tansie's advice. Tansie was right—journals were awesome. Andy's daily observations—so far a delicate haze of assurances that she could never go home, that her qualities guaranteed triumph in the wider world—were Andy's guide for a life that must surely now leave tragedy and devastation behind.

A sad truth about Emily, she recalled, was that she had never liked Andy journaling, and this was only because it was Tansie's idea and because Tansie lived in The Goddess Temple. No matter how much Andy had defended this sanctuary, her lover had questioned its virtues. In Emily's opinion, this empowering space for sisterhood and nondualistic tantric bodywork—gifted to the mountains by Tansie, Amber, and the other migrant goddesses—could be defined more succinctly as "some hippie hand job bullshit massage parlor."

In ornate font, Andy had written on the first page **GODDESS JOURNAL**. Several of the letters sprouted tendrils to inch downward to her drawing below of a pensive damsel, folded like Angus's fortune cookie under a leafy oak. Andy had struggled with where her tresses should fall, settling on the mass of her hair tumbling off the front of her head. The final effect—that of a waterfall leaping from the maiden's collar—greatly displeased the artist. But this frontispiece could not be torn out—not without defacing Andy's vade mecum, so complete and confirming with its faux-tooled unicorn, its scarlet ribbon and creamy pages.

This trying first lesson in illumination led to Andy's thoughts. These were often framed as lists, with related considerations attached in satellite bubbles or stars. Her strengths were there, burdened by adjacent flaws. Career possibilities exploded like fireworks from a doodled heart. The most recent pages were dedicated to grief and the healing that must inevitably follow. Andy's phone no longer hummed with texts from the heart she had broken, but long, bitter emails still arrived every day. She asked her therapist to give her homework to do between sessions and diligently applied herself to the task of letting Emily go.

Now she wrote *Self Improvement of the Self* and underlined it twice. Dr. Pringle brought up meditation at their last meeting, and so Andy, copying her scrawled notes, wrote *TONGLEN* under this and drew a rococo frame around the word.

"*Tonglen*," Leaf Pringle had explained, pressing her hands together, fingertips at her chin, "*Tonglen*, Andromeda, okay, let's just be present right now, okay? You can write this down later. *Tonglen* asks that we breathe in the suffering, the negativity, the pain of others, and then breathe out calmness, clarity, joy."

Andy wrote *PAIN- - - - - -JOY*. She closed her eyes and breathed through her nose for a while. One nostril seemed blocked. She opened her eyes, took up her pen, and drew a small horse near the corner of the page.

Corey was anxious. He thought about Andy all the time. Every evening he watched the kitchen door for her return, while her proximity upstairs plagued his nights. Each morning, as he left for school, he glanced at her window in hopes of more than its lattice of reflected branches.

He spoke to Malcolm. "She's not even my type," he said.

"What do you mean 'your type'? What are you, twenty yet?"

"You know what I mean."

"I thought you had a girlfriend," said Malcolm.

"Nah," said Corey. "That was just a thing. I mean, Andy and I, what would we do together? She's always like, writing and stuff. You've got to have interests in common, right? I just don't see how this can last otherwise."

"Maybe you're getting ahead of yourself?"

"Yeah," said Corey. "Shit, she doesn't even want to be in a relationship right now, right?"

"Seems that way."

"She needs time," Corey shook his head. "It's amazing what people do to each other. What a jackass. He was an idiot to leave her."

"Maybe she left him?"

"She should have."

Malcolm teased Corey, "We should kick his butt."

"Totally."

"Totally," lisped the tiny Maybelle Jolene, who was playing with her paper dolls at their feet. Malcolm reached down and petted his offspring.

"Where does he live?" he asked Corey.

A History of Saints

"Her ex?" Corey was confused. "I don't know. I don't know anything about the guy."

"He's the bad guy," the child explained. Her oval face was lit with patience, a kindly light bulb.

"Now, Maybelle Jolene," said Malcolm, "that's just your mama speaking. We talked about this, baby doll. The fact is that in most failed relationships the woman is to blame."

Corey looked at Maybelle Jolene. The little girl seemed to have no answer to this. She went back to dressing a cardboard silhouette of a huge-eyed cheerleader.

"She's like, so above me," Corey continued, mortal and doomed in his biking shorts and bare feet. In his invented plight, titans, heroes, and philosopher-kings were even now lining up to form the pantheon of Andromeda's future suitors. He explained the steep odds against him, "I'm just like, this guy."

Maybelle Jolene handed Corey the paper cheerleader. "You are like a guy bird," she said in a Delphic way, "with legs."

"Give her some time, Corey," said Malcolm. "There's no rush."

Frank woke from an unusually vivid and disquieting dream. In it, he had been showing High Cotton to a group of young heiresses. They talked about putting in bunk beds and how they insisted on paying extra for that. Frank showed them the TV. When he switched it on, a special bulletin was interrupting all programs. The news anchor described how "nothing less than a supreme being, or cosmic force, was peeling the world like an enormous orange." The girls stopped talking, then sat around Frank to learn about this disaster. A geologist was introduced to explain the situation. Referring to a childish diagram, he showed how an incision had been made from the top to the very bottom of the globe and that, from this line, everything not the internal rock ball of the planet was being rolled back like a great piece of sod. Lawns, fields, cities, and oceans were all being lifted up with the dirt beneath them. Cellars and tunnels, underground railways, and ancient cities were exposed, pulled up like so many roots. Wells and pipes bristled everywhere. What was remarkable, the geologist told them, was that absolutely nothing was being damaged. From the ozone layer through the breathable sky, all the way down to the deepest oceanic trench, the whole skin of the inhabited world was being sloughed off like "a big old rug."

"Everyone is doing just fine," said the news anchor. "Look out your window." Frank went to the window. Where the sky had been was a vast, green wall of forests and mountains. On this impossible map he could see a great part of the Carolinas folded up toward him—an aerial view of towns and highways, tiny cars defying gravity as they went about their business. The girls were crying now.

"Mike," a woman anchor asked the expert, "can you tell us what is going on? For the people out there who are feeling pretty scared right now?" A news feed along the bottom of the screen read, *World peeled like enormous orange. Churches full. Stocks plunge worldwide.*

"Well, Kaylie," said Mike, "what we're learning here is that the Earth's skin has been completely removed and transported at incredible speed several million light years to a distant solar system."

"That's incredible."

"It certainly is, Kaylie."

"Kind of like a flying carpet?"

Mike made a dismissive face, "I guess."

"But we didn't see any of this?"

"No. Because of the speed, mainly, but also because it's still daylight."

"Especially at Frank's house," nodded Kaylie.

"Exactly." The geologist pointed to a new childish diagram, "What's happening right now is that the bunched-up troposphere, the 'peel,' as it were, of planet Earth is being wrapped around a new planet that's just the right size."

"Thank God," whispered one of the girls beside Frank.

"Awesome," said another.

"So we should be…okay?" asked Kaylie, the blond helmet of her hairdo unaffected by another emphatic nod.

"Just fine, Kaylie."

"And we're seeing that right now on Wall Street," said the first anchor. "Stocks are starting to rise, and we're hearing a lot of relief. Mike, are there still concerns about this…stuff, for the future?"

"Jim, the future is looking pretty bright, actually," said the expert with a broad smile. "For one thing, we now have two suns and three moons!"

The dream ended with Frank and the girls all going out into the golden courtyard and looking up. The girls started clapping and Frank joined in. Everywhere in the sunlight were Chihuahuas.

Frank woke as this last, yellow image and the euphoria of an averted global disaster began to drift away. He heard the breathing of a nearby cat and felt the slight tug of a headache. That was an odd dream, he said to himself, wondering if some distant, partaken chemical was responsible. Opening his eyes, he saw on the adjacent pillow not a cat, but Angelica's domed head. Her eyes opened. "Morning," said Frank. The dog must have crept under the covers during the night. Angelica closed her eyes and Frank followed her example.

Seven

The Chihuahua doesn't have much time for a B-52 Stratofortress. When a noise from above causes your baby to flatten, that's "pancaking." Aerial attack is old news to your Chi. To the owl and the hawk your dog is just fast food.
—USAF Colonel Rex Marigold, *Little Body, Big Spirit: Living with the Chihuahua*

ANGUS CALLED A meeting of the household, choosing an evening Andy was not working at the restaurant. Everyone sat around the table and waited on the Scotsman.

"This is probably about those dogs," said Malcolm.

"It could be anything at all," said Frank.

Andy looked up from texting a friend. "He said something about 'democracy in action,'" she told them. She was wearing one of the Obama T-shirts Angus had recently handed out. Corey saw how the green tip of a tattoo coiled up from her collar toward the pulsing of her throat.

Angus came into the kitchen with a Chihuahua under each arm. He wore an Obama shirt as well, snug under his fishing vest. This was uniquely juxtaposed with a Sarah Palin button. For Angus, the newly announced Republican candidate was "a hottie, as easy on the eye as she was tricky on the ear."

He placed the dogs on the table and they stood rigid, at everyone's eye level, Rover wary, Angelica unconcerned. "Good evening, gentlemen, madam," he began. "The time has come for the naming of names."

Corey stood and reached over to pet Rover. The dog pancaked, and a great yellow pool spread out across the table from beneath his haunches.

"For God's sake, man," groaned Angus. "Have you not noticed this one's a submissive urinator?"

Frank watched the gold tide. It encircled some coins, darkened a flyer, came to a halt against the pages of *Instant Joy!* Rover also studied the passage of his flood, while Angelica stepped delicately out of its path. There was a flurry of activity as Andy and Corey blotted up the mess with paper towels. At the far end of the table, Guinevere, a tabby with a touch of Maine Coon, turned her face from the ugliness of it all.

"'Submissive urinator'?" Malcolm asked.

"He's of a nervous disposition," said Angus. "Never loom. You should approach him in a low crouch if you want to stroke him."

"That sounds scarier than looming."

"Can we set these dogs on the floor?" asked Frank.

"Who's reading that crap?" Angus pointed at the paperback.

"Nobody now," said Frank. "Somebody left it for me."

"Antietam?" Angus snarled, "Has he been back?"

When everyone was sitting again and the dogs left to explore the kitchen, Angus pulled a piece of paper from his pocket. "Since we live in a democracy," he began, "or at least claim to, I've decided we should name these dogs together."

"Why?" asked Frank. "They're your dogs."

"You feed them, Frankie."

"I know, Angus."

"I have only started them on their long journey from savagery to cultivation."

Everyone looked at the dogs.

"They are extraordinary creatures," Angus continued. "The white one, in particular, is almost ready to come inside."

"She was in my bed this morning," said Frank.

"She's so cute," said Andy. "She sleeps in my bed, too."

"That's interesting," said Angus with irritation. "She must be getting in somehow. I thought I had them corralled on the front porch."

"Yeah," said Frank. "All that kind of needs to come down now, Angus."

Angus ignored this. "No doubt, these dogs have had names and owners before. I have devised my own system for renaming strays to their satisfaction. A system for ascertaining the sound, the fricative associated with the handle they find most familiar."

"You've been guessing their names?" said Malcolm.

"In a way," said Angus. "What I know now is that the male had a prior name beginning with a *gah* or *kah* sound." He made these noises with emphasis. Rover was circling a bowl set out for cats. "The white dog responds to a *la-la-la* sound."

Frank frowned.

Angus took a scrap of paper from a tattered journal, "I've got a list here of the names that seem to register best, to please the wee rascals. I'll read the choices, and then can I get a showing of hands for your favorites?"

"This is fun," said Andy.

"Let's begin with the male," Angus raised a pencil. "George or Georgie…"

"That's a *jay* sound," said Malcolm.

Angus went on, "Geronimo…"

"That's another *jay* sound," said Corey.

"Jesus!" said Angus. "Can I just finish here? Captain or Captain Blackie, Gandalf…"

"Gandalf?" said Frank.

"Gorky, Geoff, Keith, Gawain, Geezer, Chris."

"Can we hear those again?" asked Andy.

Angus read the list again slowly. Rover nudged the bowl around the floor. Hands were raised and Geezer won with three votes.

"Is Geezer a name?" asked Corey.

"It's slang," said Angus, "for a bloke, an old guy."

"Oh," said Andy, who had voted for the name. "I thought it was a water thing. Geezer!" she called out. "Geezer, come here! Geezer!"

"Let's continue," said Angus. "Lady, Lulu, Lavinia, Lakeisha, Lily, Lemonpie, Lovely, Lemur."

Everyone noticed Angelica's sharp response to Lakeisha. The name took the majority of their votes.

"That was fun," said Andy.

"Totally," Corey said.

"Long live democracy," said Frank.

"It doesn't matter then, if those are the right names?" Corey wondered aloud. "Just that they come when we call them?"

"Regular bloody Wittgenstein," said Angus.

Angelica was scooped up by Andy and set in her lap. "Lakeisha," she cooed. "Lakeisha wants to sleep in my bed tonight?" Lakeisha gazed up at Andy's face. Geezer scratched at a piece of cat food lodged beneath the baseboard.

"Is it just me," Frank asked Angus, "or aren't those pretty similar-sounding names?"

"So? I'm not writing a bloody novel here, Frankie. The facts are out of my hands. Destiny fated that a tiny, practically microscopic, puppy was once named Lakeisha. Dare I conjure for your consideration a loving first owner of African American descent? And Geezer there was christened Geezer. God knows why. Anyway, they can tell the difference. Look at those ears. The Chi has uncanny hearing."

The ears were noted by all, except Guinevere.

"Geezer!" Angus shouted. The dogs looked at him.

The gold tide

Malcolm kept a binder for the songs he had written. Titles like "Tulsa Whore" and "Bitch from Tupelo" suggested a recurring theme, but Corey's torment over Andy was a new inspiration. The daily sight of his wan face, ever turning in expectation of Andy's surprisingly light tread, reminded Malcolm of love's gentler aspects. Sentimental ballads did not always have to involve .38s and shallow graves, followed by hastily improvised lynchings. He put aside his own catastrophic history with women, strummed his guitar, and borrowed from a long history of Celtic and country metaphors. He could not help, however, sprinkling this new hope with a few hard and weighty images from his own reality.

Love, with its endless associations, had ruined for Malcolm, among other things, meadows, Adirondack chairs, airports, cheese fries, sailing, the sound of rain on a tin roof, and moo goo gai pan. He played his newest creation, "The Glad Hag," for Corey.

"That's beautiful, man," Corey shook his head. "That's so fucking beautiful."

"Thanks." Malcolm put down his guitar.

"You just wrote that?"

"Yeah."

"Awesome, man. But she stays with him, right? When he comes back from the sea?"

"I guess," said Malcolm. "She's waited all that time."

Corey went back to his deficiencies, "I wish I could play guitar. I can't even sing."

"You want to sing to her?"

"You know what I mean," said Corey. "Something creative. Like she's used to."

"Have you tried poetry?"

"Are you kidding?"

"It works. Chicks love it."

"It would feel totally gay for me to even try that."

"What are you going to do, then?"

Corey jumped to his feet and scratched his head furiously. "I don't know! I'm screwed! This is fucking bullshit! She doesn't even see me. I'm invisible. Like yesterday, I told her I might go camping and she was like, 'That's cool,' and I was like, 'Well, you know, anytime you want to come along I've got like, two tents,' and she was like, 'Isn't it kinda scary out there?' So I said, 'Not really if there's two people.'" Corey paced around the room, sat heavily on a chair, leaped up again. "You see what I'm saying?"

"You asked her to go camping with you?"

"I don't know! I guess."

"What did she say?"

"Something about not sleeping good on rocks."

"Don't give up, Corey," Malcolm said. "I'm counting on you."

"There is no hope, dude," Corey said with resignation. "There is absolutely no fucking hope in this picture."

Malcolm returned to an old concern. "What do you think about Johnny Stone? For a stage name?"

"That's cool. Yeah, I like that. What about Johnny Rock?"

"Rock's a first name. Johnny Boulder?"

Corey thought carefully. "Clint Boulder?" he suggested. "Clint Stone?"

"Flint Stone?" countered Malcolm.

"Fred Stone?"

From time to time Frank got help from an illegal called Juan. Somehow they worked effectively together with no understanding of the other's language. Frank would reinforce his broken instructions with elaborate gestures. His big hands could intricately mimic such things as the operation of a circular saw despite an interfering extension cord. Juan would study these performances and reward them with a nod.

"Okay then," Frank said to Juan with a mime that involved door handles, a steering wheel, and the breaststroke. "Soon we are to be getting in the truck. Head to ocean."

Angus saluted the travelers with his coffee mug. He had come out with a string of animals to see them off, but the departure was taking a while. Dogs and cats now lie scattered across the broken asphalt for no good reason, eyes closing, their curiosity forgotten.

"You have everything you need?" Angus asked Frank.

The bed of the truck held a few tools, a couple of plywood offcuts, Frank's orange suitcase, and a grocery bag with Juan's change of clothes.

"I think so," said Frank.

"ETA?" asked Angus.

Malcolm's arrival interrupted Frank's reply. "*Buenos dias*, Juan," he said. "You headed out, Frank?"

"They're building some kind of ramp for a cripple," Angus told Malcolm. He raised his cup again. "You're a good man, Frank. You too, Juan. Have you ever visited the coast, amigo?"

Juan turned his Aztec gaze upon Angus. He was wearing a faded T-shirt that read, *Oh, Goody!*, and heavy canvas pants that crowded around his short calves.

Angus grinned at Juan for a while, then swelled slightly to recite, "'I have seen the marsh hen swimming, with her young on Taylors Creek, I have seen a curlew running, catch a minnow in its beak.'" He looked over at Frank, "Should I get him those binoculars?"

"We're good," said Frank.

"If you need anything," said Angus, holding his coffee cup to his ear, "call me."

"Right," said Frank. "Actually, I should use the bathroom one more time." The Chihuahuas sprang up and followed him.

"Hey, Frankie!" shouted Angus, "You want to take one of the dogs? Geezer? For company?"

Frank waved the suggestion off as he stepped into the house.

"He's more of a cat person," explained Malcolm.

Angus shook his head. He grimaced at the Mexican, "Juan, *vous êtes gato hombre? Perro hombre?*"

When Frank and Juan had left, Angus set to work.
"Hello, Lida?"
"Hello?"
"Lida Barfield?"
"Who is this?"
"It's Angus," said Angus, "of Carolina Court."

"How did you get my number?"

"We spoke a couple of weeks back. You called me. High Cotton—you were interested in the room?"

"Oh yes. I didn't recognize your voice. I thought you were a pervert. Is it still available?"

"Aye, absolutely. You could move in right away, in fact."

"Are you the owner?"

"Frankie? He's away on business. As I said, though, he welcomes my maintenance of the estate."

"I remember you saying that. Well, I am ready to move."

"You should, lassie. Stillness is death. Do you need a hand with anything?"

"Perhaps my wardrobe."

"Is it heavy? My back—an old sports injury."

"Not furniture. My dresses, clothes, shoes."

"But of course," said Angus. "Be glad to."

"We talked about arranging some extra closet space?"

"Aye, that's right. Not a problem."

"I don't have any furniture really, but I have a lot of clothes. A lot."

"Today's world cries for ornament."

"They're mostly vintage and quite valuable. Do you wash your hands?"

"Every day. I'm a collector myself, as a matter of fact—" Angus began.

"I will see you tomorrow then. To view the room."

"Tomorrow it is. I'll have the place swept and dusted for you, Lida," Angus said into an empty phone.

He looked around at the dense forest of coats, thin shirts, and creased pants that choked his room, fragrant with the peaty, composting scent of his cigarettes. "She's feisty, this one," he said approvingly.

The girl needed something for her clothes? With effort, he wrestled the garments off one of the racks and flung them onto a high area of books and shoes, supported from beneath by a selection of hidden chairs. There was the movement of a cat, and Angus cursed the animal as it fled his lair.

He wheeled the empty clothes rack out into the hallway and stopped at Andy's door. "Andromeda?" He knocked lightly, "Andee?"

When there was no reply, he went to Corey's door. His success on Frank's behalf had him beaming, red in the face, triumphant. By the time his landlord returned, all Frank's problems would be over. Angus wanted to call another meeting of the household at once. He would check on Malcolm. He headed for the stairs, the clothes rack dismembering a rubber plant as he went.

Eight

As much we may say of them that are troubled with their fortunes; or ill destinies foreseen...
—Robert Burton, *The Anatomy of Melancholy*

FRANK'S TRUCK CLATTERED down the steep, winding interstate, dropping out of the mountains into the Piedmont. As the radio signal weakened, a news report about something having happened at Lehman Brothers, a struggling bank in New York, was jarringly replaced by a Christian station. Frank turned the radio off and drove into America.

That was how leaving Asheville always felt to him—as though his little town was like a stockade in the Old West, crowded with exiles, surrounded by hostiles. Only when called to fulfill some family obligation would Frank and his townsfolk venture out. For a funeral, a wedding, a reunion, they descended into the bullying traffic, their modest cars speckled with utopian bumper stickers, the reluctant journey to their alien roots marked by billboards set like great pins across the map of the New South, promising big trucks and a neighborly God from high above.

Fort Asheville—a no-kill shelter for the artists, the misfits, the weird-do-wells Frank loved so dearly—where the forty-hour slog was banned forevermore. A town that took an Eden aim at play and self-expression, surely as pioneering, as American in that hope as any Mormon outpost once holding out for uninterrupted bigamy.

With Juan silent beside him, Frank was left to such thoughts. He followed the broad, dull highway that bypassed the past as it strung together the new. All those dead towns out there, and now the boom was over and they had missed their chance. Their storefront windows would stay empty, their streets would keep crumbling.

Not that the boom had offered much. Asheville's recent success had only made the city more commonplace. For years downtown had waited—dusty, vacant, dotted with eccentric souls—only to at last be gutted all at once, refitted in the standard funky way for lattes and beer, vegan cookies and condos upstairs, the sole evidence of a famous haberdasher or a celebrated department store left only in a pressed tin ceiling or a sepia photo in the bathroom.

This American disconnect between the past and the present perplexed Frank—the pride taken in bulldozing everything between the two. Even Asheville, for all its claims, was a history of demolition rather than stewardship.

Everything he saw now to either side of the interstate—the houses, offices, motels, and chain restaurants—was built to be replaced. America wanted its history *olde*—theme parks with carriages and actors in costume. The tourists couldn't get enough of that. Yet back home nothing was left to age, nothing new made to last. It was the enduring habit of a roomy country. The settlers used to burn down a place just to get the nails back.

Still, the recession was here. Change had stalled. Perhaps Asheville could keep what little character was left. Frank wouldn't give up. History mattered. Carolina Court mattered. He wouldn't let the old house down. People passed through life without trace. Like his tenants, like himself, they drifted until they vanished. What was important was what was made well enough for the future to cherish, what we fought to keep.

"It matters," Frank told Juan.

Juan looked at Frank.

They were bypassing Greensboro now. Frank gestured at the dozen lanes of speeding traffic, the acres of asphalt filling their view. "This is all… I mean, what is this?"

"Interestatal," Juan told him. "Greensburro."

"She liked the room," Angus informed Malcolm and Corey. "She's moving in tomorrow."

Malcolm looked troubled. He tightened his ponytail.

"Frank knows about this, right?" asked Corey.

"Of course."

"That's a lot of people," Corey said. "Where will she park?"

"We can make space. You'll barely notice her. High Cotton is almost a separate apartment, when you think about it."

"I guess so," said Corey.

"She told me she has no intention of using this kitchen," Angus added, "even when I mentioned tonight's dish."

"Is tonight Moroccan?" Corey asked.

His curiosity softened Angus's martial demeanor, "Close, lad. A Tunisian dish."

"Super cool," Corey nodded, "and fish is an excellent source of fish oil."

Andy came into the room.

"Andromeda, I was just telling these lads about the newest addition."

"Another dog?" Andy looked delighted.

"Hardly," said Angus. "Another damsel to keep you company. Another woman."

"Awesome."

"She'll be in the slave quarters."

Andy turned to Corey and smiled upon his awaiting face. "I have something for you," she told him. "It's nothing much."

Corey mouthed something in the deafening aftermath of this statement.

"It's upstairs," Andy said, "I can get it."

"No, no," he protested, rising to follow her, his chair falling upon a cat.

When they had left the room, Malcolm complained, "I thought you said there was just going to be Andy."

"Relax, man. Do you no see the natural balance I've restored? Anyway, there are no more rooms left now. My work is done."

Corey followed Andy upstairs. What was happening? She had thought to seek out a gift for him? Was this possible? He stood in her doorway and admired the ordered room. How affecting was the carefully made bed, with its Pier One batik cushions and a bear with a Georgia Bulldogs T-shirt.

"Can you use these?" Andy asked. She held out the package of bungee cords.

Corey took them and gazed upon their different lengths and varied colors.

"For camping?" Andy suggested.

"Thanks," said Corey at last. "Thanks. These are awesome."

"I can't use them," Andy smiled. Her teeth were even and white, her lipstick clogged ever so slightly along the inside of her lower lip.

"You can't use these?" Corey asked. "I can use these for camping." The packaging crackled as he held the gift close.

Emily had tried not to think about Andy or where she now lived. She couldn't help looking for her lover's car, though—searching oncoming traffic or, at the sight of the familiar paint color, glancing into driveways with sick expectation. On her way to her therapist she saw Andy two cars ahead at a stoplight. She hissed slightly.

Quite ignoring the expensive advice that she was about to hear again, Emily made a sudden, angry decision to follow Andy. In the movies, she told herself, you had to follow a car from a few vehicles back, never right up behind them, especially if they knew you already. She tried to keep her distance, but a U-Haul truck and the giant ass of some stupid pickup with six wheels kept hiding Andy's vehicle from view. Emily was relieved when her quarry turned onto a quiet residential street. She crept to the corner and peered up the road to see Andy turning once again. Emily stamped on the gas pedal and sped the intervening distance to come to another tiptoeing stop where Andy had made a left. There, at the top of the street, was the little blue bottom of Andy's beetle turning into a driveway. Three cats looked down at Emily's car, halted and indecisive at the junction. Emily wept and pounded the steering wheel until she accidentally hit the horn. Then she hurried away.

Malcolm had quit drinking after a DUI. He limited himself now to ten cups of coffee a day, a pack of American Spirits and two Red Bulls. Frank went through a 24-pack of Bud Light in just under a week, drank a little wine, and took the occasional Temazepam for his restless leg syndrome. He popped TUMS after every meal.

Because of love's recent anxieties, Corey had been given a prescription for Zoloft. He barely drank, except for an ale or two at the weekend. Andy smoked a little pot with her friends and liked mojitos. She still took Dexatrim when she thought she looked fat and drank Boost to supplement her tiny diet. She had gone off birth control pills when she thought she was a lesbian.

Angus smoked Camels and drank a fifth of Scoresby every couple of days. He maintained "a decent cellar" of budget wines under his bed and had not taken his lithium in months.

Lida Barfield drank bourbon and smoked Marlboros and the best quality Northern Lights or Kush. She had a pretty jewelry case in which she kept her pot, Xanax, Adderall, and Vicodin. Upon moving in to High Cotton, she placed this in the drawer of the bedside table along with several bottles of perfume and her vibrator.

Angus's clothes rack was a disappointment to her. She would use it, however, until he found the chifforobe she had requested. As Angus brought the last of the dresses in from her car she arranged them by color along the rack.

"Is that everything?" Angus asked. "No furniture?"

"Just the photograph." Lida pointed to a print of a canal in Venice.

Angus picked up the one huge, leather-bound book that comprised her library. "*The Anatomy of Melancholy*," he read aloud. "Heavy stuff for a young lady. You're reading this?"

"I'm not young, Angus. I'm nearly forty," Lida said. She looked at him, as if to a windswept graveyard. "That's an heirloom. The second volume remains, for now, with mother."

"I'm impressed," said Angus, "as I am by your choice of tipple." Lida had set a bottle of expensive bourbon beside the TV.

"Do you need a drink?"

"May I?"

"Help yourself. Pour me one. I have some glasses in that box."

"Do you need ice?"

"Absolutely. Three cubes."

Angus took the glasses next door to the kitchen and returned with ice. Lida hammered a nail into the wall with a single blow and hung the print.

"Lovely," said Angus. "That's a charming wee tool kit."

"Father gave it to me when I went off to college." Lida caught Angus off guard with a beatific smile as she took her drink. "Oh, Angus, thank you so much for all your help." She patted the bed. "Sit, sit," she said. "Sit by me."

She sat cross-legged on the pillow and sipped her drink.

"Here's to your new home." Angus switched his glass to his other hand and fished around in his pocket.

Lida watched him. "Is that a plastic finger?"

"A fortune cookie. Shall I read you—"

"No." Lida looked beyond Angus. "I know my fate."

Angus put the locket away. "What do you do exactly, Lida?" he asked, "for employment?"

"I'm trained as a nurse, but I only do that part time. I'm on call. Trauma ward. The real reason I'm here is to take care of my mother. She's in Hendersonville. I need to be close."

"Aye," Angus said. "Of course, you could be closer. Hendersonville, for example."

"Not that close. We have a complicated relationship."

Angus nodded. He was enjoying his drink, snuffling its fumes noisily.

"Mostly I work downtown at Olive to Eat Cheese."

"Huh?"

"It's a pun. Not the best. 'I live to eat cheese.' They sell olive oil and cheese."

"I know it. On the square."

"No. That one closed down. They sold balsamic vinegar and olives."

"You're an interesting creature, Ms. Barfield."

"I'm a survivor."

"Aren't we all?"

"No," she said. "I am a breast cancer survivor."

"Really?"

"Yes." She looked down at her cleavage in a consoling way.

"They seem fine."

"They are now." She lit a cigarette. "I should tell you that I'm allergic to cats."

"You should keep your door closed then, "Angus told her. "This place is infested with felines. How do you feel about the Chihuahua?"

"The Mexican dog? Why do you ask?"

"I've just rescued a pair from the wild. You'll see them about."

"Can something be done about the cats?"

"Not really. Frankie's fond of them. Personally, I share your doubts. I like cats as individuals but not as a race." Angus examined the bottom of his glass.

"Another?" Lida held out her own empty tumbler. "Fetch me one."

"Gladly, madam," Angus stopped at the table. "I was going to ask, it's nearly lunchtime. Would you like an introduction to the rest of the cast? The motley crew of this vessel?"

Lida gestured with her cigarette. "All in good time."

Corey knifed about the neighborhood on his road bike, trying to keep his mind on poetry. His frustration powered the climb of every hill until he was breathing hard and his mouth tasted of metal. Now and then he would stop, take off his helmet, and look helplessly around.

In the park children chased each other, yelping furiously. A retired couple played tennis, and a group of shirtless college students were knotted around a basketball hoop. It was hot and humid, but the sky was a single, construction-paper blue against the acid-green, scissor-sharp outline of the trees. A few birds dipped, black as ink, from one piece of shade to another. The only flowers on hand to prompt Corey's verse were the garish purple scribbles at the tips of the crepe myrtles. "This shit is hard," he said aloud. This repeated statement had spurred his ride so far, and it drove him on again. He put on his helmet and headed for the cemetery. Among the epitaphs, he recalled Angus's ability to find useful reference books at various thrift stores around town.

He followed Montford Avenue up to an old bookstore, where his search yielded a paperback, *On Love*, written by someone called Andreas Capellanus. It was all in a foreign language on one page, with English on the next, but Corey fell on a number of terse lines that had him nodding in agreement. "He who is troubled by the thoughts of love finds it harder to sleep and eat." "The person who is not jealous cannot love." "The true lover is preoccupied by a constant and unbroken picture of his beloved."

"Too fucking right," Corey agreed with this distant arbiter of chivalry. "Shit."

Impressed as he was by the *De Amore* translation, the bookstore's jumbled selection overwhelmed the poet-to-be. He put the book back on the shelf, went home, and looked up love poems on the internet.

Alone, without literary guidance, Corey settled on the first site combining love and poetry that came up in response to his search. On a screen crowded with ads, he studied the verse of recent contributors with names like Hawkswing, Aeni, and Ralph Erskins Sr. It amazed him how these people could find so many words that rhymed. The poetry was flanked with dozens of links to further pages with titles like "Kiss Types," "Cute and Sweet," "Love Recipes," and "Hot Cruises." Corey spent a long time on the site, his heart full of tender response. He printed one of the poems out, astonished by its craft.

A Perfect Pleasant Sunrise
By Erica

The first time that I saw your face,
A perfect pleasant sunrise
Came second in that age-old race
For beauty's highest prize.

When first I kiss'd your red, red lips
No confection could compare,
Nor could a rose's smell match this—
The fragrance of your hair.

You are the perfect man, you see?
A match meant oh so long ago.
Can you make this poor girl a we?
That's all I seek to know.

When Corey clicked on the author's name, her email address came up in his mail. Inspired, he wrote to her.

To: Erica62
Subject: I seek to know ☺
Dear Erica,
You are truly an awesome poetess. I read your poems and was like, damn. Honestly, I was so ready to steal your stuff but that would not be at all okay, right? So I am just going to learn from it and try and go with my own poetry from there. Any tips for a young man who just might be falling in love?
Thanks,
Corey Sullivan

Nine

On the other hand, there are perhaps an equal number of women who class all men as rotters.
—Herman H. Rubin MD, *Eugenics and Sex Harmony*

MALCOLM TOOK MAYBELLE JOLENE to the Mountain State Fair. Her shoebox diorama had won a ribbon and a place in the exhibition hall. She also wanted to see the pig races and the rodeo. They bought their tickets and took their place in the slow-moving crowd as it entered the fair, shuffling its way between the food vendors and the rides. Stragglers paused to consider pizza slices and turkey legs, then rejoined the herd, content in the knowledge that there would be pizza and turkey legs ahead.

Above the carnival, an evening sky fit for the End Times spanned the valley, a swathe of blood-stained gold with storm clouds dark to one side, emptying a distant deluge and silent lightning upon the mountains.

"Are you hungry yet?" Malcolm asked. It was Maybelle Jolene's suppertime.

She quickly shook her head at this weak attempt to distract her from the prizes but, after a few steps, realized an opportunity. She was wrong, she told her father. In fact, she was desperately hungry—close to death even. She clutched her belly. She pointed weakly.

"What is it?" said Malcolm.

When her father's ear was close enough, Maybelle Jolene whispered a plea for cotton candy.

"You know what your mama would say about that. You need some real food." He looked around. "Maybe later."

They pushed on. Their progress was aided by following the wake left by several heavily armed security guards who cleared a path through the crowd on their way to the human cannonball. Malcolm and Maybelle Jolene joined the ring surrounding the cannon. The projectile appeared at last, wearing a white jumpsuit with red and gold stars. He did some calisthenics and then picked up a microphone to explain his lineage. He had broken his father's record, he told them, and a leg once. The guards, with their black uniforms and black plastic-handled pistols, stood around the huge gun barrel looking serious.

"They're going to shoot him over there," explained Malcolm, "into that net."

"I'm not doing that," said Maybelle Jolene.

"It's not a ride, baby."

Maybelle Jolene was filled with fresh urgency as they entered the exhibition hall. She pulled Malcolm along by the hand, detailing her school project—the unexpected challenges, her teacher's curiosity, the childish failings of her schoolmates.

Shoebox dioramas filled one whole aisle. Most of the boxes, Malcolm noticed, were for men's work boots from the discount shoe store. Varying degrees of care had been taken in the depiction of each scene—the girls had chosen to mitigate the severe confines of a shoebox with comforting detail, while the boys' work captured in broad strokes the lively, fatal world that lie beyond the home.

A History of Saints

His daughter's diorama had won a pink rosette. The projects flanking her own showed crusaders storming a castle and an orange farmyard with tilted livestock. Maybelle Jolene had reproduced the culminating scene of the 1984 TV adaptation of *The Burning Bed*. Dollhouse furniture and PLAYMOBIL figures did not detract from her vivid depiction of an abuser's last moments. The little figure of Francine Hughes, as played by Farrah Fawcett, watched her plastic husband, wrapped in cotton wool smoke and paper flames, from a suitable distance, her face implacable under a luxuriant thatch of extra hair. Aside from the conflagration, the bedroom was cozy and well appointed.

"Your mom helped with this, right?"

"Nuh-uh," the artist shook her head. "I did it all. She didn't do nothing, 'cept tell me the story of the justice viable homicide. Ms. Pindle says Mama must have watched that movie at an impressionist age. Can we see the pigs with babies now?"

"Sure," said Malcolm. "Let's just take a look around first. It's a lot cooler in here."

The rules posted beside the vegetables stated that "unsightly or deteriorating displays will be removed at the discretion of fair management." As they wandered the aisles of produce, Malcolm tried to imagine the state of such evictees. The vegetables that remained were small and withered, their haggard forms outlined by paper plates, as though this were the first, proud crop to follow some apocalyptic drought. Two deteriorating carrots, thin as yellow pencils, rested together under a blue ribbon.

Unlike the guzzling parade waiting for them outside, these exhibits spoke of hard times. If the produce display was ominous, the flower arrangement aisles warned of far worse—as though a tornado had just howled through the steel barn, robbing every vase of all but a few battered stems. A single blade of ornamental grass, plastered to a glass bowl, had won "People's choice."

They looked at the photographs of foggy lakes and flowers, of insects in focus, and then at the wood carvings of Indian chiefs and old-timers with corncob pipes. Malcolm was stirred by the bitter struggle all around him. None of this had been easy. Life was hard, God knows. He knew that. He was reminded of weathered Okies, of dying hoboes and the protest songs of Woody Guthrie. Yes, this effort deserved ribbons and medals and rosettes. There was hope and courage in this tiny mutant gourd, that deflated pumpkin. Those squash might have been plucked in their infancy, but others would go on…

"Can we go now?" asked Maybelle Jolene. "I'm hungry."

Justice viable homicide?

Malcolm bought her a corn dog for supper, then a funnel cake and a bag of cotton candy as big as her body, then some Dippin' Dots and half a gallon of lemonade. She rode one of five ponies that trotted in a tight circle under a little tent; she became temporarily wedged in the humid fold of an inflatable dinosaur slide; she rose and fell, swooped and soared in a fiberglass elephant and a fiberglass bumble bee.

"I don't know, man," Malcolm told her as they watched a singer performing under a food tent. "If I'm not in Nashville next year, I might try this place."

"You can sing as well as him."

"Better, baby," said Malcolm. "Better. Don't play with those electric cables, honey."

"Can I have some more ice cream?"

"I think you've had enough."

"Puh-leeze," Maybelle Jolene's eyes were wild in her imploring face. "Please, please, please, please, please?"

Before they left, they visited the rodeo. Maybelle Jolene wove around her thoughtful parent, jabbering to herself about some girl at school, clasping her empty lemonade cup like a bucket clutched to her chest, noisy with ice. They watched the pretty teenagers in cowboy gear galloping around, now under a clear night sky, with Old Glory and the Stars and Bars fluttering above them. Twice Malcolm had to stop his daughter from climbing into the ring.

On the drive back Malcolm started to sing as words came into his head, "*Rodeo girl, rodeo girl, ride my way, be my pearl.*"

"That's good, Dad!" screamed Maybelle Jolene. "That's super good! I want to be a rodeo girl. Please, Dad, please, can I be a rodeo girl?"

"Ride your horse toward me now, forget your job, ignore that cow."

Maybelle Jolene clapped her hands, cackling with frenzied delight.

Corey received a prompt reply from Erica62

To: mtnbikerboarder
Subject: Re: I seek to know ☺

Dear Corey,

I would be happy to help you with your poetry. How nice to be young and in love. Who is the lucky girl? I wish you all the best in your courtship, but don't be surprised if it doesn't work out. Life is not all roses—or maybe I should say that with every rose comes that mean old prickledy stem. Tell me something about yourself. Are you tall? I am having trouble imagining you. What do you do for a living? I see you are sensitive, but I am guessing yours is honest toil? Do you work every day in the great outdoors, using only your strong hands? Ask me anything you want about poetry, or, indeed, life. It is possible I am older than you suspect, despite the youthful voice of my sonnetry, but age is only a number, and in my heart I am still a swooning maiden. Corey, do not despair if your exquisite verse falls upon a silly, deaf ear, for the oceans teem with bright and silver fish.

Your guide in love,
Erica

A little confused, Corey wrote back.

Thanks, Erica.

I totally appreciate your help. I am six foot one and still in school. I did do some landscaping work for my uncle one time. I don't think Andy has a hearing problem, but I am going to write a poem anyway and send it to you to check it out if that's okay? I was afraid it would just be way too gay to do stuff like this, but you have to speak from the heart, right?

Thanks for your help.
Corey

As Andy was leaving, a dusty Mustang pulled up abruptly alongside her VW Bug. Andy waved politely. Her new roommate got out of her car, collected her shoulder bag, and came over to Andy's open window. "Lida Barfield," she said, taking Andy's hand while appraising the tall girl in the little car.

"Lied about what?"

"That's my name. Lida."

"Oh yes," Andy smiled. "I'm Andy. Nice to meet you. Do you need any help moving in?"

Lida traced a stray hair away from her forehead. "That's kind," she said, "but it's all done. Angus helped me. I have very few possessions."

"Me, too! It makes life like, so easy."

"I have been that way since the Balkans," said Lida.

"Is that where you're from?"

"No," said Lida. She looked past Andy to examine the contents of Andy's car. "I like your bag."

"Thanks. Yours is awesome."

"It's a copy but a good one."

"Are you an actress?" Andy asked Lida.

"That is a charming notion. No, I am a nurse, a nurse of heroes. I work at the VA. Trauma ward."

"That is such a good thing to do," said Andy.

"You are quite pretty," said Lida in a clinical manner.

"I cannot compare to you," Andy protested, noticing Lida's odd effect on her speech.

"I have a necklace you should have," Lida told her. "It belonged to my grandmother. It would suit your coloring." She ignored Andy's protestations. "Come by my rooms upon your return." She turned on her heel and left. Andy watched her go, not even sure for a moment why she was still sitting in her car.

Julyan Davis

After Corey completed his poem, he emailed it to Erica for her to critique. To his surprise she did not reply. He sent another message to check that she had received the first. She wrote nothing back. It made him sad. Now he was full of doubt about his efforts. He went back to the poetry website and decided to contact Ralph Erskins Sr. on the matter. He was pleased to see Mr. Erskins was the day's featured poet.

Haiku for Basho
By Ralph Erskins Sr.

Please come back, Pickle.
You were right, okay? Suitcase
In the dead of night.

The title of the new poem was strange, but Corey liked its punchy brevity.

To: ralphsr
Subject: I need help!

Dear Mr. Erskins Sr.,
My name is Corey Sullivan. Can I send you a poem I wrote for this girl to see what you think about it? Or if I should just give up on this poetry idea? I need help from a real expert.
Thanks, Corey

Frank and Juan waited in the buffet line behind Mrs. Reed. Frank's aunt carefully jostled a pork chop toward her already crowded plate, cajoling the reluctant meat along with a few gentle words. Frank put a hand on her thin, folded back. "You need some help there?"

It was Sunday, and the cafeteria was packed with the church crowd. Behind them a tall, overweight family—a line of great bowling pins—watched this delay with the same impatient, ancestral head. Although he had smiled at them and nodded his sympathy, Frank's attempt to speed things along prompted no flicker of gratitude. Genetics had sculpted thin, identical lips onto each jowly face. Fresh from worship, they scowled upon the old woman and the Mexican in front of them.

"These are so good." Mrs. Reed smiled at her nephew. "GOOD," she told Juan.

Mrs. Reed's invalid husband waited with his brother and Frank's cousin at the table. Frank took his aunt's bony fingers in one hand and Juan's coarse grasp in the other. They bowed their heads.

"Lord, we just ask your blessing on this food," said Frank's cousin, "and thank you for bringing Frank down to see us. And his friend here. We thank you, Lord. Amen."

"I should break a hip more often," Frank's Uncle Jim said from his wheelchair. "Guess that's what it takes for a body to get noticed."

Frank appreciated the brevity of the prayer. When he was a child, listening to the litany of requests that began each meal, he imagined Christ going all around the world like an attentive waiter, summoned from table to table, taking orders. Frank still wanted someone to push out a chair for the poor guy. Had anyone ever thought to do that? Ask Him to join them, "Hey, take a weight off, Lord. What can we pass You?"

Frank's family ate in studious silence. Eating, especially for his parent's generation, with their childhood glimpse of the Great Depression, was serious work. They chewed thoughtfully, slowly making headway through their piled plates. The TV in the corner showed a hurricane bearing down on Galveston, interspersed with chaos on Wall Street.

Finally, Frank's Uncle Jerry spoke. "Now don't go making that thing so steep Jim gets to kill himself going down it," he told Frank. "Don't build it flat, neither. Ramp has to be to code, pass code."

Frank's job was almost done, but Jerry was still giving this direction. He came by each day to stand beside his handicapped brother under the shade of the pines, the two of them throwing out observations as Frank and Juan sweated in the sun.

"Well, I think it looks just fine," said his aunt. "How's your house coming along, Frank?"

They all knew what Carolina Court meant to Frank. Once, when his mom was still alive, he brought down a photo album, showing the house before and after his renovations. There was even a newspaper clipping and a photocopy of an award from the Preservation Society. His family was unimpressed. They were happy to live in modest ranch homes, surrounded by austere lawns decorated with machine parts and retired cars. To them, Frank's intricate porches and flower beds looked like a lot of work.

"It's good," said Frank. "Got a couple of strays now. Chihuahuas."

"Chihuahuas?" Uncle Jim shook his head.

Frank's aunt beamed. "Those your little dogs, Juan?"

Frank was glad his family had accepted Juan, but he wasn't surprised. On his own the Mexican posed no threat, and as a visitor he deserved their hospitality. His parents would have done the same. For his relatives, there was no reason fellowship and prejudice couldn't flourish side by side. They were as eager to help a stranger as they were to build fences. Division offered solace.

"Used enough wood on that ramp," Uncle Jerry complained.

"Cain't use too much wood," said Frank's cousin. He nodded at Frank.

"Can too," said Uncle Jerry.

A History of Saints

Frank searched for a reply in the silence that followed. "A termite will eat pressure-treated wood," he said.

They all looked at him. Juan took a sip of iced tea.

"Yup," said Frank. "If they have to. I mean, if there's nothing else around. Termite guy told me."

"This some Asheville termite guy?" Uncle Jerry was skeptical. "Don't matter anyway. Chemicals'll kill 'em. Make them sterile, for sure. Just bugs…"

Mrs. Reed laid her hand on Jerry's arm. "Well now, Frank and his friend will just come back and build Jim another ramp if this one gets eaten up. You'd do that, wouldn't you, Frank?"

Jerry snorted.

"Absolutely." Frank turned to Juan. He made a nibbling gesture with one hand and a ramp gesture with the other. "If termita eat ramp, we come back, build another." He worked an invisible hammer. "Okay?"

Juan looked at Frank carefully, then at the tiny old man in the wheelchair with the skin cancer bandage across his bald head.

"You'd come back, wouldn't you, Juan?" said Frank's aunt.

Frank's cousin stopped eating to watch Juan.

Uncle Jim stared at the Mexican, his eyes wide with abject hope, as if Juan's alien approval here, now, on this Sunday, might work such a miracle of longevity. Even Jerry seemed relieved to see him nod.

To: mtnbikerboarder
Subject: Re: I need help!

Corey,
How you doing, kiddo? I didn't expect to hear from any guys off this site, but that's okay.

How long do you think my nose is, son? Nah, just kidding, that's swell! I'll play Cyrano for you (ha ha). Send your verbiage along and I'll get the chainsaw out! Smart thinking BTW, the dames go wild when they open up that purple prose. See here though, once you send the first you better keep writing.

Glad you like the old doggerel from this aged poetaster! I got a taste of the bard killing time in the navy (and what did I see, I saw the sea!) Rhyme and meter run through this old tar's veins. I'm on my seventh book of poetry and it's all Jap stuff right now.

Right, left, right, boom, boom. Those sweet little haikus will have your girl up against the ropes. Seventeen syllables and she's yours. Sounds like you're a sonnet man, though, right? Starry-eyed buck like yourself? Well, of course you are! Let's run this flag up the pole and see what the gal thinks.

Yours in ink,
Ralph

If Erica's reply had been confusing, this was incomprehensible. After reading it several times, though, he decided that Mr. Erskins was not rejecting his request. He sent Ralph his poem with thanks.

Ten

Qui non zelat amare non potest.
(The person who is jealous cannot love.)
—Andreas Capellanus, *On Love*

Having discovered where Andy now lived, Emily followed a related line of inquiry to The Goddess Temple. The temple was a shabby green house in West Asheville, with a screened front and a rusted camper van in the driveway. Emily picked her way over a scattering of building materials that had decorated the front yard for a decade. A toilet bowl had been turned into a flowerpot, and a few boards had been rearranged to hold dirt for some dead vegetables.

The shrine was populated by never less than four, often transient, goddesses, one of whom, Andy's friend Tansie, answered the door. She was pinch-eyed and still in her pajamas. "Oh hey," she said.

Emily nodded and followed her into the house. The little home, for so long noisy with the blue-collar family that built it, was quiet this morning, the only sound the little trickle from a tabletop fountain. Emily loathed the temple, but she needed information. Although she fearlessly defended her sexual orientation and her subsequent disavowal of

Catholicism, wearing these decisions like armor through the world, Emily shared the unyielding moral code of her Sicilian grandmother.

Tansie led her to the kitchen. Oriental rugs and saffron pillows were scattered through the house, while complicated odors fought for cultural dominance. The kitchen doubled as a greenhouse and laundry room. Herbs in pots crowded the shelves around the washer and dryer, pressing themselves against the filthy windows. Emily looked around, her face white and her lips a pressed red line, while Tansie made tea for them both.

Tansie's lower back was partially exposed. Emily noticed a helpless, innocent mole satellite to a blue tattoo. Emily didn't like body art. She felt Andy had desecrated her perfect white body with that tattoo of a stupid unicorn with leaves seemingly growing out of its stupid, goddamn ears.

"Would you like a cookie?" Tansie asked.

Emily shook her head.

Tansie gave her a smile. "Let's sit in here," she suggested. They went into the front room. Aside from a brick fireplace with a wood stove, any sign of the cozy parlor it had once been was gone. The goddesses had pulled up the carpeting and painted the floorboards pink.

Tansie arranged herself on a large pillow while Emily hunkered down on a low stool, her black boots unforgiving beside Tansie's bare feet.

"Have you heard from her?" Tansie asked.

"No," Emily said.

"I'm sorry."

"Is Gina still here?"

"Uh-huh. I think she's upstairs, unless she went out."

"Has she heard from Andy?"

"Gina?" Tansie was surprised. "I don't think so. Do they know each other?"

"She was here that time Andy and I came 'round," said Emily. "She was flirting with Andy the whole time."

"Really?"

"Really."

"I thought you said Andy wasn't gay anymore."

"No," said Emily with loud exhaustion. "She just said that to get out of being with me. She's totally gay."

"We're all bi here," Tansie assured her.

"Yeah, yeah," said Emily.

"You can be really judgmental sometimes, Emily. D'you know that?"

Emily looked over at a dance pole and a disco ball in the corner. She rolled her eyes.

"These cookies are really good. Are you sure you don't want one?"

"Can I smoke in here?" Emily asked.

"Please!" Tansie protested.

"Okay, sorry. It's just like, there are ashtrays everywhere."

"Those aren't ashtrays. Those are for the hookahs."

Emily was about to say nothing when she heard sounds above them.

"That's probably Gina now," said Tansie. "She has to take Toby out."

Emily watched the ceiling.

"There's nothing between her and Andy," Tansie assured Emily. "I'd know."

Emily made her hissing sound. "So how's it going anyway?" she asked. "The 'temple'?"

"Actually, it's been kind of slow," Tansie said cheerfully, "but a friend is going to make a better website, and Matt is going to start teaching classes."

"You have a guy in here?"

"Oh yeah. He's awesome. He's a tantric master."

"And he's bi, too?"

"I don't know. Probably."

"Right," said Emily.

A goddess came down the stairs, followed by a large, saggy dog. Toby wobbled down the steps with the dexterity of an old table. "Hey," Gina waved, recognizing Emily. "I'm just taking Toby outside. He needs to use the bathroom."

"Yeah?" said Emily. "Well, maybe Toby can just hold it for right now."

Toby stopped. The dog stared at Emily and Tansie through the stair rails, the sound of his labored breathing filling the room. He made his way down to one of Emily's boots and gave it a lick.

"Toby's pretty old," said Gina.

"It looks like his hips are shot," said Emily. "Have you heard from Andy?"

"Who?"

"Andromeda."

"Oh," said Gina. "Oh yeah, I heard you guys broke up."

"Where d'you hear that? From her?"

"Maybe."

"Maybe?"

"I can't remember."

"Or you just don't want to say?"

Gina wasn't really awake, but the tension was too much for Tansie. "She hasn't been here, Emily! We don't know anything!"

Emily stood up. Toby got out of her way just as quickly.

"Who's she with now?" Emily barked.

"We don't know who she's with!" Tansie cried. "We haven't seen her!"

"She hasn't been here," confirmed Gina, at last aware of the interrogation.

"So she is with someone else now," said Emily slowly. "If she comes back…if she comes back here, what are you going to do?"

The goddesses didn't understand. Nor did Toby. Tansie squirmed on the silk pillow.

"You're going to call me. That's what you're going to do."

Frank circled his tired eyes several times with his fingers. "Well," he asked Angus, "are you going to at least introduce me?"

"It was top of my list. As soon as I can catch her—the girl's hardly ever here. She's a mystery. Furtive, even."

"Great."

"In a good way, mind. Low maintenance. Except for this chifforobe thing."

"Chifforobe thing?"

"It's a kind of wardrobe."

"Yes," said Frank. "I know."

"She has an unusual turn of phrase," said Angus. "As it turns out, High Cotton has a wee shortage of closet space. In the time being, I will find luxuries to placate her."

"Okay, well…"

"How was the coast? I hope you took Juan to the beach. *Todo el mundo amore la playa, non?*"

"Angus, I really appreciate all the—"

"Say no more, Frankie…"

"Can we just take a break for now? Now we've got girls and dogs and every space filled?"

Angus indicated Carolina Court with his arms. "Stillness, calm, *dunkelheit*. Your home is fully stocked and making you money."

"Did you collect a check for me?"

Angus fished about in his shirt pocket for a folded check and presented it to Frank. "That's for the first month and the deposit together."

"She's paying this much?"

"It's by far the finest accommodation on the property, as you're well aware."

"Well, okay," said Frank, surprised to realize his mortgage would now be more than covered with the addition of this monthly income. "Thank you, Angus."

To: mtnbikerboarder
Subject: Re: I need help

Corey,
Your poem had some good stuff in it, kiddo. I made a few changes, tightened some of it up, but you can pick and choose what you want. Lucky gal- it's clear you've got the hots for her. One thing, you're sure she's into that kind of stuff? I've seen a thing or two and all's fair in love and war, but you might want to slow it down a little. Just a thought. Let me know how it goes, Romeo,
In ink,
Ralph

Again, Corey was confused. Did anyone like camping anymore? Mr. Erskins was probably too old, Corey decided. He downloaded the attachment and was pleased with many of the alterations his new mentor had made. The poem was much shorter than Corey's first version, but he liked the new format.

Angus moved with ease through his natural habitat—the untidy stalls of his favorite thrift store, Junque U Like. He pushed a shopping cart in case he made an important discovery for himself, but he was there to find something for Lida. The dogs rode in the cart.

There was a lot of vintage clothing in the market, but Angus moved past this. He stopped at a salt and pepper shaker set fashioned after a pair of once brightly colored mushrooms. There was a lamp with a Cherokee maiden as its base. Angus picked it up and showed it to the dogs. In the next booth he smiled at a small oil painting by a local artist—an intensely blue mermaid was draped like an anchovy filet over some rocks, the sun setting behind her and a tiny, doomed ship entering the scene from the left. Angus put it in the cart.

On a crowded dressing table, he spied something else that made him nod with satisfaction and added this to his purchases. In a booming, butchered Jamaican accent he sang to the Chihuahuas, "*I carry mi ackee, go a Linstead Market, not a quattie worth sell! Lawd, what a night, not a bite, what a Saturday night!*" The dogs watched him for a moment, then looked out over the startled shoppers as though the serenade made absolute sense.

On his trip Frank had time to reflect on his years of growing inertia. When labor was scarce his casual approach to work had been tolerated but not anymore. Competition was suddenly keen. He had returned ready to work harder, only to find that with the renting of High Cotton—and at the steep rent Angus had somehow wrangled for it—he might be able to survive almost exclusively as a landlord.

Still, a twinge, a niggling urge toward self-improvement remained. Should he go back to school? Many of his friends and neighbors were retraining for new careers, seemingly all in medicine, as though the future world would be one great, strange hospital and healthcare the single economy—nurses and doctors and orderlies changing shifts with their patients at a given hour, disrobing as the lame and diabetic rose from their beds to switch their gowns for scrubs.

No, the idea of learning about all those drugs and bones was impossible to Frank. He was wary of education. It was expensive, and his own, convoluted studies at college had led to nothing useful, unless a degree in wildlife management had made him better than most at feeding strays.

He decided instead to focus on the house. With this new income, he could make the last repairs and finish painting the place. In the meantime, he would tighten his belt and get through these slow times. There was a problem he could also address. It was hard for Frank to tighten his belt. He had put on a lot of weight over the summer.

If there was to be a midlife metamorphosis, a reinvention of Frank Reed, it should be that. Angus, of course, had volunteered his help—with his dusty medical manuals and global cooking, but it was hard to take nutritional advice from him. The Scot was not trim and ate in a random and foraging way. Angus shopped at a store that sold only goods on the brink of their sell-by date or in cans and packaging disfigured by the travails of shipping—fierce sauces from Indonesia, canisters of rejected chicory coffee, Korean noodle bowls, a sack of freckled bananas, or a rare boon of lychees.

Still, Frank conceded that Angus had a point about his eating habits. And he had the example of Andy and Corey, too,

A History of Saints

who both made a quiet religion of their diet. They shopped at Halcyon Meadows, the supermarket where Malcolm busked and where Lakeisha and Geezer had grazed in their wilderness days. Frank wondered how his young tenants could afford it. The place was expensive—a tithe to be paid for moral affirmation, for a precious extension of mortality. As customers considered salmon cakes from Finland and cheeses shipped from Tuscany, signs everywhere assured them they were saving the Earth with paper sacks and organic wine.

Summer was turning to fall. Frank set a goal to lose the extra weight by Christmas. Somewhere around the house was a plastic thing to maximize the efficacy and discomfort of sit-ups. Frank hunted it down and found in his search a set of small dumbbells and a Pilates tape. It was a start. He made a list to take to Halcyon Meadows. Apples were a good idea. Bananas, too. Wasn't there some chart about a food triangle and color in your diet? Blueberries providing the best source of blue food?

As the house was quiet, he put the exercise tape in the VCR. He found a yogurt in the fridge and sat with several cats on the sofa to watch the pounding introduction to the Pilates routine—tanned young men and women pouring into a studio gym, ecstatic to be involved.

Julyan Davis

Andy found a single sheet of printed paper slipped beneath her door.

All Tied Up

Bright galaxy, you interest me,
Hiding away and yet so close. Oh,
Yes! I watch you come and go,
I know it shows.

Under the stars the two of us might lie,
Watching the flight of a shooting star
Naturally in separate tents, but sharing the same
Mind frame.

A change is good, always for the better
Without change, life can seem the same.
Is it time for you to take that path once more?
Through a new door?

You are an intellectual humanoid,
Beautiful and wise in your quiet ways,
Kind to animals, I notice and see.
Be kind to me.

I'm tied to you! What can I do
With these? Were they a gift
To let me tie you up? If you want me to
I'll capture you.

Then I could take you on a trip,
And you might struggle at first.
I could drive until you felt the same
And there was no blame.

Don't run from your new home,
Off to some place you can't be seen.
Don't say, "I'm sorry, this can never be."
My heart is tied to you, you see?

Andy read this, then carefully read it again. She shook her head. "Oh, Emily," she said aloud. "I guess you found me." She sat down on her bed and cradled the Georgia Bulldogs bear, but slowly her sympathy faded. This would have to be discussed with Leaf Pringle. Emily needed help. Things had gone too far. Andy got up and hurried to the window. Was she being watched even now? She tore up the poem and seized her phone to text her stalker, *Now u r putting poems undr my door? R u serious?*

Eleven

Every owner dreams of a free Chi, but who wants to find their little rascal smoking in a corner beside a chewed electrical cord? The Chi whines from the playpen, "Let me out." The loving owner says, "Safety first, madam."

—USAF Colonel Rex Marigold, Little Body, Big Spirit: Living with the Chihuahua

A<small>NGUS TOOK APART</small> the corral on the front porch, taking care to retrieve each screw. Whistling cheerfully, he worked with unusual precision. Any observer would have guessed this just another morning in the life of a professional small dog corral man. He wrote numbers and arrows and words like, *LEFT UPRIGHT*, on each post, before setting them to one side by the roll of chicken wire.

Lakeisha watched all this steadily. Angus noticed her attention. "Incarceration needs to be a known reality," he reminded her, "for us all. This can be quickly reassembled, 'Keishy." Resuming his whistling, he slipped the screws into a sandwich bag and taped this to one of the posts. In a near-transparent hand, he wrote *Dog Corral* on the sandwich bag. He sat the strange package in a chair.

"At last," said Frank, padding outside with a cup of coffee. "Thank you, Angus." He examined the silver mummy of the dismantled jail. "'DO' what?" he read.

"Would you have room for that in your basement?" Angus asked.

"Not right now," said Frank.

"Then I'll add it to the yard sale!" Angus clicked his fingers at Lakeisha. "You like that idea, don't you, lassie?"

Frank and Juan had returned to learn that Juan's mother, back in Juarez, was ill. The news catalyzed Angus. At once he had suggested a yard sale to raise money for the cause.

Frank's first inclination was to protest, but it then occurred to him that the event might help clear out his tenant's room. It might even succeed in earning a little for his friend's mother. "They'll be fighting over that," he observed, "but only if you label it better."

Angus looked at Frank. His bloodshot eyes widened. "I'm a fool," he laughed. He picked up a box cutter and started to cut open the package.

"What?" Frank asked, like a man questioning the weather.

"Signposts, Frankie, for the sale! There's enough in here for every street corner."

Andy watched Lida Barfield sort through her luggage. Tops and pants were hauled out to receive the most cursory glance, then tossed onto the bed. Despite the praise Andy gave each article of clothing, Lida's expression suggested that her search was rewarded with soiled sackcloth, stuffed into her suitcases by lepers in the dead of night.

"I love that!" cried Andy.

"Take it," said Lida, as though the tiny top would fit the other girl.

"Oh, I can't," Andy protested. She held up the necklace she had just received. "You're too generous already."

"Nonsense," Lida cast the blouse aside. "If I was to make a list of all the shit I've given away—clothes, furniture, sunglasses, cars, even—it would go on forever. You tell yourself you're in love and yet," she made a silent movie gesture to encompass her print of Venice and weighty Jacobean tome, "what do I have to show for it?"

Andy made a sympathetic noise.

At last Lida found something she liked. She pressed it to herself, modeling the dress for Andy. "I wore this in Cologne. It was Eric's favorite. He said I looked chic. He tried so hard to impress me, to impress the world. Just another poor, dumb jarhead full of dreams. Gone now, of course. But enough about me. Tell me about you, Angie."

"Actually, it's Andy. It's short for Andromeda."

"Andromeda?" Lida considered this. "That's not bad. I like that."

Andy laughed. "There's nothing much to say about me. I got here about a year ago. I'm from Augusta. I want to be a dancer if I can."

"Aren't you too tall?" Lida put the dress on a hanger, pursing her lips with revulsion as she was forced to hang it on Angus's clothes rack.

"I guess."

"You don't want to look like a bull in a china shop, do you? No, you should be a model. Hasn't anyone suggested that to you?"

"Maybe, but this is Asheville, y'know. Anyway, I'm too old now." Andy studied the necklace, feeling a little downcast. Lida's bovine simile was a blow, unmitigated by the compliment that followed it.

"How old are you?"

"Twenty-five."

"Well, I'm sure you will succeed. You are very pretty, and this town is full of stinky, hippy girls with no idea how to dress. Do you have a man in your life, Angie?"

"No," said Andy. She didn't want to talk about Emily. She was haunted by the image of her ex searching the hallways of

Carolina Court, poetry in hand, checking each door until she had guessed Andy's room. It was terrible to imagine. Andy had never hurt anyone before. This new side of her was too much to bear. Lida was right, she was like a bull in a china shop—a great, thoughtless cow creature, breaking people's hearts.

Frank emptied the brown paper grocery bag and looked at his lunch. In Halcyon Meadows he had spent a full hour wandering from aisle to aisle, mystified. Where he usually shopped you could get meat and two vegetables, a biscuit or cornbread for under five dollars. Not at Halcyon Meadows. The preprepared food here was much more expensive and difficult to match into a simple meal. Each dish seemed dedicated to a different nationality's cuisine. At either side, ladies in exercise gear or business suits were ordering tiny portions of this and that, as though supermarkets had always been this way. Frank came away with some spinach leaves, an exotic version of potato salad, and a single salmon cake. To supplement this tiny meal, he had bought a round loaf studded with every kind of healthy seed. At no extra charge they had dropped this into a slicing machine. Frank was eating one of the little circular end pieces that resulted, when Geezer and Lakeisha trotted into the room, followed by Angus.

"What have you got there?" Angus descended upon the loaf.

"Bread."

Angus helped himself to a larger slice from the center. "May I?"

Frank nodded. "Did you make those?" he asked. The Chihuahuas were sporting decorative jackets.

"I did," Angus talked through a mouthful. "They're not finished. This is a trial run solely to judge comfort. They'll need these soon enough. There's no winter in their native habitat."

"Really? I thought it could get cold down there in the desert."

"Not like here. Of course, there's a great range of clothing available for the smaller breeds, but it's bloody expensive. These are actually made from wee little T-shirts for infants."

"They fit quite well."

"Hardly, but that can all be adjusted."

"What kind of paint is that on the shirts?"

"Household paint. In your basement. D'you not recognize the colors?" Angus pointed at Geezer. "The downstairs john?"

"Those paints are still good?"

"Some." Angus took another slice. "Are you going to eat that salmon cake?"

"Yes." Frank sat down and drew his little servings about him.

Angus picked up Lakeisha, then looked at his hand. "I should have used a hair dryer," he said, wiping his fingers on his pants. "I could have tried to paint these damn things before I put them on the doggies, but in cases like this, it's always easier to paint the costume filled. Think of the Ballets Russes, if you will."

"Okay," Frank parried the suggestion. "Do those marks mean anything?"

"Nothing," said Angus. "They're primitive hieroglyphs, nothing more. Are you trying to starve yourself to death, Frankie?"

"I'm trying to lose some weight."

"Good man. You could shed a pound or two."

Corey was losing weight fast. As days passed, and there was no response from Andy to his poem, he became more and more troubled. Her unchanged sunniness toward him was confusing. How do girls respond when they receive love poetry? Perhaps the camping references had put her off? Camping wasn't for everybody. Ralph Erskins Sr. clearly had doubts about it, and Andy already told him she didn't like sleeping on rocks. He hadn't listened. He was a fool. He guessed that she had decided to ignore the whole thing and that her usual sweetness was just her way of showing appreciation for his futile gesture.

One morning, however, he saw Andy looking sad as she prepared her simple breakfast of herbal tea and a handful of goji berries. Her sigh gave him both hope and new concern.

"Are you okay?" he asked.

"Have you ever destroyed a human being?"

Corey stared at her.

"I mean like, completely?"

After a moment's panic, something told the young man this wasn't a critique of his lyric verse. Corey took a breath. Here was a chance to show his moral temper. "Destroying people is totally not cool, Andy. It's super negative behavior."

"I know."

Emily stood in a bush. She lit another cigarette. "Big mistake," she said. "Big mistake, Miss Andromeda Megan Bell."

From the shrubbery she could see Andy's car. A glint of sunlight on the windshield was blinding. Even the sun was against her, thought Emily. To add to this celestial sabotage, birds kept landing on the ugly branch that already obscured her view—stupid birds with stupid faces, throwing back their heads to sing for no damn reason at all. Beyond these annoyances rose Carolina Court, its windows steely with the same unkind light. And behind one of those windows sat Andy, holding hands with her lover, the two of them laughing, no doubt—laughing between passionate kisses—at silly little Emily Nazario.

So they were exchanging poetry, were they? Andy's accidental text, clearly meant for her new lover, had given Emily all the evidence she needed. It also confirmed the little she'd been able to extract from those dumb goddesses over in West Asheville. How long had this been going on, she wondered. Perhaps Andy knew this big, old house pretty well already. Maybe she'd been sneaking over to see this girl for months, dreaming of when she could ditch crazy Emily, move into some fancy mansion with… A squirrel paused on the branch, directly in front of her face. The rodent stared at her. Emily flicked her cigarette at this new outrage.

Stupid birds with stupid faces

Frank sat on a shady bench, reading the paper. The twitching of a cat tail was a distant movement—the hopping of a mockingbird along the fence rail another. The door to High Cotton was closed and its occupant still a mystery, but not a disconcerting one. She was a private creature, thought Frank, and he admired her wish to be left alone. He would meet her in due time. The dog corral was gone and the dogs dressed for winter. All was well with the world.

Andy sauntered past. She waved at Frank.

"Is that good exercise?" he pointed at the yoga mat under her arm.

"Totally," she smiled. "It doesn't just stretch you out, it's awesome for toning."

Frank could see for himself the truth in these two claims.

"Is it expensive?"

"That's what's so cool," said Andy. "The classes are all free. You can leave a few bucks if you want, but you don't have to. I guess it's a kind of service for the community, maybe, because there is just like, such a high density of yoga teachers in this area."

"That's cool. Is there a class for beginners?"

"Uh-huh," Andy nodded. "'New to yoga,' 'Slow flow,' stuff like that."

Frank patted his midriff. "And I could start to lose this?"

Andy frowned. "You might need 'Crunch' or 'Bikram' for that." She offered to take Frank to a class.

"Maybe I should just go on my own to start. You stick to the advanced stuff."

"Awesome," said Andy. "I'll get you a list of classes." She continued on her beatific way.

A little while later a young woman entered the courtyard.

"Well, hey!" said Frank, rising from his seat in the shadows. "We finally meet," he smiled. "I'm Frank."

The girl was clearly spooked by his sudden appearance. Frank sought to reassure her. "Your room okay?" he asked.

She said nothing.

"High Cotton? You settling in?"

Emily nodded carefully. In case she ran into anyone at Carolina Court, she had prepared a cover story—a search for a friend living somewhere on the street. She was not ready for this, though. All at once Emily was in a deeper, unrehearsed subterfuge. Two curious cats advanced on her. She watched them circle her legs.

"Angus said you had some allergies?"

"No," said Emily. "Not really." This was a mess. She stood frozen, resisting an urge to run.

"Well," said Frank. "Okay then. You just let me know if you need anything."

"Thanks," said Emily. Was she now expected to enter the house? She could see three possible doors. She needed an excuse to leave. At once. With her luck so far, Emily guessed Andy had likely forgotten something and would join them at any minute.

Poor girl, Frank was thinking, no wonder she keeps to herself, she's a nervous wreck. She looked unkempt, too, hardly what Angus had described. Were those black smudges on her face?

Emily tucked her shirt into her pants. This guy thinks I live here, she told herself. Make the most of that, Nazario. Christ, maybe he thinks I'm the bitch Andy's seeing? "Is Andy around?" she began. "Andromeda?"

"She just left for yoga," Frank said. "You two hitting it off?"

"She seems nice," said Emily.

"I'm sure she likes having you around."

"Yeah?" Here was a lead.

"Well, y'know," said Frank. "Feminine energy." He sounded like Angus now. "Kind of balances things out."

Emily thought carefully about what to ask next. "I think we could become close friends," she said. "Maybe we already are?"

She wiped her nose. There were a number of sooty fingerprints around her face, and this act drew half a cavalier moustache across her upper lip. (Emily had come directly from her struggle to put out the fire her cigarette had started in a neighbor's leaf pile.)

"Cool," said Frank. The girl's searching tone was confusing.

"You know, like the way we do stuff together all the time? Hang out together?"

"Yeah," said Frank. "Well, that'd be cool, right?" Was his new tenant another lunatic?

Something brushed his leg. He looked down and saw an immensely small lion. He looked again. It was Speck, the tiniest of the long-haired cats. Apart from the face and neck, her entire body had been shaved. From the center of a circular mane, her tiny features gazed up at him, tolerant, trusting, newly alien. "Oh for Christ's sake," he groaned.

Emily took her chance. She gestured back to the street. "I forgot something." She hurried from the courtyard.

Frank found Angus upstairs on the internet, investigating boar hunting and traditional culinary preparations of wild pig. Angus was sitting in the doorway, his desk holding open the door to the choked room, pressed by his recent purchases to become the unavoidable sentinel of the staircase. The hair trimmer from Junque U Like was lying beside the computer. Frank held out the cat. "Is this you?"

"The wee creature quite enjoyed it," said Angus, tapping Speck on the head. "He'll certainly stay cool now."

"She. It's nearly fall, Angus."

Angus thought about this. He tapped Speck on the head again, *"Born free, as free as the wind blows..."*

"Don't do this again, not ever. Not even in the spring, okay?"

"I could make her a jacket...," Angus began.

"Please, just leave her alone. Leave all the cats alone."

The Chihuahuas, sturdy in their painted suits, lay camouflaged against the clothing that littered Angus's room. They watched Frank as he gestured with the tiny, shaved cat.

"The act was merely a gift for Lida, Frankie," said Angus, "to control the cat hair situation."

"Oh," said Frank. "I just met her, by the way. No problem with cats. Completely nuts, maybe, but no problem with cats."

"Isn't she fascinating?"

Frank resisted a desire to confiscate the trimmer on the desk between them. "That can go in your yard sale," he said.

"Really? It still works, Frankie."

Twelve

So, on the other side, many a young lovely maid will cast herself upon an old, doting, decrepid dizzard...if he hath land or money.
—Robert Burton, *The Anatomy of Melancholy*

Perplexed and uncertain, Corey returned from a lengthy bike ride past twisted trees and glittering rivers. As he bounded upstairs in his orange Lycra suit, he glimpsed Malcolm in his room. "Hey, man," he called out. "Can I show you something?"

"Sure," said Malcolm. "What you got?"

Corey went to his room and returned with a copy of his poem. He took a precarious seat on an amplifier to await the musician's opinion.

Malcolm read the poem, squinted a little, read the last stanzas again. "That's cool, man," he said. "I didn't know she was into that stuff."

"Camping? Yeah, that was my first mistake." He blinked and took a nervous swig from his water bottle.

"I mean like, bondage, kinky stuff."

Corey blinked again. His mouth fell open and all the water inside spilled out over his knees. "Unnnnhh," he said. A wave of comprehension toppled him from the speaker. "Gaaaah," he added from the floor.

"He's going to be sick," said Maybelle Jolene.

"You okay, man?" Malcolm went over to the felled poet. He tried to help him up, but Corey flapped a long, muscular arm at him. After such a blow, to rise was impossible. His terra-cotta–colored form took up the entire rug, contorted in agony like some Roman athlete downed on his flight from Pompeii.

"What's going on?" asked Angus, enthusiastic in the doorway.

Maybelle Jolene diagnosed the patient at her feet. "He's probably eaten a funnel cake," she told Angus, "or Dippin' Dots. Pretty soon he's going to throw up everywhere."

Malcolm handed him the poem. "He wrote Andy a poem," he explained. "She hasn't replied."

"Poetry?" said Angus. "God bless him! The lad has a soul, after all." He read the poem and made a couple of buzzing kazoo noises. "This is a disgrace," he said.

"I didn't mean to sound like a pervert," Corey moaned.

"Pervert? I'm talking about the verse. Did you write this drivel?"

"I had help from a master," said Corey. "Ralph Erskins Sr."

Malcolm and Angus looked at each other.

"Ralph who? Where d'you find this bloody McGonagall?"

Hearing the commotion across the hallway, Frank rolled off his book-covered bed and came to see what was going on.

"The poor devil was trying to write poetry," Angus told him. "Tae Andee!"

"Is he alright?" asked Frank.

"Take a look at this," Angus handed Frank the poem. Corey protested weakly at his verse's growing audience.

"'Without change things can seem the same'?" Angus quoted Corey's seldom-disputed claim. "Jesus."

"There's some stuff in there about tying her up, stuff like that," said Malcolm.

"Kidnapping, too," added Angus.

"Oh dear," said Frank.

While the three older men and the child pored over the poem, Corey dragged himself across the rug to Malcolm's futon. "Just bungee cords, is all," he mumbled.

"At least the lad's got passion," said Angus. "Some imagination. Our own Marquis de Corey, conjuring up saucy diversions in the dead of night, then reaching for quill and ink. A skill of the true gentleman! To pen a sonnet, ride a horse, fight a duel, aye, even inflict a mortal wound upon a rampant boar…"

"I'll go with that last one," said Frank.

"You need to write the poor girl an apology," Angus told Corey. "Explain what in God's name you meant."

"I was just trying to use camping metaphors and smileys."

"Dinnae give up, laddie!" Angus did a little dance. "We are here to help. Romance will bloom within this Court." He froze mid-jig and stared at the ceiling. "Is Andy here? In the hoose?"

"She's at work," said Frank.

Maybelle Jolene crossed the room and put a tiny hand on Corey's shoulder.

"I will never write another poem again," he promised her.

Lida Barfield's presence—or rather her mysterious absence—around Carolina Court concerned Malcolm. So did her vehicle. The Mustang spoke of unnecessary and costly drama. Its dashboard was untidy with receipts and parking tickets, discarded lipstick and sunglasses. The muscle car was the kind of ride driven by Malcolm's natural predator.

It was reassuring that the new lodger kept herself apart from the rest of the household, but he made a point to avoid her, choosing to leave and return via the front door. The courtyard—mouth now to her den—he ceded to her.

One afternoon though, returning from town, he found himself on the same path as his fellow tenant. He slowed his steps to keep behind the small figure, but the distance between them kept closing. She was wearing the sort of boots that Malcolm often wore to a gig—tooled and worn leather, the toes upcurled and capped with brass that was a little loose and rang out at each step. At the great stone steps that led from the street to the house, Lida stopped and turned. She looked him up and down.

"Hey there," he said. "I'm Malcolm. I live here, too."

"Yes," said Lida.

"You liking it here?"

"I am," she said. "The location is particularly convenient."

"Yeah, totally. I hardly even use my truck."

"Is yours the green one?"

"Yeah," said Malcolm. "The green one."

"You will let me know if my vehicle has blocked you in?" Lida asked in a commanding way.

Malcolm nodded.

Lida put out her hand, "Lida Barfield."

Malcolm had to take the first step to reach her hand. From a distance, the gesture looked like he had taken a bow.

It took Corey longer than he hoped to write his apology. In the meantime he took pains to avoid Andy. He would hurry out, praying not to be delayed in the hallway by Angus. He thought about dropping school and leaving town. He imagined his note as the single item left in his empty room, kind of like how David had left that sock when he moved out. Instead he put the apology into an envelope, this time slipping it under the bathroom door into her bedroom.

A History of Saints

Late at night, in near darkness, Lida Barfield watched reality TV shows. On coming home, she would shower, then put on a robe and slippers and open a bottle of wine. Until her shows came on she would sit on the edge of her bed and look across the room. Sometimes she turned to the vast book beside her pillow—Burton's *The Anatomy of Melancholy*. She would stare at a randomly chosen page, her eyes barely moving, as though she was absorbing the lines rather than reading them. Then she would watch *Cheaters* and *Are you Hot?*, *Next*, and *The Pickup Artist*. All this tanned and toothy activity Lida watched much as a naturalist might study wildlife. Except for the occasional drag on a cigarette she held herself very still and upright. She rarely blinked.

When this was over she would open her laptop and resume her hobby. Lida was an active member of a website called yourtrophybride.com and was currently maintaining several threads of promissory discourse.

Dear Misti, she wrote, I'm sorry I didn't get back to you sooner, but it's been nuts. We had six buyers today. Before lunch! I'm worn out. I thought a month in Florida would be enough of a break, but now I'm not sure, baby. I need to sell this dealership and retire. Like yesterday. Damn, I sure could do with one of those back rubs you mentioned. Listen, I'm an old-fashioned kind of guy. You know that. I like you a lot. You're beautiful, and so crazy smart for your age. You should own that tanning place by now.

This online stuff is kind of weird to me. Is there any way we could meet in person? Maybe somewhere halfway? I wouldn't ask you to come all the way up here. Maybe somewhere in North Carolina? I'm meeting some clients in Asheville. I'm just talking about a drink, nothing more. I'll reimburse you for the hotel. I just want to look into those eyes. Think about it, will you? I'll say goodnight now, baby doll, hoping you'll dream about this old fool for love, Joe.

Lida sent the message and took a sip of wine.

Chrystal baby, she began. *What a day! Don't ever buy a jet! I'm sorry I didn't get back to you sooner...*

Frank walked into the class with Andy's yoga mat under his arm and a five-dollar bill in his pocket. He wore his sweatpants and a loose T-shirt. Although he gave his classmates a nervous smile, he sensed a ripple of surprise travel across the women. Something was wrong. There were no other mats in the room, there was strange pulsing music, and the ladies were tying little silver belts of coins around their waists.

"Can I help you?" a pale woman approached him.

"I'm here for the class," said Frank.

She touched his yoga mat and shook her head, "That class is over," she said in a foreign accent. "The hours have changed."

"Ah," said Frank, relieved the anticipated ordeal was postponed. "Okay."

"Please stay," the woman said. "Don't go."

Frank held up his mat. "I came for the yoga…"

"You try class, yes? One time? You are not feeling to have been driven from this place."

"I don't," said Frank. He felt he should say more. "What kind of class is this?"

"'Tribal Fusion with Lark.' I'm Lark," said Lark. "It's Egyptian belly dance."

"Oh well…," he began.

Lark stopped Frank. "Belly dance is not only for women, yes? I have taught men as well." A line of foiled recollection creased her brow. She noticed that several of the women had overheard her. "Ah yes!" she told the class. "Belly dance is not exclusive. Men have danced alongside women since ancient times. The role of the man in the troupe was to protect the female."

The women looked at Frank.

"I really came here for the yoga," said Frank, "and I haven't even done that before."

"But you are willing to try? You are not afraid, no?"

"Belly dancing? Seriously?" But he was already letting her slip the mat from his grasp.

"What do you seek?" Lark asked him.

"Seek?" Frank turned to the ladies now circled around him. "I guess I just need to lose some weight, is all."

"This totally kicks yoga's ass for that," said one girl, and the group laughed triumphantly.

Frank shrugged. He had driven over here, after all. "Well, okay," he said.

He took off his shoes and found a place among the others on the dance floor. He was shown how to put on a hip scarf. As Lark spoke to them, he noted himself beyond her in the mirrored wall. He looked incongruous, to be sure, but he felt comfortable. He liked the tinkling energy in the room and the way he had been so quickly accepted into their ranks, uniting as they all had against the feeble yoga class.

Their teacher brought each of them a flowing dance veil. Everyone received a different color. Frank's was violet. The girl next to him was given a batik veil of vibrant orange. "That's awesome," she complimented Frank's veil.

"Thanks," said Frank. "Yours is, too."

Lark came up to Frank. "The man should project power," she told him. "You should share your high spirit with audience, but you must let them know you are not to be challenged. You are their protector. You look fierce, yes?" She gave him an example of a scowl.

The music was turned up, and Lark formed her class into a circle. Everyone held their veils behind them, arms outstretched. As a little boy, Frank had played Superman like this, running around the yard with a bathroom towel flapping behind him. Or had he been Batman?

"The veil should be an extension of your body," said Lark, "to show the lovely movement of your arms, ladies." She gave Frank a smile. "And gentleman, to be emphasizing your strong shoulders, no?" She began to sway gracefully, the chiffon moving like water around her. The class copied her motions. Frank closed his eyes. His belt tinkled and he felt his veil sweep the back of his calves.

"The veil is mystery, the beginning of the dance. You are great bird, Mister Frank!" Frank moved his arms up and down to Lark's directions. He imagined himself a condor, although technically birds don't move their wings up and down separately. Was Lark Polish, he wondered, Russian? When he opened his eyes, the girls were all twirling. Frank found the effect magical, impossibly Technicolor under the fluorescent lights.

They danced in a ring around the room.

"Please, Mister Frank," called Lark. "No limp wrist! And fingers together."

Hearing his heavy tread above the music, Frank made an effort to keep on his toes. He found a comfortable, prancing step. When he caught a glimpse of himself in the mirror, he decided not to look that way again. Instead, he watched the dancers, the troupe, running like flames before him, sweeping brightly behind him. He returned every smile of encouragement but also remembered to give an occasional scowl. He would look after them all. He would be their fierce protector.

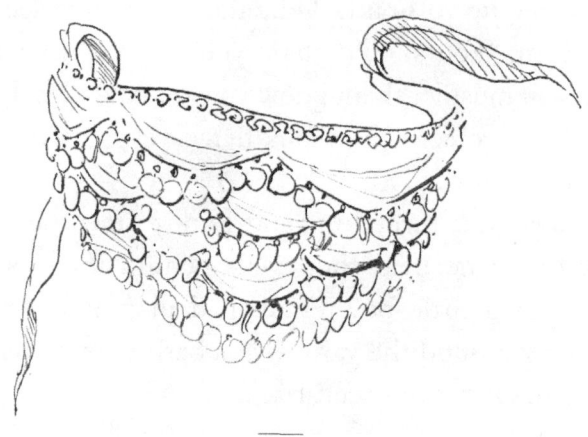

Thirteen

Nemo duplici potest amore ligare.

(No one can be bound by two loves.)
—Andreas Capellanus, *On Love*

Frank was in the courtyard dealing with a dead goldfish, when the door of High Cotton opened. A woman, seemingly dressed as a 1960s flight attendant, looked out at him. She wore a little blue hat, a blue jacket, and a pencil skirt. She waved a gloved hand and walked over. "You must be Frank," she said.

"Hey," said Frank, reaching up to shake her hand. "You're a friend of Lida's?"

"I am her," said Lida, looking perplexed. "I am she."

"You are?" Frank rose with difficulty from a circle of cats that had been feigning disinterest in the crime scene. "I thought…" He scratched his head. "So you're Lida?"

"Yes."

"Well, that's weird, but okay. Nice to meet you finally."

Lida looked at the fish in his other hand.

"One of them killed it," said Frank, nodding at the dispersing cats. "It's life."

"I should have introduced myself sooner," said Lida, "but I have been busy attending to my mother."

"Oh yeah?"

"She is infirm."

"I'm sorry."

"Thank you. She can be demanding."

"It's tough getting old."

Lida adjusted her little cap. "Assuming one lives so long."

Frank, still confused at this new Lida, was having trouble getting his bearings. He felt out of place—a gardener suddenly addressed by the lady of the household. "Well," he said, "at least you have plenty of years ahead of you."

"We shall see. I fear my cancer is returning."

"I'm sorry?"

"It's not important. As you say, 'It's life.' I count my blessings, every day. After all, people are starving everywhere, even in Mississippi."

"I guess so," said Frank. Lida's turn of phrase was making Angus seem normal. "Did you just say you had cancer?"

"Of the breast. A genius saved my life."

"A doctor?"

"Yes. I was acquainted with him through my nursing career. I'm pleased with my room," she went on, "although I have not yet received the furniture Angus promised me."

This brought Frank back to reality. "Uh-huh," he said. "The…chifforobe, right?"

"That's right. A large one."

Frank tossed the goldfish into the bushes. "I'll make sure he gets you one."

"You have a lot of cats."

"They're not really mine. Angus says you're allergic?"

"I have a lot of allergies. It's ridiculous the things I am allergic to. They're the least of my troubles, of course, compared to ductal carcinoma."

"Sorry about the cats," said Frank. "They just show up here from all over."

"Because of the cat food?"

"It's kind of a chicken and egg thing. They showed up first, though."

"I am not sure if it is a chicken and egg situation, Frank," Lida lightly corrected her landlord. "Without food the strays will not linger."

Together they watched a cat's stealthy advance upon an azalea. Suspended in its branches, like a wilted yellow balloon, was the carcass of the little fish.

I read what I wrote and it was like oh shit, I totally get it. You are mad or just think I'm some kind of pathetic pervert, right? All I wanted was to write you a poem to say how awesome you are and how I feel so tied to you and connected. I am completely not into what it sounded like, or kidnapping, either. I should never have tried this poetry stuff, especially on a real artist. I guess I was just trying to impress you. Can we just start all over and you forget that I ever made this mistake? Can we just exercise these ghosts? Just be cool roommates until maybe or maybe not one of us one day looks at the other and sees everything they will ever need in another humanoid?

Andy read this twice. She guessed Emily as the apologist on the first reading but then Corey as she read it again and realized where she had found the note—close to the bathroom they both shared. Corey—not Emily at all—was writing poetry to her. Emily had not discovered her new home. Emily had not been stalking her, after all.

She was sorry she'd thrown the poem away because she had no idea what Corey was referring to in this reparation and because she'd never received a poem from a man before. Emily had left her lots of romantic letters and notes, all spontaneously written out on paper towels or the backs of envelopes and left in places for Andy to discover. Corey's had been carefully printed out like a professional poem from a real book of professional poems.

She was flattered but pensive. She thought back over all her past exchanges with Corey for any signs of his heartache but couldn't recall any. He was just a regular guy. He had offered to clean her bike and to change her oil. He promised to show her a trail he enjoyed and once said something about camping. She'd not found him unattractive, yet suddenly her memories were very vague. She needed to get a good look at him again.

Not that anything could happen between them, of course. Andy had only to consider the impossibility of her life right now—there was Emily stalking her... Oh no, that hadn't happened. Still, there was the trauma of that breakup, and there was her family getting on her case about finding a real job. There was the problem of how her nose was kind of funny-looking, which nobody really understood, not even Leaf Pringle. And besides all this, she was so fat and huge right now she just hated herself.

She folded his apology and put it away. Poor Corey. Full of humanoid compassion, she went downstairs. Should she see her suitor she would be gentle but quite clear that she was like, so totally between people right now. Still, she felt a desire to reassess her roommate before she did. Corey's declaration had reached Andy at a time when her psyche ached for reassurance, for admiration, for a cuddle.

When you were a kid, did you attend a lecture on learning how to walk? Did you pass an exam on breathing? The hell you did. J.J. Antietam deleted *The hell you did* and replaced it with *I don't think so.*

He continued, *Your learning curve was your own: action-orientated, dynamic, hands-on. And it lasted! Here at The Self Center* *we teach by NOT teaching. We are <u>NOT</u> in the teaching business. Once you are part of our vibrant community, our teachers will coach you through workshops and interactive experiences in which you will experience life-changing...*

J.J. paused for the word he was seeking. He drummed his long fingers impatiently on the keyboard, then lay his polished bald head on his desk and cursed in frustration. He did not enjoy writing. His happiest arena was a more active one—the pacing guru encircled by rapt faces, his audience following every spidery gesture he made, gasping at his revelatory truths, delighted by his scathing wit. He should be a star on the TED Talk circuit, not tweaking some dumb vision statement because that ditz Melanie couldn't build a website if her life depended on it.

With a fierce shove, he pushed his rolling office chair away from his desk, whisked up a remote from the coffee table that doubled as a Japanese sand garden, and came to rest across the room in front of a large television. He clicked through the channels. Every single news station was in an uproar. Congress had just rejected the bank bailout bill. In turn, the stock market had immediately crashed. "Oh baby!" said J.J. Antietam. "Baby, baby."

He crossed a thin leg, sheathed in black denim, over the other and hugged his ankle. "Here we go," he laughed aloud. "Here we go, people!"

The kitchen was busy. Angus was throwing together an unlikely supper, while Andy listened to Malcolm recount a family loss. Frank had taken apart an old radio in the hopes he could repair it. A cat sat among the silver plastic wreckage, trying to flick each little screw Frank was collecting off the table.

"What happened then?" Andy asked Malcolm softly.

"My mom called me at work. 'Malcolm, it's about Mindy.' I said, 'Is she okay?' And she was like, 'Not really. It's another tumor even bigger than the first.' I said, 'Can they operate?' And she said they could, but it was about quality of life at this point. She was sixteen and there was only so much longer she could go on, what with the other stuff."

"So they put her to sleep?" Andy asked softly.

"Not right away."

At the stove, Angus snorted. He shook his head violently, as though the overheard conversation was a persistent horsefly.

"They watched her for a while," Malcolm went on. "Just in case, maybe, but then they asked if we could come in, if we wanted to be with her in the last moments, after they stuck her with the needle. They did that, and we petted her, and she just went kind of flat after a while. You could really feel like she had floated up and gone out the window."

"Was that your only iguana?" Andy asked after a while.

"We've had a few."

"Christ, Malcolm," said Angus. "You're not one to spurn a tale for fear of reception." Having finally worked a can opener around a mangled can of squid parts, he emptied the contents into a pot of bubbling orange matter.

"Was Mindy buried or cremated?" Andy asked.

"Cremated," said Malcolm. "It seems kind of weird to bury those things."

A History of Saints

"This is not bad," said Angus. "If you ignore the aftertaste, it's pretty good. Any takers? Where's Corey?"

"Corey went camping," said Frank.

"He did?" asked Andy. "I was looking for him earlier."

The three men exchanged glances. Behind Andy's back Angus mimicked a swooning maiden.

"Yeah," said Frank. "He'll be back in a couple of days, he said."

"Oh," said Andy.

Angus brought his dish to the table and sat down. "I don't know," he said. "This may not keep that long. Once you open a can like that one, you have to respect it being past the sell-by date." He scowled at the cat in front of him.

"Leave the cat alone," said Frank.

"I was just going to pet its wee head." Angus spooned some squid into his mouth and chewed thoughtfully for some time, his eyes twinkling at Frank with inexplicable mirth.

Frank took a sip of his beer and waited.

At last there came an audible gulp. "Frankie and I have some news," Angus told the others.

"We have?" said Frank.

"The hootenanny," Angus reminded him.

"Oh yes," said Frank. "That."

"The what?" asked Andy.

"A gathering, Andromeda," Angus explained. "This will be no ordinary yard sale. We plan to follow it with an evening of music and laughter. Malcolm, your talent will be required. I'll provide the wine and wee nibbles."

"And no hookers this time," said Frank.

Angus looked dismayed. "I told you, I didn't know their profession," he said. "I thought they were just two heavy lasses waiting for a bus."

The door opened and Lida entered the bright kitchen from the black night. She was dressed for baccarat in Monte Carlo. She waved a hand at the fan's glaring, wobbling

127

lights, as though it was customary for such fixtures to obey her dismissal.

"Aha!" cried Angus. "It's Anouk Aimée, ready for her tea."

Lida eyed the room with distrust. "This is the kitchen," she observed. It was her first real view of the room since Angus had given her a hurried tour of Carolina Court.

"The engine of the ship," said Angus. "Will you join us?"

"Hello, Angie, Frank." Lida looked at Malcolm, "… Marlowe?"

Malcolm nodded. "Malcolm."

"I heard your voice," Lida told Angus. "I've been looking for you."

"I am seldom far from the Court," said Angus. He enjoyed the formal repartee Lida brought to their conversations. "We have victuals here, milady, flavored with the spices of Eastern Timor. Will ye join us?"

"Frank assured me you would provide a wardrobe. Isn't that right, Frank?"

"That's right," Frank grinned. "You promised her a wardrobe, Angus. A chifforobe. A large one."

"I'm not the landlord," Angus fished for a chunk of tentacle. He looked up at Lida. "If I had a wardrobe, I can assure you it would be yours. Some of us are content to manage with a humble clothes rack."

Lida looked from Angus to Frank then back to Angus. "So I am to expect nothing for my clothes?"

Malcolm had found a cat under the table and was stroking it emphatically, as though the gesture might placate this standoff.

"I've got some room in my closet," said Andy.

"Thank you, Angie," said Lida, "but that will not do."

"I'll keep looking," said Angus. "Your concerns are mine, Lida. Dinnae forget the cats I planned to shave for you."

Frank looked over at Speck. At some point, Angus had managed to dress her in a Christmas stocking with leg holes.

Speck looked back at him. Her expression failed to match the scarlet *JOY TO THE WORLD* embroidered along her new winter wear.

"I didn't ask you to shave anything," said Lida.

"You see?" Frank told Angus.

Angus withdrew his whistle from his vest. Lida crossed her arms. Angus played a few notes in her direction.

"Here we go again," said Frank.

"Your name is heard in high places," Angus began, *"You know the Aga Khan, He sent you a racehorse for Christmas, and you keep it just for fun, for a laugh, ha ha."*

The serenade left Lida cold. She turned sharply on a pointed heel and walked out.

"Oh," said Andy. "I think you upset her."

"She's pissed, alright," said Malcolm.

"She'll get over it," Angus told them.

With a shrug, Frank went back to fixing his radio. "You make peace with her, Angus, alright? She's seems to be going through a lot."

"I feel so sorry for her," agreed Andy.

"Really?" asked Angus. "What has she told you all now?"

To: AndromedaB

Subject: Final words of a freind

Andromeda Megan Bell- I know you will not read this- just like u have not read my texts or other messages so this will be my last ditch try to reach out if only jst to say goodbye. What we had yes even though it was very momentarily something special. You were my first love- I know you don't believe that no matter how many times i say it but it was true.

Emily emptied the rest of the wine bottle into her glass and lit another cigarette. She went on.

You are so fragile like a china cup, broken and glued back together so many times that it is just totally stupid to even bother fooling with the shards and pieces of your ego. Yes you, who are so beautiful and prefect and all your talents as well on top of that. HHA HA i have to laugh. I know what you are thinking. You always listen to everyone-except me of course- you act like you are so confused and cant commit to anyone or anything but all your negative self hate is destroying your life. Have you really talked to oyur therapist about this? I don't believe you have.

I know what really happened btw. I know I can come off as too intense- but isn't that what love is after all? I know that my true love drove you away, but I also know you cant be alone. Your not that type. Okay. So I know. YOU MET SOMEoNE ELSE. I don't care who she is andy it really dosnt matter at this point

Something tells me you've gone back to Granitetown. Don't ask me why- I can sense these things. I am tied to you that way. I am leaving too. I've had my fill of this fake town with its lies and promises and tattoos and fake smiles and so I say, enough already, goodbye Asheville and all your hipppy bullshit. And to you, Andromeda i say farewell also. As we were once lovers in ancient eygptitian times so will we be again, I believe.

Until then,
Yours sincerely,
Emily Nazario

With this sudden, sober close to her deception, Emily hissed slightly and, after a moment's hesitation, hit send.

Fourteen

[A] vexation of the mind, a sudden sorrow from a small, light, or no occasion...
—Robert Burton, The Anatomy of Melancholy

ANDY WAS PAINED by Lida's crisis. Fate could be so cruel. Wasn't it enough that her new roommate could be facing another battle against cancer, without the trial of not having enough hanging space? She knocked on her door the next day.

Lida looked tired. Her lipstick was smeared. "Don't worry," she assured Andy. "I have faced far worse things. Nate and I lived out of a suitcase for nearly a year."

"Nate?"

"A past love," said Lida. "He's in the diplomatic service now, quite high up, but when I knew him, we were just free spirits."

"You've done so many things."

"Yes," said Lida. "I have weaved...woven quite the tapestry, I suppose."

Andy saw a chance for worldly advice. "Did he write you poetry?"

"No. I have only loved one poet. I never speak of him."

"Did he hurt you?"

"He hurt himself. He was born without an epidermis."

"Oh my God!" said Andy. "Really?"

"No. That's just an expression. He was overly sensitive. I will never forget his hair." Lida looked away, then scratched her ear. "He had the best hair."

"Corey wrote me a poem," Andy confessed all in a rush. "That's never happened before. On paper, like a real poem. I've never had something like that happen before."

"I have dozens of poems," said Lida. "They're in my storage unit." She crossed to the window and opened the curtain a little to look out onto the sunny courtyard. "Corey?" she asked.

"Yes," said Andy. "He lives here, too."

"Ah yes," said Lida. "Of course. The boy." It was noon, but Lida was still wearing her turquoise nightgown and matching chiffon bed jacket. She toyed with the ribbon at her throat. "Are you in love with him?" she asked Andy.

"Oh no!" Andy began.

"You seduced him, perhaps?" Lida stayed at the window. Before Andy could speak, she went on. "Love is a terrible thing. It leaves no prisoners. 'I accept the fact that love is love.' Are you familiar with the works of McKuen?"

"I didn't seduce Corey," cried Andy. "I hardly know him. I don't want to—"

"I don't know you well, Angie," said Lida. "Hardly at all, and yet…your eyes. They tell the truth. I believe you."

Andy was relieved, "You do?"

"I do."

"You do?"

"Yes." Lida looked at Andy with a strange, forlorn smile, then swiftly crossed the room to fling herself emphatically onto the bed beside her guest. Whatever effect she intended by this gesture was spoiled as her elbow struck the unyielding corner of Burton's *The Anatomy of Melancholy*. She gasped something and rolled off the side of the bed.

"Are you okay?" Andy called out. "Are you alright?"

Lida climbed back onto the bed, rubbing her elbow vigorously. "It's nothing," she told Andy. "Welcome to my fucking life." She tried to punish the massive book by pushing it to the floor, but it seemed determined to share the coverlet with them.

"Did it get your funny bone?"

"Kind of," said Lida. "It doesn't matter."

"I love old books," Andy searched for any distraction from this new blow to her roommate's existence. "I keep a journal. I write in it every day."

The chiffon around Lida's shoulders trembled in an emerald cloud as she continued to massage her injury. "I need a Xanax," she said. "Like now. You want one?"

'Yes, please," Andy said eagerly.

Lida opened a drawer and offered Andy a pill from her little silver case. "So," she said. "He wrote you a poem? He doesn't seem the type."

Corey had found a high mountain bald to play the penitent. From here he could meditate upon the calamity of his life. He set up his tent close to an old campfire site and sat down on a great shard of granite, watching the horizon as though a solution might arrive from that direction. It was colder at this altitude, but Corey had brought all the gear he needed to keep comfortable in his time of reflection. In the silence he would find the internal peace he sought. In the face of a star-filled night he would be able to weigh the true, minor scale of this episode against the enormity of time and space. As it turned out, however, the place had excellent cell phone reception. Corey spent the evening talking to his friend Mike.

"Dude," said Mike. "You might as well come home. She's going to be there when you do, so you might as well get it over with."

Throughout the conversation, Corey had spoken with strange calm and gravitas, as though his starry backdrop required such a performance. "Mike," he said, "You are right. She is just a woman…"

"Totally, man…"

"If this shit is to be, then it is to be. I have a life, Mike, I have a life." Corey walked in circles around his little fire, tidying its ashen edge with his toe. "If she's the kind of person who would judge a guy because he screwed up a poem, I mean, how many guys would even write a poem? If she is that kind of person, then I can do better. I deserve better. What kind of woman would judge a man for exposing himself the way I do?"

"Totally."

"But no more poet stuff. No way. That shit is over for me. This woman has to love me for what I am, Mike."

"What's that?"

"A guy. Just a regular…," Corey paused. "What the fuck? Someone's fucking dog is tearing up my tent, man!"

"No fucking way," Mike said supportively.

Corey picked up a stick. "Just a minute, man," he told his friend as he strode over to his tent. "Hey!" he shouted. "Go on! Get out of here."

"What kind of dog is it?"

"A real monster," said Corey.

A History of Saints

Andy looked at a new blank page. She wrote the word *Evening* in the ornate cursive that continued to evolve as her journal progressed. The title was intended to merely appoint an hour to her thoughts, and yet, Andy wondered, perhaps this was already the evening of her life? For what guarantee was there that she would live to grow old—or even see middle age? Lida's constantly endangered life was a grave example.

Outside, the dry leaves were restless in the chill wind that swept the courtyard. Inside, a mortal dancer sat at her diary. Earlier, as Andy lay folded in the bathtub, she'd found near a buttock what were surely the first dimpled fingerprints of cellulite—already Death's grasp reached out, relentless, inevitable, to disfigure his intended bride. Even by the kind light of the candles she had arranged around the tub, it was too much to endure. Andy had taken a washcloth and draped it over this sad section of her lengthy thigh. She was able to tug one corner of the fabric far enough to hide a further discovery—an ugly red dot that could only presage a pimple.

What could she add to the word *Evening*? Nothing. It spelled out everything she felt. She underlined the word. Then she underlined it again. Then she filled the space between the two lines with a wavy line. Then she capped the new, wider line created with two decorative finials.

Despite all this, the page looked empty. Andy wrote *You will live.* Then she wrote *You will love again.* Below this she added *What does he see in me?* and *Born without an epidermis?* She drew a picture of herself as a shriveled old woman and then circled the face with flowers. Her next tattoo might be just this simple, moving portrait.

Corey lay in the darkness. The bear attack was over. The fleeing animal had knocked him over—knocked the wind out of him—but Corey felt no broken bones, no torn flesh. He checked his body with his hands. His clothes were not sticky. He wasn't matted with blood.

Mike was still on the line. "What's going on, man?" Corey could hear the tiny shouts from the phone some feet away. "Corey?"

Corey crawled over to the phone. "I'm okay, Mike."

"What happened?"

Corey let out a deep breath. "I was attacked by a bear, man."

There was an appreciative silence for a moment. "Fuck! No way! Are you okay? Are you alright?"

"Yeah," said Corey. "I think so."

"What about the dog in the tent?"

"That was the bear, man."

"Are you like, mauled?"

"Pretty much," said Corey, checking himself again, "but it didn't break the skin."

"Shit."

Corey let out another meaningful breath and looked up at the pierced firmament.

"Can you get down from there?" Mike asked, "Do I need to call someone?"

"I can make it," said Corey. "I'm coming home." He lay there a little longer. A meteor scratched the night sky.

Corey felt the great elation of the survivor. And more, for surely this encounter canceled out his botched start at chivalry? Weaponless, save for a little stick, Corey had been tested by a true predator of the wild. Alone on a mountaintop, he had overcome every instinct to run and instead had driven his sizeable, shuffling adversary away into the night.

Now he whispered his thanks to the bear. If he had left Carolina Court as a failure—a pervert, even—he was returning as a hero. He saw his battle might be more of a guy thing, for Andromeda clearly loved all animals, but it occurred to Corey that a carefully worded account of the action might convey his intent from the first, in a gesture dedicated to his lady's vegan ways, to spare the beast's life.

When Frank returned Andy's yoga mat to her, he hadn't mentioned the belly dancing, only that he had missed the yoga class. After returning to Lark and the troupe though, he ached for Andy's opinion. He'd confided in Elaine, and she was supportive but had expressed some surprise in the concept of masculine belly dance. Frank guessed his tenant would know more about the ancient art. When he met Andy in the kitchen and she offered Frank her mat again, he told her everything.

"Awesome!" she cried. "That is so awesome! Are you going back?"

"I have. Tonight is my third class."

"That is super cool," said Andy. "I could never do that."

"Of course you could," said Frank. "You'd be perfect."

"I don't have the right look."

"And I do?"

"You know what I mean," she said hurriedly, her face turning red. "I'm too tall. I need to be shorter, curvier."

Frank laughed, "Well, I am that. Really, though, there are all kinds of girls in the class."

"Are you the only guy?"

"I am," said Frank. "I'm their protector. That's what they told me."

"They're right." Andy smiled, then added, "I actually didn't know men did belly dancing."

"Hmm," said Frank.

"I might…," Andy began. A friend had invited her to contribute to a dance piece, but Andy was not sure if she was emotionally ready. She stopped herself from telling Frank more.

"Yeah, apparently it's pretty rare," Frank went on. "Lark says—"

"Is Lark your teacher?"

"Yes!"

"Oh my God, she is totally awesome!"

"Yup!" Frank flapped his arms. "It's 'Tribal Fusion with Lark!'" He made a turn or two, bowed, and sashayed his way out of the room.

Laughing with delight, Andy applauded Frank's exit, then went back to the task of weighting a block of tofu with a plate and a water-filled saucepan.

The screen door creaked, and Corey limped into the kitchen. Andy looked up, her face filling with beautiful alarm. She came toward him. "What happened?"

Corey was a mess. There was a gash on his cheek and a dark bruise around it. In hiking down off the mountain in the pitch dark he'd taken a heavy fall. The bundled tent he carried in his arms snagged on the branches of a tree, and Corey had tumbled face first into a creek bed.

"I was attacked by a bear, Andy," Corey said slowly. "A bear."

"A bear?" Her eyes widened. "A bear? Oh no!"

"Madam Barfield," Angus smiled. "Will you forgive me for the other night?"

"For what?" Lida asked. It was a warm October day, the leaves and acorns falling around them.

"I was just teasing. I have every intention of finding you that wardrobe."

"You have a stink bug on your neck," Lida observed.

Angus found the creature and cast it aside, sniffing his fingers.

"So," he asked, "you forgive me then?"

"Of course."

"I have a wee gift for you." Angus had been back to Junque U Like, where he had found the hair trimmer, and had settled on the oil painting of the mermaid as a suitable peace offering. He handed the tiny canvas to Lida.

"Thank you," she examined the gift. "Is that a dolphin?"

"It's a mermaid. There's a little ship in the distance."

"Yes, I see."

"I'm assuming it's the labor of a local talent," Angus added.

"So it's an original?"

Angus checked Lida's face for sarcasm. "Absolutely. There's the signature, *Pin* somebody," he read.

"I will put this in a special place," said Lida. "After all, I still have that big empty spot."

"Not for long," Angus promised her. "I will find you the chifforobe to fill it." He retreated with a bow, "Seize this fading day, milady," he said, signaling the orange canopy above them.

Lida shook her head at this glib reference to mortality.

Frank waited for his lunch at a Bavarian restaurant. The low-slung log cabin sat close to the old highway that was once the artery to the north. The road had long been bypassed by an adjacent interstate and the motels that lined it for decades were gone or closed, but this one restaurant remained. It was Frank's escape. The place reminded him of childhood road trips to the mountains—the exposed cabin logs that threaded each dining area; the matching beamed ceiling, hung with *biersteins* and perennial Christmas decorations; the windows framed with flowery curtains, plates and figurines along every sill; the little bar and cheerful waiter—it all pleased him.

Frank ran a hand over a soft wolf pelt that was stretched across the defunct fireplace beside his table. He gazed upward at the white throat and shining muzzle of a deer trophy. The creature still looked attentive. A flag was draped over her neck, and a collection of bottles crowded the mantel. An old

German pop song played for all the stuffed animals and Frank. The restaurant was empty.

"You alright over there, Frank?" the young man behind the bar asked. "Need anything?"

Frank leaned back over his dwindling beer. "What do you do when you find yourself living with a crazy person? No—two. Two crazy people."

"Two now?"

"I think so. I think that's all."

"Crazy how?"

Frank could not begin to explain Angus and Lida. In his mind he saw small, costumed animals wandering around the house, Angus disguised as a mattress, Lida dressed for some Hitchcock intrigue, but these things were hard to describe.

"One is too many. You should move out, man."

"It's my house."

"Oh yeah. Well, I guess you just have to ask them to move out, find someone else? My mom used to say to me about people like that, she'd say, 'Joey, you be careful now, crazy people will make you crazy.'"

"It's not that easy, though," said Frank. "I mean, maybe if I was someone else it would be easy. I find that kind of stuff hard. And then…," Frank stared blankly across the room as though he was just another poor trophy on the wall, "who would come in their place?"

"There are plenty of regular people in this town, Frank. Not everyone's nuts."

"Really?" Frank ordered another beer. He should be eating salad, he knew that, but he had come here for the comfort of sausages. His little table was crowded with two secondhand books on belly dancing. He opened one and searched again for any mention of a man, a protector, among all the photos of half-clad houris.

"Now you're talking, dude," said Joey, looking over Frank's shoulder as he replaced his beer.

Fifteen

A faithful friend is better than gold.
—Robert Burton, The Anatomy of Melancholy

Corey lay in his bed, propped up with pillows. He considered bears. They came in all shapes and sizes. Most were brown, a few were white, his was black. The Kodiak bear lived only on Kodiak Island. Why it did that Corey didn't know. It was probably an awesome island for bears.

He heard a gentle tap at the door. "Corey? Are you awake?"

"Andy?" he said weakly. "Hey."

Andy's doting figure loomed into view. She carried a tray. "How are you doing?" she whispered.

"I'm...alright," said Corey, turning his head slowly toward her. His neck still hurt.

"I brought you some green tea," she said, "and a magazine to read."

"*dancetrain*," Corey read aloud.

"Sorry, it's all I have right now."

"Thanks."

Andy took a seat beside the bed. She watched Corey thumb through an article on audition rejection in LA's competitive dance scene. "I didn't realize it was you who wrote me that poem," she said. "I thought it was someone else."

Corey looked up at her.

"My ex," said Andy.

A pang of jealousy impaled the patient. "Nah, it was me," he said.

"That was really nice of you. When I thought it was from… that other person, I threw it away. I'm sorry. Do you have another copy?"

Corey's heart lurched from jealousy and shame to relief. He still kept his eyes on a leaping Black man in a leotard, though. "I don't," he said. "It wasn't any good anyway. It was stupid."

"I thought it was beautiful," Andy assured him. "What I remembered."

"It was about camping. I actually had help from Ralph Erskins Sr."

"I've never really been camping."

"I know. Anyway, if you had come with me, chances are you would have been killed."

"By the bear?"

Corey nodded. "Thanks for bringing me this stuff," he said.

"It's nothing. Is there anything else you need?"

The Black dancer had an earring of some kind, but it was out of focus. Corey looked at the image until it fell away into pixels, into one strange, miraculous surface of ink and the sheen of the magazine's paper. "Maybe we could go out for a beer or something sometime?" he heard himself mumble. "Get something to eat maybe, get a drink or something?"

"Sure. Okay."

Angus wandered the streets of Montford. He carried his several brightly painted signs for the yard sale and hootenanny, crafted from the dog corral posts. Ahead of him, at the end of their leashes, the dogs led his search to place the ornate markers. There were few good spots left. Obama signs were everywhere as Election Day drew near. As much as Angus himself had promoted the candidate from Illinois, he was quick to replace the most prominent placards with his own.

He complained to the Chihuahuas about the state of the sidewalks. Variably of old brick or cement, they were rucked and fractured in places, brutally repaired in others.

"Bloody disgrace," he muttered, smoking a cigarette with no free hands. He wore a military trench coat and a bright yellow sou'wester fisherman's hat.

The neighborhood shared Angus's random, piecemeal appearance. Plastic pipes poked out of once-lovely stone walls, telephone wires hung in great tangled loops at the eaves of historic homes. Every now and then, between the little cottages and turreted mansions, an empty lot had grown wild—a rusted gate ajar to nothing, steps leading into an accidental meadow full of wildflowers and weed trees. Each street in turn was a testament to the ups and downs of prosperity.

"Anguth!" A figure crossed the street, pushing an empty shopping cart. It was Trey.

"Trey!"

"Look at those liddle dogths!" Trey abandoned his cart to pet the animals.

Angus quieted Geezer. "It's Trey. Hush! This man saved your life!" He cast away his cigarette and shook Trey's hand with both of his. "How are you? How's your tongue?"

"Fuddily enough," said Trey, "as it turds out, my tug is not fuddy recovered."

"Dear God," said Angus.

"These thigs happen."

"You're right, my friend. I knew a fellow—"

"Where did you buy those liddle dog coads?"

"The jackets? I made them."

Trey stared at him in wonderment, "You made theb?"

"And these," Angus drew a yard sale sign out from under his

arm, like a bright play sword. Then his eyes opened wide at an idea. "You must come to the hootenanny!"

"A hoodedaddy? When?"

"Saturday. It starts at six."

"This Sadurday? I wish I'd knowd thooner."

"You're busy?"

"I can rearrage my appoidments," Trey looked hurt. "You should have called me."

"I lost your number," Angus lied swiftly.

"I'll be there, Anguth."

"Bring your mandolin!"

"I will," said Trey. "I may not thing, howeder." He took the yard sale sign carefully from Angus and examined its craftsmanship. He pointed at his cart. "Do you need thad? To caddy the signs?"

"A kind offer, Trey, but I have the dogs with me."

The two men smiled upon each other, both delighted at this unexpected reunion. Aside from a soiled blazer, Trey was dressed for the beach. The bells of the basilica struck the hour. The dogs waited.

"You could put theb in the card, too," Trey suggested.

"They do like riding in carts, Trey," said Angus. "Great Scott, man, but it's good to see you!"

"You, too, Anguth."

"And you could collect the cart on Saturday."

"She's been good to me," said Trey, looking fondly at the rusted buggy, "but I don't need her eddymore. You can have her." With this parting gift he went on his way.

It had rained that morning, and wet leaves, yellow and scarlet, were pasted to the shining road. Angus watched their afflicted benefactor diminish, careless of the puddles in his flip flops. He put the signs and the dogs in the cart. "'His life was gentle,'" he told the dogs, "'and the elements so mixed in him that Nature might stand up and say to all the world, *This was a man!*'"

As they rattled along to finish setting out the signs, Angus expanded on the qualities of his leathery, mottled friend. When he had said enough about Trey, Angus mused on the varied lives to either side of their path, pointing out the evidence of his neighbors' mettle, so very much on view.

Lakeisha and Geezer glanced back at their teacher as Angus noted each home in turn. Playful neighbors had already littered their yards for Halloween with plastic skulls and had draped giant spiders in webs above their porches. True gardeners, like their own landlord, were out preparing their flower beds for winter, while others had scorned such frivolity, preferring to remind the world of the virtues of rain barrels, tilled earth, and composting bins.

The sun broke through the clouds. Vapor rose from the warmed asphalt, and Angus tossed his now unnecessary hat onto the dogs. He laughed at some unvoiced thought, but their happy class was to be spoiled in its last moments.

Having placed the final sign at a street corner, they approached a blue house. Angus noted its austerity. "The gentleman ahead," he told the dogs, "is a minimalist." A square man with no hair sat in a stained, plastic chair at the absolute center of his lawn. Behind him five bushes were sculpted into tornadic green cones. Beyond these, a picture window was busy with snapping Pomeranians, their frenzied barking at the sight of Lakeisha and Geezer muffled by the glass. The man watched carefully as Angus approached. "Those your dogs?" he asked.

"They're communally owned," replied Angus. He stopped at a mailbox painted the same blue as the house. The name *EVANS* was printed on both sides. Angus took a stab at a Welsh salutation. "*Nos da hyfryd!*"

The man looked sharply at him, then went back to watching the dogs with narrowed eyes.

"Chihuahuas," said Angus.

The man shook his head. "White un's a Chi. But that other one? That there's a Min Pin, no doubt about it."

Angus bristled at once. "What the hell are you talking about?"

"Black un's a Min Pin, jes' with lil ol' legs."

"They're both—"

"White un's full Chi. Funny head is all."

Angus glanced again at the name on the mailbox. "Now you hear me, Evans!" he began.

Evans pressed himself up from the tightly fitting chair. "But that un's Miniature Pinscher, plain as my face." He enunciated the breed again loudly, "MIN-EE-AT-CHURR PINCH-CHURR."

"Don't cross me, man!" Angus warned him. "Are you familiar with the Patagonian purr-kick? One step closer and you will be. I've taken down bigger men than you—"

"Where d'you get that buggy, anyway?" Evans came toward them. "I had me a buggy jes' like that 'til it got stole."

Angus pushed the cart and its tumbling dogs away. "I was given this by a friend just now," he shouted over his shoulder. "A man who could break you in half, you Welsh bastard!"

Evans was not deterred. Angus started to run, steering the shopping cart down the hill. All the way home he cursed and raged, red with fury.

Busy with snapping Pomeranians

A History of Saints

Leaf Pringle watched as Andy searched her journal for another personal failing that they could discuss before the hour was up. They had talked about Emily's email and Andy's horror that she'd driven her ex away from Asheville.

"She's probably gone back to New Jersey," Andy mourned, "even though she hates it there and her family can't accept her life choices." Her antelope neck, from her pink ear to her pink top, was still gold from the summer. Her nails were all bitten short. As usual, Andy's long figure was bundled precariously at the lip of the chair cushion, as though taking up the comfort of the armchair was more than she could ever deserve. Her book bag and water bottle were tidy at her feet.

Andy might appear ready for flight, but Dr. Pringle knew she was quite content. She had other similar patients. With her foibles shed in weekly confession, Andy could leave to welcome anew the weight of her preferred disorders.

Andy's face was troubled now as she consulted one of her lists. Dr. Pringle braced herself, hoping the frown referred to some dietary issue. She just wasn't ready to discuss the shape of Andy's nose again.

What Andy wanted to talk about was Corey. Also her nose. Neither was an option, though. Her therapist had stated emphatically at the last session that she was not a plastic surgeon. As for her confusion about Corey, to ask if she should go on a date so soon—and with a male humanoid, for that matter—would surely make her look shallow and foolish in this time allocated to grief.

"Are you still enjoying your new home?" Dr. Pringle asked.

"Oh, it's great," said Andy. "My roommates are really interesting. It's really interesting there."

"That's good."

Andy nodded as she took a sip of water. Her lashes dipped with satisfaction at this little drink. "This one girl is a survivor.

She's a trauma nurse. I think I mentioned her, from the Balkans? And the landlord, he's so nice and he's actually taking belly dance instead of yoga. Angus, he's kind of like a street person but super intelligent, he's going to have a hoot-thing on Saturday because Lakeisha and, oh, I've forgotten—what's the word for a little old man? They're not in the cage anymore so the whole porch is free now, and this other guy, he got like, attacked by a bear, well just scratched, really."

"I see," said Dr. Pringle after a moment. "Well, okay. That's good then. We have about ten minutes left if you've found something in your journal?"

"Do you think I'd make a good nurse?"

"A...trauma nurse? Was that the expression you used? It would be a big change, of course, a big commitment."

"Maybe just a regular nurse?" Andy managed to perch still further forward as she confided, "Actually, I've been looking after the guy who was attacked by the bear."

"That's kind of you. And the nurse in the house, she was unavailable?"

"She said she was tired. She's not really in the house, she's in the slave quarters."

Dr. Pringle started to make a note but gave up. She said, "Right, well—"

"She's beautiful," Andy went on, "She's been through so much. I've never met anyone like her. She dresses like an old-time movie star."

"Are you attracted to her?"

Andy reared back from the suggestion. "Oh no! It's not like that! I just meant..."

"It's alright, Andy."

Andy saw an opening, "The thing is, Dr. Pringle..."

"Leaf, please."

"Leaf. The thing is I'm not even gay."

"Well, we talked about that. You were experimenting?"

"I could be bi?" Andy wondered. "I probably am. I don't know any more. It's confusing. What if I want to date a male humanoid?"

"A 'humanoid'?"

"A male one."

"Are you ready for that? I thought we were still working through your feelings about Emily."

"Of course," Andy said softly, slowly folding in contrition.

"Perhaps we should talk about that some more?"

"Typical Welsh bastard," Angus went on.

"Is that like, in England?" asked Malcolm.

"Next to it." Angus waved the geography lesson aside.

"And you weren't pestering him?" said Frank.

"He just came at me," said Angus. "Man's a bloody maniac. Seemed to think my shopping cart was his! I tell you, he was lucky I had the dogs with me. If I had been on my own, well, let's just say I strike without compunction. D'you know *Secret Fighting Arts of the World*, by Gilbey? I have it memorized."

"That's your shopping cart?" Frank asked. "On the porch?"

"Absolutely. Trey gave it to me."

"Can that go in the yard sale? Would you mind?"

"Jesus, Frankie, I've only...," Angus paused. He thought for a moment. "Aye, you're right. Anyway, with the state of these sidewalks I might as well be pushing the thing over bloody cobbles. A man has to think of his ears at my time of life. Fair enough. It might fetch a dollar or two for the cause. All for Juan, right?"

"And Juan for all," said Frank.

The three musketeers sat around Corey's bed. Their invalid, d'Artagnan, looked confused.

"Trey's coming to the hootenanny, mind," cautioned Angus. "He can't see me selling his gift."

Malcolm had an idea. "What you want to do is like, set it to off to one side, like it ain't even for sale but you just used the buggy for bringing the other stuff in. Don't put any tag on it, but when you see someone sniffing around, you just call out the price to them."

"Brilliant," said Angus. "Pure genius."

"The fact it's apparently not for sale will make it even more desirable," said Frank.

"I'm actually doing a lot better," said Corey.

They turned to the patient.

"I don't know, man," said Malcolm. "A freaking bear. That would have freaked me out."

"In the wild, definitely," agreed Frank. "At least here in town you can just step back in the house." Asheville was crowded with bears. They wandered the city, their delinquent children in tow, trudging from trash can to trash can with their pointy, searching front paws and clownish, splayed back feet trying to keep up, like two actors out of sync in a fur suit.

Corey took a book from the bedside table and opened it to show them a portrait of his enemy. They all leaned forward to study the humorless mouth, the flat head, the tiny button eyes set wide apart.

"*Ursus americananus*," Corey informed them.

"*Americanus*," Angus corrected, "although I appreciate why you'd want to insult the beastie."

"Creepy," said Malcolm.

"You seem just fine," Angus put a hand on Corey's knee. "The only thing that matters, lad, is how are you doing with the fair Andromeda?"

Malcolm nodded.

"She threw the poem away," He told them. "I don't think she even read it. She thought it was from her ex."

"Lucky, dude," said Malcolm.

"And…?" said Angus.

"She's looking after me." Corey held up *dancetrain*. "She gave me this."

Frank took the magazine from Corey and opened it.

"And...?" said Angus.

"And I kind of asked her out," said Corey. "I think she said yes."

Angus clapped. "*Sweet Sir Galahad came in through the window...*" He looked over at Frank, leafing through the magazine, "Frankie, did you hear that?"

"Yeah," Frank looked up. "That's great, Corey." The three veterans exchanged high fives over their smiling protégé.

"When I told her I let the bear live," Corey told them, "she was like, totally impressed."

"A little bullshit goes a long way," said Angus.

Corey looked affronted.

"Listen to the master," said Frank.

Sixteen

Et ipsae quidem omnes habent exigendi modos.
(These women have all manner of extortionate ways.)
—Andreas Capellanus, *On Love*

To: freedb&b
Subject: Concerns

Dear Frank,
You have welcomed me into your home. How long have I wandered in search of such a refuge, to recover from injuries both physical and psychological? A while. Shall I just say that?

I cannot thank you enough for the peace High Cotton has already brought me. You have created a rare living space for kindred spirits to share, a gathering of searching souls. Angie is sweet, Corey is truly inoffensive, Marlowe is on a path towards gainful employment, I have no doubt. You seem to be a guiding force, and Carolina Court reminds me of long ago days where monks and nuns would gather, separately of course, to meditate and study. However, I am thinking of moving out.

This evening I spoke to my mentor, Lady --------------, (for personal reasons, I must conceal her name). I met her in Oxford, where I spent a year completing my training as a trauma nurse. Her estate, with its ever-vigilant Borzois, heroic walks and almost constant laughter, was my first haven. She was the one who suggested I write you.

Life is so complicated, Frank, so uncertain, and yet certain values remain. Trust. Acumen. Reasonableness. And that brings me with sadness in my heart to the issue at hand. As I look across my little sanctuary, I see my beautiful clothes sagging on that shitty little rack Angus gave me, in danger of collapsing at any moment onto the dusty floor and the ten million cat hairs that blow in daily from the courtyard. This cannot be.

Frank, are you familiar with mental illness? It's clear you and Angus are old, dear friends, but I am already seeing warning signs that say 'Lida, evacuate! Run. You have seen this all too often before.' Alcoholism, delusions of grandeur, even Napoleonic Syndrome.

Angus is like the worst kind of twice-baked potato, loaded with everything your personal mental health doesn't need right now. My years in medicine have taught me all too well. Ask me if I have seen suffering and I will answer, yes.

The first day I met Angus, memories from my own past, memories I have tried to bury, came back to haunt me. My father was a TV personality. Have I told you that? I understand if you feel Angus deserves a home (at times the homeless do), but I feel I must voice my concerns. Angus may be a danger to your life, your liberty and the pursuit of happiness. I've already said too much. How I hate being the medical expert sometimes. Forgive me. I will say no more. Can you at least ask him if he even plans to find that chifforobe?

Be blessed,
Lida

A History of Saints

Frank read Lida's email again. He appreciated her kind words about Carolina Court. The vigilance of the borzois intrigued him, but the cat hair issue seemed unlikely—or indeed the threat posed by Angus. Frank was left only with questions. Was his tenant leaving or just awaiting furniture? Who was Lida's mysterious mentor? Would Frank have recognized her father's career? And who were Angie and Marlowe?

Ever-vigilant Borzois

Corey sent Andy a text.

C: Do u like picnics?

A: Sure

C: Would u like to go on one? With me? Saturday?

A: That would be awesome what about the hoot thing?

C: We could be back in time for that

A: Awesome

C: Cool i know a good place

A: What can i bring?

C: Do you have any allergies or stuff?

A: No i can eat pretty much anything as long as its vegan

C: K i will bring stuff

A: I will bring desert

C: K tx i will bring plates

A: R u feeling better? I can hear u moving around your room

C: Yeah tx i heal pretty fast

A: Will there be bears at the picnic? :)

C: :)

Tansie searched for her keys outside The Goddess Temple. It was dark, and the goddesses were all away. She jumped, dropping her keys with a clatter, when Emily stepped out of the night. "Shit, Emily! You frightened me."

"Have you got your phone on you?"

"What?"

"Show me your phone."

Tansie gave her the phone. "It's totally uncool sneaking up on people like that, Emily," she protested.

"Have you heard from her?"

"Andy? No. She's—"

"I need you to send her a text."

"What do you mean? Don't you have a phone?"

"Of course I have a phone," Emily snapped. She stepped close to Tansie. Her face was white and fierce under a purple woolen cap. She handed her back the phone. "I need the text to come from you."

"Can we go inside? It's cold out here."

"I'm fine," said Emily.

"What do you want me to say?" Tansie opened her phone.

Emily was silent for a moment as she rehearsed her message once more. The night before she had woken with a start, convinced that Andy had failed to grasp the message within her email. It was vital that Andy believed she'd left Asheville for good. "*Hi Andy,*" she dictated to Tansie. "*Are you okay? We miss you. Don't come by the temple though. We are all sick...*"

"We are?"

Emily ignored this. "Keep going," she went on. "*Emily came by before she left town. She seemed so sad. She said she will never come back.*"

"You left town?"

"Yeah," said Emily. "I'm in Trenton right now. This is just a fucking hologram you're talking to."

Tansie flinched. "Why are you so mean?"

Loud barking sounded from inside the house. Toby had heard the keys fall and finally reached the door. "I should let him out," said Tansie. "He needs to go pee."

"Just finish the text," ordered Emily. "*She says she will always love you.*"

"That's it?"

"That's all," said Emily. "No, wait!" She snatched the phone, quickly added *r u seeing anyone?*, then hit send.

"You're crazy."

Emily stared at the phone's tiny screen.

"Can I have my phone back?"

"Wait a minute!" Emily already regretted her unplanned query. How long would it take Andy to reply? To her relief the screen lit up.

Hey tansie i miss u guys
2!! R u okay? I feel so bad
about emily i know she left
town no i am not seeing
anyone altho i might have
a date bc I am a humanoid
after all ☹ wdyt? Am i a
bad person?

"What does it say?" asked Tansie.

Emily closed the phone slowly and then hurled it onto the pavers. She stamped on it several times, grunting loudly. In her short romantic life so far, Emily had developed a skill at destroying phones. Two now had been ground underfoot, one tossed from a car window, another thrown from a bridge to vanish with a tiny, soundless splash into a brown river below.

"What the fuck!" shouted Tansie.

Toby's barks were deafening.

Emily pulled her billfold from a back pocket. "You want another phone?" She shoved a handful of bills at the goddess. "Get yourself one. Just don't call her back when you do. This never happened. I was never here."

Tansie took the money. "You're nuts," she said and went inside. The screen door slammed behind her. Toby fell silent.

Emily brought her arms up around her head and at the same time slowly dropped to a crouch. Her mouth made strange circles and lines as tears ran down her face. After a while she felt among the leaves for the sharp pieces of Tansie's phone, gathering them up carefully in a cupped hand. Then she went away.

Angus had enlisted all hands to prepare the porch for the sale and hootenanny. Elaine swept the summer's pollen off the weathered floor as Angus and Frank arranged a few plastic folding tables. Malcolm raked the yard. It was the last perfectly warm day of the year.

"We need to keep these tables close to the railings," Angus told Frank, "otherwise we could stall the natural flow of traffic."

"And we could put up even more signs, directing buses and coaches to the back of the house," said Frank.

Angus had placed fresh placards for the public at each corner of the lot, even a poster on the fridge alerting the household to the evening event, with a dubious quote attributed to Brigham Young about the joy of dancing.

"You may laugh," said Angus, "but I've had remarkable turnouts in the past. There's a strategy to a successful yard sale, or indeed, the simplest booth at a flea market." He adjusted a plastic table by a fraction. "It's a matter of theme, expectation, discovery. What people often forget is that the junk sale enthusiast seeks bargains."

"They do?"

"Absolutely. They don't come here to pay full price for anything." He nudged the table back to where it was. "You might think to yourself, how can anybody want this crap? I don't want this crap. Ergo, who the hell would? That's your first mistake."

Malcolm looked up from his raking. "What's the second mistake, Angus?"

Angus appeared not to hear this. "I also put an ad on craigslist, Frankie."

"Aw," sighed Frank. "Really? I kinda wish…" He was already concerned at what the next day might bring.

"I think you'll be pleased at the results." Angus grubbed around in his ear. "Amazing I never thought of it before, really. A whole new audience. The elephant in the room."

"What kind of crap are you planning to sell to this elephant, Angus?" asked Elaine.

"Knickknacks, primarily. Bits and bobs."

"And the buggy," said Malcolm.

"In a sane world, we could sell off a few of these felines," added Angus, stepping over Chiquiquita.

"This is your chance to sell your balls, Angus," said Frank. "Those hairy things."

Angus considered this. Malcolm and Elaine waited for his response.

"I got a strange email from Lida," Frank went on.

"Hardly surprising."

"The new tenant?" Elaine asked.

"You haven't met the Barfly?" said Angus.

"Barfield," Frank translated for Elaine. "Her name's Lida Barfield."

"You're in for a treat," Angus told her.

"Yeah," Frank went on. "Well, she's still pissed at you, Angus. She said she might be leaving, or…maybe not. It was kind of hard to understand. Anyway, she definitely wants that chifforobe thing."

"This is the girl who had cancer?" Elaine asked.

Angus answered, "Says she had."

"Why would she invent something like that?" said Frank.

"She's not exactly normal. As far as the Barfly is concerned, I have one word for you." Angus spotted Lakeisha nesting in a pile of sunlit leaves. He went down to crouch over her, rolling her back and forth under his hand like a length of pastry.

"Which is?"

"Munchausen's." Angus smiled broadly. He picked a leaf off Lakeisha's eyelid.

"Damn," said Malcolm. "What's that, Angus?"

"The cancer stuff is just to win our sympathy. She's fit as a flea. As far as I can tell, nothing she says is true. Her whole story is made up. I'll bet she's never been ill in her life."

Malcolm whistled. "Shit, man," he said.

"Mad as a badger," said Angus.

Frank and Elaine looked at each other.

"Now, Angus," said Elaine, "that's quite an accusation."

Angus left Lakeisha alone to address them all. "Let us consider the facts before us," he began. "The Barfly arrives with her strange belongings—a book, a print, a hundred dresses. From where? The Balkans? Hardly. We may never know her true origins. My ear is attuned to many accents, and yet I cannae place her. We've only been told she is here to care for her mother, and yet this sickly woman is some forty miles away? Strange, no?

"Every day, when I go out to collect the mail and sort it into the necessary piles—aye, accept it as a token of gratitude, Frankie," he told Frank, who was shaking his head at the recollection of this daily meddling, "do I find hospital bills, correspondence of any kind, for our reclusive 'survivor'? Nothing. She claims to be an out-of-state trauma nurse. Is that even possible? Is there such a thing? And yet she simultaneously works at that tourist trap downtown? I've been watching her. Eye candy she may be, but furtive. The rest of the time she's holed up in her room. She's potty, alright."

Malcolm seemed the most impressed by this diagnosis.

"That's amazing," said Frank. "Now I have two mental health experts living under the same roof. Lida said something about you being the worst kind of baked potato."

Angus laughed as he returned to the porch, "Sticks and stones. I've heard it all before."

"You've been called a baked potato before?"

"In as many words."

"Well, you found her," said Frank, "you keep her happy. With Wall Street going under I'll need that rent for sure. Are you drinking already?"

Angus had pulled a sagging cardboard box from under the table, crowded with several bottles of wine. "New wine needs to breathe," he explained. "I will hide these, of course, until the dancing begins. And I expect you to dance, too, Frankie. With abandon."

"You'll be dancing, Frank?" asked Elaine. "I'd love to see what you've learned so far."

Angus froze in his task. "What's this? What's this?" His good humor was maniacal by now.

Elaine's eyes widened at her mistake, but Frank could only shrug and smile at having his secret revealed. "I've been taking dance lessons," he admitted.

Malcolm paused again in his raking. "Awesome, dude."

"Swing?" asked Angus. "Tango? I considered flamenco dancing once myself—all that stamping." He stiffened and, with a sneer, struck the porch boards a sharp blow with his foot. Chiquiquita jumped, then made a slow, stately exit to assure them all her fright had never taken place.

"Belly dance," said Frank.

"Like Andy?" asked Malcolm.

"She doesn't do belly dancing," Frank reminded him. "This is... I don't know. It just happened. I went to the wrong class." He spoke to them all. "I'm still not even sure if I should be doing this, if men even do this stuff."

"Baladi?" said Angus. "Nay, it's a strong tradition. I knew a zenne dancer myself. Funny feller. Turkish, of course. He learned it in Istanbul—that whole underground gay nightclub scene. Tremendous exercise, of course, for the midriff and buttocks. I imagine you have some healthy young lassies around for scenery, eh?" He winked at Elaine.

"I can't dance," said Malcolm. "Not at all. Maybelle Jolene wants to be a dancer."

"'Gay nightclub scene?'" asked Frank.

Lida had sorted out five sugar babies from the bowl. The others were discarded. With a thin smile, she now read a reply from Melody, perhaps the most ambitious of the babies.

Hey Joe,

I would totally like to meet you for dinner. Asheville is a big drive for me, but I think it would be totally worth it. This may be the time to set expectations, though. A really important thing for me right now is like dignity. I am a feminist and have been since I was 5. When I moved to Atlanta it was of course to find myself and start a business and that is still my dream.

As you know I am looking first and also primary for a mentor. I only had to look at your profile to see you had a rich, business mind full of the tools that could teach me to realize my dreams and create a business model of my own, helping other women overcome the challenges I have always faced in the workplace and the real world. I want you to teach me those skills and also golf like you mentioned which looks so cool.

It's awesome that you think I am super attractive, but please do not think I am just about superficiality or looks. I talked a lot about my body last time but that was just joking. The problem for me right now is tuition and other daily expenses which are extremely close to beyond my budget. I don't want to discuss figures right now, but I think before I make any commitment you should know that my rent alone is $750 which does not even include utilities. Also, my car needs an oil change and the back tire looks kind of funny.

That's all for now!! I have to run! Let me know what you think. I hope your horse gets better.

Hugs, Melody

Lida rubbed her elbow. It still ached when she straightened her arm. She would reply to Melody later. She closed her laptop. Only the streetlight outside now illuminated her room. She lay back on the bed, folding her arms across her chest and rested for some time in this corpse-like way, breathing gently, the moody, abusive rectangle of Burton's compendium beside her. After a while she got up and took a colorful glass pipe and a lighter to the window. A cat stole across the flagstones. Then another. As she lit her Hindu Kush, she saw a tiny flame answer her own across the courtyard. A dot of red glowed against the outline of a figure. Lida recognized her stalker. She had seen this person before—and not just at night. She smoked her pipe and watched.

Seventeen

The Eskimos and Laplanders—who don't know any better—rub noses, as a token of salutation. In Polynesia they don't even go that far.
 —Herman H. Rubin MD, *Eugenics and Sex Harmony*

Angus stood among the trestle tables. He watched the street through his binoculars, the flecked surface of the road jiggling in his fractured view until a car tire wheeled into sight. First one and then a second spotted and rusting vehicle slowed to park in front of Carolina Court. A woman passenger pointed at Angus. He waved back. "If I'm not mistaken," he told the dogs, "the cavalry has arrived."

The Chihuahuas began to bark.

"Hold your tongues!" Angus yelled at them. "Everyone's asleep! For Christ's sake, welcome these good people." He hurried down to meet their visitors, the dogs at his heels. A tall woman approached, holding a Ziploc bag.

"Beth Ann?" Angus asked.

The woman shook her head. "Ruby."

"I'm Angus. Can I help you unload?"

Ruby waved the bag. "It's all in here," she said. "Are you Australian?"

Angus stared at the tiny bag. "That's it?" he asked her. He looked over at another woman, likely Beth Ann, squeezing herself out of a car. She was carrying a seemingly empty grocery bag. "This is it?" he asked them both.

Frank was reading in bed, pinioned under a coverlet weighted by books and sleeping cats. Angus tapped on the door as he simultaneously stepped into the bedroom.

"What's going on?" Frank asked.

Angus's face was full of foreboding. "We seem to have disgruntled hoarders."

"What? Where?"

"On the porch."

"What? How many?"

"Three. Ruby, Beth Ann, and someone—a friend, I didn't catch her name. Possibly—"

"I don't need to know their names. Why are they disgruntled?"

"Your sale has not met their expectations," said Angus. "On craigslist I asked them to bring things to sell, but apparently—"

"My sale?"

"They've brought nothing, Frankie! They were meant to set up their own tables, donate a part of their proceeds to Juan's mum. They're only here to buy."

"Well, of course they are!" Frank tossed his book aside. "They're goddamn hoarders! Don't let them into the house, okay?"

Angus glanced back into the hallway. "They're still outside," he assured Frank.

Frank extricated himself from the crowded bed. "Make sure they stay out there," he said.

"Where's Speck's stocking?"

The cat was lying, undressed, on the bed. She was staring at Angus. Across her tiny body, tufts of hair had begun to return in varied lengths.

"She doesn't like it," Frank said. "It made her hot."

"It's chilly today, mind."

"Will you just let me get dressed?"

When Frank came outside Angus was sitting alone.

"Where are they all?" asked Frank.

"They left." Angus looked grim. "I had to be brisk with them, Frankie. They were cluttering the place up."

"Off to a good start then. Did they leave anything at all?"

Angus reached over and lifted up a Ziploc bag. "A selection of fucking bread loaf ties. She wants five dollars for this. Said she'd be back later in case it hadn't sold. Who can fathom the mind of such people?"

"We're qualified." Frank sat down. "Is that it for your secret weapon then?"

"I fear so."

"Right."

Angus swayed on the rocker. They watched the street.

"It is a lot colder today," said Frank. "Do you think that'll deter your crowds?"

"Not a chance. This is the lull before the storm."

Frank looked around. For all Angus's talk of yard sale strategy, the results were unimpressive. His tenant's final preparations were half-hearted and last-minute—the previous evening spent trudging up and down the stairs with his "bits and bobs," muffled complaints sounding through the house about the lack of help. Nor was anything arranged in a way that suggested Angus's promised "themes," so certain to encourage exploration and discovery.

The bread ties rested on a number of bags filled with tattered magazines. Old coats and shirts were dumped in piles or wadded between dusty appliances. There were some hats and a cracked bicycle helmet for a child. Between two strange, domed shapes that Frank finally recognized as the garnered cat fur, he was relieved to see the hair trimmer.

Scattered under the tables were shoes and records, picture frames and toys, some cardboard boxes holding loose seashells. Geezer's original cat harness was a pink tangle on the floor. At the bottom of the steps Trey's shopping cart sat off to one side, empty and temptingly tag-less as Malcolm had suggested.

The only table in any order was the one offered to Frank and the others to decorate with their own contributions. Andy had found her old copies of *dancetrain* and arranged them in a neat fan shape beside an old snowboard of Corey's and a brand-new *Field Guide to the American Bear*. Beside this, Frank had placed several books of his own, neat between two bookends depicting the Greek masks of comedy and tragedy. They included Angus's gift of *Eugenics and Sex Harmony* and the urine-stained *Instant Joy!* For now, Frank had decided to keep Colonel Marigold's *Little Body, Big Spirit* in case some Chihuahua health issue arose.

Maybelle Jolene, excited to be a part of the event, had volunteered a plastic mermaid with a battery-driven tail for them to sell, along with a stuffed toy eagle and her prize-winning conceptual shoebox piece. Malcolm had placed these next to an orange metal bucket surrounded by nativity scene figures. A handwritten request from Angus read, *JUAN'S MOTHER DEATHLY ILL IN JUAREZ MUCHAS GRACIAS POR LOS DONATIONS!*

Frank took a tiny, broken seashell from a box and examined it. "Where did you find this stuff?" he asked Angus.

"Yard sales, primarily. At the end of a morning they're giving it away. I just bide my time. Dumpsters, too."

"And yet you feel it has resale value?"

"Morning, guys," said Malcolm, coming out to join them. He took an empty chair beside Frank.

"In this setting?" Angus went on. "Absolutely. A fairly well-kept home of this age and proportion? A passing driver says, 'Hello, hello? Estate sale?' I don't drive by, I swoop in. Anyway, one man's trash…"

"Where is everybody?" asked Malcolm. "I thought you said it'd be like, crazy out here."

"They're coming," Angus assured him.

Frank thought of telling Malcolm about the dismissed hoarders. He decided to enjoy his coffee instead.

Angus took up his binoculars, scanning first the large, unfocused face of his landlord and then, beyond it, the yard. "Frankie, have you ever considered a grotto? A folly, as it were, to grace your gardens?"

"Nope."

"A hermitage?"

"Not really."

"You know what I mean, right? The great gardens of England? The sweeping view across a lake to a tiny, wee cave…"

"Yeah," said Frank. "I know the history. This yard's a little small for that kind of thing."

"What about in that corner over there? Did you know old men were once paid an annual stipend, aye, good money, to be hermits? Ornamental ones?"

"I don't need a hermit, Angus."

"It's a profession I'd consider."

"Aren't you kind of…noisy? For a hermit?"

"Not at all." Angus put Lakeisha in his lap, then set the heavy binoculars on top of her. "Many of these fellows were known for offering their wisdom to passing guests. Or not. The quieter ones were just for display, creeping about, doing their thing."

"Here comes somebody," said Malcolm.

Later that morning they heard footsteps inside the house.

"They're up," whispered Angus.

Corey had told them about the planned picnic. Angus, Frank, and Malcolm listened intently to hear what they could of the young couple beginning their day together.

After a while Andy came outside. She was dressed in a pale summer frock and sandals. "Oooh," she said. "It's cold out here."

Her shabby roommates beamed at her from their circle of lawn chairs.

"How's it going?" she asked.

"It's picking up," said Frank.

"We sold your magazines," Angus told her.

"Awesome."

"To Frankie," he joked.

Andy smiled, then frowned. "I think I need to change my clothes," she said. "It's cold!"

As she hurried back inside, Angus whistled. "'My queen and lady,'" he sighed. "'Her beauty superhuman.'"

There was one customer on the porch. "How much are these?" the woman asked. She held up one of Angus's cat hair balls.

"For you, madam," said Angus, "fifty cents each. Seventy-five cents for the pair."

"Is this alpaca?"

"Chantilly-Tiffany, some Angora, tabby."

"He'll throw in the hair trimmer if you buy both," said Frank.

Andy had suggested a place for their picnic, but now she couldn't remember the last few turns to the spot. They had been driving for a while. As they repeated a long, looping stretch through fields dotted with dark barns and distant farmhouses, Andy apologized again.

A couple of raindrops appeared on the windshield.

"Oh no," said Andy.

"Don't worry," Corey assured her. "There's like, a 30 percent chance of rain." He was feeling nervous and glad to cover his apprehension with the role of the patient driver, dismissive of nature's efforts to thwart their plans.

"I hope it stops," said Andy.

"It totally will."

"Okay." Andy was nervous, too. She had changed into a sweater and jeans, but her fingers felt cold and she rubbed her hands together. Although she never drank in the day, she wished she'd brought a bottle of wine. "There's the river!" she said with relief, pointing to a sheet of silver water.

Between them both, they'd brought enough food to feed four, but neither had an appetite. They wandered the riverbank around the truck in different directions, pausing to look out over the river, each wondering what to say next.

"This is awesome," said Corey.

"It was different before," said Andy.

Early in the summer, Emily had shown Andy this spot. The river was soft and verdant then, with dragonflies buzzing over the green water. But now, under a clouded sky, it was a brown stretch of shoals, its edges untidy with boulders and dead trees. Andy could not help feeling this wintry view was deserved—bringing Corey here was just another betrayal of Emily.

"How about over here?" called Corey.

Andy arranged the picnic beside their backpacks and colorful water bottles. They congratulated each other on the snacks they'd purchased, and this led to a discussion about their favorite restaurants. Both agreed they really liked Thai food and sushi best. Andy was shocked that Corey had not yet gone to Eco Eatery. She described their tacos passionately. Corey promised he would go. Perhaps they could go together? Andy clapped her hands with anticipation.

This local itinerary secure, they listed the foreign countries they wanted to visit one day, when they had gotten passports and cool travel gear. Corey was shocked to find how many travel plans they shared. They enjoyed food, the notion of buses, even walking in parks. By now, his shy glances at Andy's face had changed to rapt study.

Andy hugged her knees and smiled. Corey lay easily with all his weight on one elbow until a growing numbness in his fingers and then tremendous discomfort in his shoulder forced him to switch position. Always mindful of hydration, he drank a little water.

Andy was talking about her hopes and dreams. "I don't know if I want to be an artist or a dancer," she said. "I suppose I could be both? Or a writer, even?"

"You're so talented you could be all of those things."

"I guess."

"Are you going to play your guitar tonight?"

Andy shook her head. "I'm not good enough yet."

"I pretty much know what I'm going to do in life," said Corey. "Personal trainer. That kind of area. Fitness science of some kind. Nothing as interesting as you. Unless I make a total paradigm shift or something. I really like outdoor stuff."

"Outdoors is awesome."

Corey nodded. He looked around with appreciation at the kudzu vines and broken trees. "How did you find this super cool place?" he asked her.

Andy winced, then sighed. "My ex showed me. A few months ago."

The conversation, so far skipping happily along, plunged ankle-deep into icy water.

"Right," said Corey. "It's a cool place." Somehow, all too quickly, they had arrived at the dreadful matter of his rival. Now he must steel himself for the truth. It was time to face his predecessor and to learn just how much Andy's ex dwarfed Corey in his inevitable attributes. He tried to sound nonchalant, "You say that guy is still hanging around?"

In the pause that followed he felt faint and weak. If only he had read more of Mr. Capellanus's treatise on love—or even bought it. He was a knight unarmed.

It took Andy a moment to realize what he was asking. "Uh, no," she said. "Not anymore. Actually, he was a she. She's gone now."

"Like, a girl?"

"I'm not gay," said Andy. "I mean, it's complicated. I wanted—I thought I might be. I had a bad time, the guy before." She took a big sip from her bottle and studied the wet grass tufted around the backpack. "It's complicated." Andy felt sad again. Her stupid life experiences were ruining everything. Self-conscious under Corey's surprised scrutiny, she covered her nose.

Corey nodded slowly. He was confused, but his nausea had vanished.

"Shall we eat something?" Andy said.

"Yeah," said Corey. "This looks great."

Corey watched Andy prepare a plate for him. The way her long, white hands effortlessly opened a tub of hummus was miraculous. How strange life could be, he thought. Like Andy said, it was complicated. Here he was imagining her ex as some like, huge, ripped guy or genius, or even worse, some huge, ripped genius, and all along his competitor had just been a girl.

His silence worried Andy. "Are you…?" she asked. "Does that freak you out?"

"No, no. I totally get it." Corey was suddenly hungry.

As Corey munched on kale salad and mock chicken, Andy spoke more about Emily. She could still see her busy little figure downstream, climbing over the rocks and walking out along the fallen trunks, as though intent on defending their special place against precisely this future. She had become a ghost for sure, Andy realized, and just like those Corey had described in his apology, definitely the kind that needed exercising.

She described how she'd met Emily waiting tables and how they moved in together to save money. She started talking about The Goddess Temple but then decided Corey might not understand all that. Emily had left town, she explained, and gone home to her family. She didn't go into detail about the texts and emails—that wouldn't be fair to Emily, but nor did it feel right for her now, with Emily's phantom watching them, to be reassuring Corey that it had all been just a mistake.

While Andy struggled with her past, Corey ruminated on the world of lesbians and gender stuff. There were some lesbians at college, but they didn't look like Andy. They looked more like geeky guys, with strange, guy-like hair and soft, blurred faces. He could totally get why they would be attracted to other girls though, especially someone as hot as Andy. He wondered how Andy might feel going back to the whole dating guys thing. Yet here she was with him now. She was so beautiful. She looked sad, he noticed.

Andy picked at her plate, barely eating. She had nothing left to say about Emily.

"Are you okay?" Corey asked.

"I think it's raining," she said.

The weak October sun had dipped below the tree line. Corey took the blanket he had brought and wrapped it around Andy's shoulders. She thanked him, then added, "You must be cold, too."

She held up the blanket and Corey nodded and smiled and sat beside her. They huddled together under the fleece, their shoulders touching as they watched the river and the circles the raindrops made. Andy thought about how kind and sensitive Corey was. When he turned to say something to her, Andy did the same, and their hands were suddenly close enough in the grass for their thumbs to touch. Now and then, each looked up to meet the other's eyes. Corey could smell her perfume. At his signal, his thumb led an outrageous advance, stroking the length of her thumb.

Andy's damp hair, heavy against the sides of her head, reminded Corey of something—the lovely ears of a spaniel or perhaps a setter? He reached out to caress the wet curls. As he stroked her head in this way, his fingers happened to pull down and then release the rubbery tip of her ear.

"Ah," she whispered softly, as though this was some little Eskimo tradition she had learned in childhood—so treasured then and yet quite forgotten until this kind reminder. She tilted her cheek toward him and Corey nuzzled her neck.

As she started to say something, he brought his face up to hers and kissed her.

"It's raining now, for sure," said Malcolm.

"The evidence of an intervening deity is as fucking scant as ever," said Angus. "An act of charity capsized. The hopes of our lad and the fair Andromeda just as likely scuppered in this pissing weather. That's a cat harness, madam. Yours for a quarter."

Over the course of the day Angus's mood had worsened. Very little had sold. Beth Ann's frantic return to collect her precious loaf ties only made things worse.

For the sake of the stragglers braving the weather to visit the sale, Frank was determined to balance Angus's rumblings with his own good cheer. "I'm glad Andy changed clothes," he said. "She'd have been miserable in this."

"I preferred her in that wee costume," said Angus, but without his usual lust. He took the coin from their sole customer and added it to the bucket. "Not much of a haul," he said. "Even in pesos. I still think Juan should have been here. The whole family. Those wee brown bairns, gazing up at you? We would have sold all of this crap."

"Like I said," Frank told him. "He's very grateful, but he's a proud guy."

Angus shook his head. He started to speak, but his assessment of the unhappy results of pride upon Juan's mother was interrupted by a voice from the street.

"Hello, Frank!" J.J. Antietam stood under an umbrella. A cloud of cigar smoke surrounded his head. He wore an elegant gray coat and a long scarlet scarf.

Angus growled. The Chihuahuas got up.

"Take it easy," Frank told them. "Hey, J.J.," he waved. "How's it going?"

"Doing a little downsizing there?"

"We happen to be raising money for a dying woman!" shouted Angus.

"Just a little yard sale," Frank called back. "You need anything?"

"I'm good," said J.J. "It's good to see you surviving, Frank. Tough times ahead. Hard times for us all."

Behind J.J., Frank saw activity in a dense thicket of bamboo. A pair of black hands, a hunched form, could be glimpsed through the swaying cane. The others saw it, too. Moments later, a menacing Neanderthal figure broke free of the undergrowth, stumbling out onto the street. Clearly, in crossing the neighborhood, it had taken a short cut through the overgrown lot. Slouched yet swift, armed with a strange club, it now stole up on their visitor.

"Holy shit! Look out!" shouted Malcolm.

J.J. turned around, then stumbled as he fell back from his attacker.

"Trey!" called out Angus. "You're early."

Trey waved his mandolin. "The eardy bird cadges the first worm! What you god up there? Eddy bargains?" He helped the astonished Antietam to his feet and patted him on the shoulder. Then he hurried after the cigar that had fallen in a puddle and returned it to its owner.

"Who is that?" asked Malcolm.

"That's Trey," Angus explained. He hurriedly looked over the railings. The shopping cart was gone. "You sold the buggy?" he whispered. "Good work, man!"

"Nuh-uh," said Malcolm. "I thought you had?"

"Come up here, Trey, come on up!" Angus beckoned. "I have a bottle open!"

Nimbly, Trey skirted Antietam and pranced lightly up the path through the drizzle. He seemed delighted to revisit the garden where he'd helped capture the dogs, running over to the tree that had felled him, laughing, hugging the responsible branch, pointing it out, then charging up the steps to join the three men on the porch. He made a bow toward the new owner of the cat harness standing beside them, her mouth open. When he recognized what she was holding, he laughed again.

"Is he okay?" Malcolm asked Angus.

"In what sense?"

Eighteen

Semper amorem crescere vel minui constat.

(Love is always known to be waxing and waning.)
—Andreas Capellanus, *On Love*

Angus poured their guest a brimming glass of wine. Trey's arrival had perked him up. "This is Malcolm," he told Trey. "He lives here. I believe you've met Frankie?"

Trey smiled upon them, his face glistening from the rain. "Good evening," he said.

Angus pointed at the dogs. "And of course, you know these wee rascals."

"Is it my imagination, or have they growed since the udder day?"

"No, my friend. Of course, their jackets make them appear marginally thicker, but weren't they dressed when—"

"If we're going to start this thing early," Frank told Angus, "I guess we'd better put all this stuff back in your room."

"Let Trey look around first," said Angus.

"Yeth, pleade." Trey made his way over to the tidiest table, where Frank's small library remained intact between the bookends.

"Call me crazy, Frankie," said Angus, watching Trey, "but I'm going to make a suggestion. Do we really need to tidy this up now? Can't this junk wait until morning? As people stream in we may have a few more sales, eh? Raise more money for the cause?"

"How mudge have you raid so far?" asked Trey.

"Thirty-two dollars and change."

"You can leave it out here if you want," Frank shrugged. He wasn't ready to argue with Angus. "It doesn't leave much space for your hootenanny, though."

"They can squeeze together. Our real issue remains chairs."

"You're not using my dining chairs."

Angus emptied the wine bottle into his glass and took an appreciative sip.

"Are these nativity fidurines for sale? They're quide charming."

"Those were just tae evoke pity, Trey," said Angus. "Let me think about it. I'm going to get the old orange flute." He hurried off, full of glee.

"This is extraordinary," said Trey, peering into Maybelle Jolene's shoebox. His wet shirt clung to his wide back, the skin purplish through the transparent cotton.

"My daughter made that," Malcolm told him. "That show, *The Burning Bed*?"

Trey looked back at him with a disbelieving, Ahab eyebrow. "A powerful piece of teddyvision, indeed," he said. "How odd is this chide?"

"She's just six," said Malcolm. "She got the idea from her mom."

This reminded Malcolm of a new concern, and he turned to Frank. "I don't know, man. Maybelle Jolene's mom says Maybelle Jolene wants us to do Halloween all together, like, as a family."

"Really?" said Frank.

"At least Maybelle Jolene's mom told me she asked for that. What d'you think?" Malcolm always referred to his ex-wife in this lengthy way, as though to speak her given name would conjure her at once in writhing, sulfurous form.

Angus reappeared. "What's this?" he asked Malcolm.

"Maybelle Jolene's mom is talking about us all doing Halloween together."

"She must want something from you," said Angus.

"Maybe not," said Frank. "It might be a good thing."

"Mister Jacky is going to be there," Malcolm frowned. "He's going as a superhero or something. Superman or someone." His ex was dating a towering podiatrist she'd met at the gym. Maybelle Jolene called him Mister Jacky and now, reluctantly, so did Malcolm. "If Maybelle Jolene really wants me to go, I guess I will. And if Mister Jacky is dressing up, I guess I should too. I might go as a stormtrooper."

"My third wife liked to dress up," said Angus. "One time as a caterpillar. Poor benighted woman."

Frank persisted with his optimism. "Well now, if Desiree is dating this Mister Jacky, maybe things might get better for you guys."

"A caterpillar, for God's sake. At her sister's wedding."

"Where would you fide a thormtrooper codume in this town?"

"There's a costume shop on Lexington," said Malcolm. "I don't mean like, a Nazi—just one of those *Star Wars* guys."

"Oh."

Angus picked up a couple of chocolates and looked at them. Frank raised a hand, stopping him from passing them out to the dogs.

Trey carefully took the chocolates from Angus. "I love those liddle guys," he said. "Chocolade will make them die, Anguth. Then their death would be a weight you would have to caddy the rest of your life."

"He's right, man," agreed Malcolm.

Angus fed the Chihuahuas pretzels instead, then took up

his flute and blew a few notes. He seemed impatient to begin. "Who knows 'Five miles from Gundagai'?" he asked.

His fellow musicians looked blank. "I picked it up at the Grace Emily in Adelaide. It's one young Geezer should hear. The scatological version, of course."

With this, the hootenanny began. Malcolm performed his "Bitch from Tupelo" and then "Bitter Pill" when Trey asked for an encore. To lift the mood set by these compositions, Angus sang "Rose Garden," doing his best to affect Lynn Anderson's soft country twang. The rain went well with the lyrics, and Angus's performance convinced them all that fickle life must surely limit any promises he made. Malcolm laughed at the mess his own life was. He sang "The Glad Hag."

Frank, comfortably slumped in his chair, ate potato chips, and watched the others. Trey fascinated him—his virtuoso accompaniment, the huge hands that almost hid his delicate instrument from view. The homeless man had kicked his flip-flops aside. His splotched feet slapped the floorboards as he played. Every now and then Trey would stick his tongue out. Frank wasn't sure why.

Lakeisha and Geezer remained close to Angus, watching him intently as they waited for further snacks.

At six o'clock Elaine arrived. Frank took an umbrella out to her car and helped unload two large platters.

"I've got nothing done today. Not one thing," Frank told her without regret. "Not one single thing."

"You've managed to drink a little," Elaine laughed.

"Wait 'til you see Angus."

They hurried the food onto the porch, and the band stopped playing to greet her. Angus snatched up a tiny quiche. Crumbs falling from his mouth, he introduced Trey.

Trey made a great bow. He stuffed his shirt into his shorts and sat back down, blinking at Elaine.

"How did the sale go?" she asked.

"We sold Corey's book on bears," Frank told her. "Some seashells, that cat harness."

"And Trey is buying the nativity scene," said Angus.

"God bless you, Anguth. I thuspect I will also purchase the chide's diowama."

"Thanks, dude," said Malcolm.

They played on, and for a while it seemed it would be only their little group, the bad weather certain to keep everyone else away. Then came a commotion of giggling and shrieks. Two burly girls, both dressed in taut Lycra, came running around the side of the house. They squealed as they dodged a cascade from a broken gutter.

Frank recognized Angus's guests from the summer. He gave Angus a look. Angus shook his head. "I didnae invite them," he mouthed.

"Hey y'all!" said the white girl, catching her breath. "'Member us? I'm Kelsey. This is Jasmeena."

"Come join us," said Elaine. "Sit by me."

Kelsey waved at Angus, "Hey there!" Angus's name had clearly escaped her.

"That's Anguth," Trey told her. "I'm Twey."

"Hey, Anguth!" cried Kelsey. "Hey, Twey! How y'all doin'? Good to see you again! We saw your signs, and Jasmeena was like, 'That's the old Australian guy! The one who owns that awesome house!' And I was like, 'Awesome!'"

"Damsels of the night," smiled Angus. "Fair strollers of our streets. Welcome back."

The girls sat by Elaine, eyeing Angus as he filled two wine glasses for them.

"I trust you are surviving these trying times?" Angus asked them. "The economic downturn?"

With a snorting laugh that jiggled her frame, Kelsey assured him the recession had hardly touched her trade. A number of similarly sized circular and oval tattoos stamped her fleshy shoulders, as though she was a page in an enormous, widely traveled passport.

"We doing just fine!" laughed Jasmeena.

"My hairdresser told me the same thing," said Angus. "Certain professions—"

"You have a hairdresser?" asked Frank.

Angus lunged forward and grasped Jasmeena's bare knee. "What about this election! Nat Turner's revenge, eh?"

Jasmeena looked confused.

"A Black man in the White House? It's looking likely, lassie."

"I guess. Maybe. It don't matter. It won't change nothing."

"Nonsense! This is it. He's bright, he's funny. He da man, yo! The chance tae face America's last bugaboo. Aye, and noo excuses left tha' a Black feller cannae get ahead, am I right?"

The girls watched Angus closely, trying to follow his brogue.

"A toast!" Angus let go of Jasmeena's knee and raised his glass high, "Aye, a toast tae the… Andee!"

Everyone turned. Andy, smiling and bashful, filled the doorway. They all got a glimpse of Corey behind her. The dogs hurried over to greet them.

"Is the hoot thing over?" Andy asked.

"It's barely started, lassie!"

Trey rose and put his mandolin carefully aside. He shook hands with the young couple. "Twey," he said. "Twey."

Malcolm strummed his guitar, wondering if he should play "The Glad Hag" again for the new arrivals.

"Now who's this?" asked Frank.

A truck had pulled up to the stone steps. They watched a man and woman get out. Bent under the driving rain, they struggled to wrestle a third figure from the back seat.

"That's Harley Hicks," said Malcolm, "from the farmers market. He said he might come. That must be his family."

"Those peeble need help," said Trey. He leaped out into the downpour. Down to the group he ran, missing not one puddle, to greet them with his customary emphasis. The woman answered his bows with a curtsy. Under the glow of the streetlight, through the rain it stained yellow, Trey aided them in bearing back to the porch a bucket, a guitar, a dulcimer, and an old man. The dogs growled gently.

"Hey, Harley!" called Malcolm.

"How you doin', Malcolm? This here's my cousin Hessy, and this is my uncle, Ol' Minyard."

Old Minyard was carefully lowered into a rocking chair. He pointed a skeletal hand at the young people and whispered something.

"Brought you some apples," said Harley, looking around for somewhere to put the bucket.

Hessy shook hands with everyone. "I ain't tarred anymore like I was this mornin'," she told Jasmeena. "Shindig'll perk a body right up. I declare, some of these days I'll have a road t'walk own 'stead'a walkin' in th'mud. These'n your'n bitty fice dogs all dressed up so pretty?" Her eyes were smiling, but her jaw seemed at odds with her enthusiasm—determined to stay shut, clipping her speech to a series of peremptory barks.

Jasmeena had caught the word "dogs." She shook her head.

Hessy thanked Trey for his help. She was a small, triangular woman. With her heavy black skirt and waist-length gray hair, she tapered to a silvery point as she gazed up at him. Trey clearly impressed her. She asked if he was kin to Clara Bow.

Angus brought two of Frank's dining chairs outside for Harley and Hessy.

"What ye goin' to sing fer us, Poppy?" Hessy asked Old Minyard.

The ancient man did not seem to hear this. He was still looking around the porch in astonishment. A set of plastic, movie star teeth flared in his crinkled face. "This some kind of 'state sale?" he asked.

"What ye goin' to sing fer us!" Hessy shouted.

"How 'bout 'Lil Becky'?"

"That un's extry long," said Hessy. "If'n y'goin' tell it all."

"What's it about?" asked Frank.

Old Minyard laughed. "'Bout a boy kilt his cousin, cuts her up in pieces, burns her up in t'wood stove, 'cept fer a bitty piece o' foot—toe mebbe?"

"Driwned her in t'crick, 's how I heard it," Hessy corrected.

"Say what?"

"Driwned her in t'crick!"

"Perhaps something a wee bit more cheery?" said Angus.

"Sing 'Mole in the Groun',' Ol' Minyard," said Harley.

Old Minyard wasted no time in responding to this. His face constricted, then relaxed. His eyes opened wide. "*I wish I's a mole in the groun'*," he began in a slow, questioning way, then bellowed,

Lord, wish'm a mole in the groun'
If I's a mole in the groun', I'd root that ol' mountain down
Wish I was some mole in the groun'
Oh, don't like no railroad man
No, don't like a railroad man
If I'm a railroad man then gone kill you when he can
Drink up your blood like wine

I been in the bend so long
'been in the bend so long
I been in the bend with the rough and rowdy men
Capie, where you been so long?"

"Mole in the Groun'" continued in this vein for some time. Huddled close together, shielded against the weather by the piled-high garments and defunct appliances, they watched the balladeer sing one inscrutable verse after another. Trey ate handfuls of nuts and nodded along in approval. Jasmeena sat with her mouth ajar. Kelsey stretched and yawned.

Frank had switched to wine. His T-shirt was decorated with potato chips and quiche crumbs. His stomach rested cozily upon his thighs. How good it felt to have all these fine people sitting around him. What a pleasant day it had been. It was as though every part of his fortunate life had been gathered close about him, a reminder that he kept Carolina Court if only to host events like this. He noticed his dining chairs were under the lovely mountain folk. Beside him, the dogs finally lay down. Chiquiquita's face appeared at a window, then went away.

Corey sipped a beer. His thoughts drifted off to kissing Andy earlier in the day. They'd kissed again in his truck, but it hadn't felt the same the second time. In the truck, he'd been aware of how awkwardly his body was turned, how his knee was pressed against the steering wheel, how the rain hammered on the windshield.

Corey's surprise at Andy's ex being a girl had vanished. All his previous fears had vanished too. Now his head felt empty. He was tired.

Andy stared at Old Minyard's hands. He wore a wedding ring. She wondered if she would ever get married and, if she did, if it would it be to a man or a woman. At her wedding she would have flowers and music definitely, but not music like this. She preferred it when there were instruments as well as singing and when she could understand the words.

Old Minyard was probably the oldest person she had ever seen. No matter what products she used now, her skin would be like his one day. The older she got, the more she would look like a dinosaur. Ol' Andromeda Dinosaur, that is what the cruel neighborhood kids would call her as she hobbled down the street. She looked at the freckles on the back of her hand and again at the terrible claws of Old Minyard. If she was going to die, she told herself, she was determined to live life first.

Ol' Andromeda Dinosaur

Oh, look see a lizard in the spring
Yup, wish I was a lizard in the spring
If I was'n lizard…

Angus was fidgeting. He looked around at the audience, his face full of growing concern. He drained his glass and jumped to his feet.

"Bravo! Bravo!" he clapped. "Aye, who dissnae wish they was a lizard sometimes, eh? Or a mole, for that matter?"

This interruption startled Old Minyard. He smiled, however, when Angus came hurrying toward him with one of Elaine's trays.

"Those divils on horseback?" asked Hessy.

"Courtesy of Miss Elaine Hulsebus over there," said Angus.

The old man ate with relish. "Won't eat a hog's ear," he assured them all. "Lotta people will. Wouldn't eat one fer nothing—them hairs'll stick in your throat."

Angus turned to Andy. "Andromeda! Are you going to get your guitar? Play with us?"

Andy reddened. She began to make an excuse. Then, steeling herself to live life, she straightened her shoulders and announced, "Actually, I'm going to be dancing pretty soon, in a couple of weeks, in Marshall. It's a super cool venue. I'm doing at least one piece, maybe two. You're all invited, of course!"

"That's great, Andy," said Frank. "We'll be there for sure."

"Yeah," said Malcolm. "I'll bring Maybelle Jolene. She wants to be a dancer."

Trey asked Andy, "D'you know the local thurrealist there in Marshall? Tom thumbody? His burdesque work?"

Andy shook her head.

"Now I done me some of that!" said Kelsey, sounding as sassy as she could. "I love me some burlesque! That's a whole lot of fun, up on stage, swinging these big ol'—" She stopped herself at this, covering her mouth with both hands in a gesture she knew would delight Jasmeena.

The hootenanny rambled on, switching from old and new songs to garbled anecdotes. Angus got more wine from his room. When they noticed Corey was falling asleep, everyone assured him it was fine for him to go to bed.

Angus helped him to his feet. Inside the house, he quizzed the young man about the date. He put his hands on Corey's broad shoulders. "Did ye kiss her? Did she kiss you back? We need to know!"

Corey nodded. "Yeah. It was nice."

"Nice? Is that it? Nice?"

Corey started to say more, but Angus raised a hand. "Don't disappoint us, laddie. You're our last hope." He went back outside, shaking his head.

A little while later, the front door opened. Lida stepped out onto the porch, wearing a full-length fur coat. She carried a bottle of bourbon, a glass, and her cigarettes. As the men started to rise, she stopped them with a regal hand. "I heard the music," she said.

Hessy and the hookers pawed and smoothed her coat and Lida tolerated this admiration for a moment, then brushed them away. "Cretan," she told them. "A street market discovery."

Hessy muttered something about skins.

Lida considered the crowded porch. "What is all this?" she asked.

"It's Angus's yard sale," Frank slurred, "but I'm afraid there's nothing out here like a chifforobe."

"The chifforobe is unimportant, Frank. I have given up on that."

"It will be found!" shouted Angus.

"I doubt it," said Lida.

"You all need a chifforobe?" asked Hessy. "Harley, ain't ye kept Gatha's? Ain't hit still in t'barn?"

"Yep."

"How much?" asked Frank.

In her snarling, snapping way, Hessy explained it was a precious heirloom, passed down from her ancestors who had settled the mountains and fought and wed the Indians and then killed each other in the Civil War, and was therefore ten dollars.

"Done!" said Frank.

"Ah Frankie!" protested Angus. "You dinnae have tae pay for that!"

"I'm not," said Frank. "You are." He hauled himself out of his chair and wobbled over to Juan's bucket. He took out two five-dollar bills and handed them to Harley. "You can replace those," he told Angus.

"Fair enough, fair enough," Angus smiled. "And I'll help you collect the bloody thing."

Andy applauded. "Yay!"

To celebrate this swift and unexpected resolution to her complaint, Lida lit a cigarette. The action excited Kelsey and Jasmeena. Seeing their eager faces, she tossed them the packet. As they picked out a cigarette each, Lida spoke. "Clearly you are prostitutes."

There was a hush.

Jasmeena said, "Yeah? You got a problem with hoeing?"

"On the contrary, I respect your honesty. And you're clearly unafraid to flaunt the skimpy, garish costume of your craft."

"I swan they ain' dress fer no hunch weather like this," observed Hessy.

"We ain't ashamed to be a pair of hoes," Kelsey assured them all. "Not one bit."

"That's right," said Jasmeena.

Old Minyard sat up. "Best plant those flowers while t'moon's in the first quarter," he warned them, "less'n you need them seeds."

Hessy cackled.

Elaine was watching Lida, entertained by how she had refused a chair, preferring to stand while everyone else sat, holding court over them all in her expensive coat. Lida's defiance reminded Elaine of her younger self. She said, "That *is* a great coat. You found it in Greece?"

Lida turned to Elaine. "It's a Karamitsos. Perhaps you are unfamiliar with the long-established Greek furrier tradition?"

Trey took up his mandolin and began to play. Frank smiled with recognition at the slow first notes of the tune. He looked at Malcolm and Malcolm smiled back, picking up his guitar.

"Ah yes," said Lida. "Sirtaki." She appraised Trey, from his bare feet to his discolored head. "What happened to this man?"

"That's Trey," said Angus. He raised his arms and clicked his fingers to the music. Hessy found her dulcimer.

Trey's mandolin led the other instruments, and the building tempo of the Greek dance soon filled the porch. The melody was new to the younger women, but they smiled and clapped in unison as Angus rose to dance.

Frank lowered his head, ecstatic with some memory he could not place. "Ah," he said. "Oh!" He got up and stumbled into the house. A few moments later he was back, tying a belt of coins around his sweatpants.

"What's this?" Angus cried. "What's this?" He gave Frank a sweaty hug. "Make room for the man!"

Frank wiggled his hips and the coins tinkled. He grabbed a pair of pink leggings off a table to use for a scarf and, draping these behind him, began to sway heavily back and forth to the music.

Elaine stood up and cheered.

A History of Saints

A little unsteady, his eyes closed, Frank danced all he had learned, his amazed guests and tenants invisible to him. Whatever damned "Baladi" Angus said it was, Frank now performed it as best he could. He swished his belt and twirled his hands as Lark had taught him.

Lida stepped to one side. With her cigarette and whisky tumbler, her hands were full. Still, as if to extinguish any doubt she was incapable of merriment, she made a fierce little stamp with her foot. Angus, his arms above his head, began to dance close, pungent circles around her. Lida stamped again.

Frank's pink leggings were a red flag to Kelsey. She hurried through the chairs onto the tiny dance floor. Andy followed her with Jasmeena and Elaine.

This varied troupe crowded around Frank—Andy lofty above them all, Angus bumping into everyone, Lida dark and stamping, Kelsey wishing she could show her titties just one time. The Chihuahuas, maddened by the noise, leaped up at Frank in high, searching arcs as if to understand his transformation.

Frank opened his eyes to find himself surrounded. He took Andy's hand. "I'm your protector!" he shouted.

"You are!"

The dance rose to a crescendo and came to a stop.

Now it was Old Minyard's turn to sit open-mouthed. Hessy turned to him. "Hit's jest Asheville, is all, Poppy."

Trey played another dance, but it was clear Frank's performance had been the apogee of the evening. Soon it was time to carry Old Minyard back out to the truck. The rain had stopped, and the girls ambled off to work. Elaine left her hors d'oeuvres for the rest to finish. Andy talked quietly to Lida for a while, then went to bed.

For some time, Lida sat and smoked. The dogs were curious at the fringe of her coat, but she did not pet them. Her presence—and her unblinking expression—unnerved Malcolm.

She finished her drink and rose to say goodnight. "I am in intense pain," she said, touching her brow. "Frank, thank you for your kindness this evening. Angus, you once mentioned a back injury? Take care helping Frank tomorrow with my furniture. You," she pointed at Trey, who popped his tongue out briefly. "Your condition is treatable. You must believe that." With this she departed.

"I guess we're getting that chifforobe tomorrow," Frank told Angus.

"I guess so."

"A neurasthenic perthodality," Trey diagnosed Lida.

"If that means scary, you're damned right," said Malcolm.

Trey stayed with Angus and Frank long past midnight. He played for his hosts and for the dogs curled in their laps, until even Angus began to doze. When his friend snuffled and sighed, Trey reached over and took the cigarette from between his fingers.

He gathered some shirts and coats from the tables. These he draped generously over the sleepers to guard them from the chill. Then he put a few dollars in the bucket and carefully laid the nativity figures in the shoebox bedroom. Tucking his mandolin under his arm, he carried his purchases off into the night.

Nineteen

In almost any home in America one may note, perhaps, the worst possible selection of food known to civilized man.
—Herman H. Rubin MD, *Eugenics and Sex Harmony*

In subsequent years and, indeed, for the rest of his life, Frank would explain his present circumstances and past decisions with an account of the swift series of events that began now.

He could have begun with Angus's arrival at his door that spring or with his tenant's furtive promotion of High Cotton in the classifieds. He could have started at the capture of the dogs or the shaving of his cat or the promise of the chifforobe, but his account would always commence here, on the morning after the hootenanny, at the moment when Angus realized Trey's shopping cart had been stolen.

And why not? For if you were justifying to a stranger the aftermath of a veritable hurricane in your life, as Frank always felt he was, and telling such a story with a wish to be both concise and compelling, you would begin at the moment just before the worst winds arrived—not with those early gusts, odd perhaps, but signaling little against a blue sky.

Frank woke to the peeps and whistles of birds declaring a new day. In the cold light he saw a pile of clothing heaped in a chair across from him. The red hand of Angus protruded from the folds. Frank tried to move and realized he, too, was draped in garments. The pair of pink leggings lay on his head, protecting his ears. A warm Chihuahua stirred in his lap.

He carried Lakeisha into the house and put her on his bed among the cats. He took off his belt of coins. As he stood at the toilet, Frank nodded and smiled. The hootenanny was entertaining. As far as he could recall, the evening had also closed the tiresome dispute over the chifforobe, ending the feud between Angus and Lida. He went back into his bedroom and carefully adjusted the animals, making room for him to climb in beside them.

"Well, he's hardly passion's slave now," said Angus.

Frank defended Corey. "He was just tired, is all."

"In my day, kissing a lassie didn't wear a fellow out."

"Kids are different now," agreed Malcolm. "They're like, wored out with exercise and being healthy and stuff."

Frank made a pile of his unsold books. "It *was* their first date, Angus."

"Exactly!"

"What about all these seashells?" Malcolm asked.

"In the trash," Angus told him. "Unless you want to strew them about your flower beds, Frankie? A decorative effect for the winter months?"

"Not really," said Frank.

Angus looked at his landlord. "You're sad," he said, "and I know why."

"I'm not sad."

Angus waved him over to Juan's bucket on the last remaining table. "Look at this. Come see."

Frank looked at the dollar bills.

"The widow's mite," Angus flicked the most recent currency with a discolored finger. "But we made more than you think, Frankie. I count twelve more dollars this morning. Trey's parting gift."

Malcolm joined them to look at the money.

"He seems like a nice guy," said Frank, "covering us in clothes and everything."

Angus trembled with emotion, then coughed violently. "A fucking saint!" he managed to say. "A silver man. A true—" His coughing overcame him.

"It was real nice of him to buy Maybelle Jolene's thing," said Malcolm.

"Where does he live anyway?" asked Frank, curious where their art collector had taken his purchases.

Angus sat down to recover. He was wearing three coats, and it looked unlikely he would rise again easily. When he could speak again, he told Frank, "Different places. His choices are made seasonally."

"He had a real fancy mandolin for a homeless guy," said Malcolm.

"That was a present from his mentor." Angus made a futile reach for his coffee cup across the porch. Frank brought it to him.

Angus took a sip and smiled at Frank. "It was good to see you dance, laddie. To see you enjoying yourself. You've been troubled, aye, I've seen it, but yesterday was different. You were different. And the yard sale made you happy, too."

"I guess," Frank began.

"You've raised money for a friend in need, but charity begins at home. Never forget that."

"Okay."

"I was watching you all day..."

"You were?"

"You're a natural. The way you interact with the common

herd. Extraordinary. Effortless. And I know you could use every wee bit of extra cash."

"Not really. Thanks to you finding Lida—"

"I'm not saying weekly, of course, but a sale like this twice a month, once even? Until the spring when they'll come in droves every weekend. It's something to think about. Yesterday was just a start, mind. We didn't make much. It began badly with those bloody hoarders. That was my mistake, not yours. But look what we sold in the end. With your houseful of antiques, I can imagine this becoming a real moneymaker for you."

"I'm good," Frank said. "I don't need the money right now."

"For now, maybe, but you heard that little shit Antietam yesterday. He's right. It's likely to get worse before it gets better."

"Maybe."

"Think about it, mind. I could do with a wee bit of cash myself."

Frank missed Angus's motive behind the proposal. "Maybe in the spring we could do another," he conceded, "if we need to."

"It's your location, y'see? Catching all the foot traffic this side of town. It was pissing with rain and yet still they came. Christ, we even sold a fucking shopping cart!"

"We didn't sell the cart, Angus," said Malcolm. "Remember?"

Angus squinted at Malcolm.

"I told you last night. I didn't sell it. It was just gone."

"Where is it then?" Angus demanded.

Frank looked over the railing at the empty spot in the flower bed.

"Must of got stolen or something," said Malcolm.

"Daring," said Frank. "Right under our noses. In broad daylight, too. That's what you get for making it priceless."

Angus wrestled to free himself from the folding chair, splashing coffee around him. "Show me!" he roared.

Malcolm pointed out the patch of exposed mulch filling the cart-shaped vacancy. Angus stared.

"It was right there." Malcolm told him.

Now Angus was perfectly still. Frank and Malcolm watched the man between them. A quivering nostril hair was the only sign of life in the Scot. His stained eye was frozen. Parts of his cheek were pale, parts flush. Then one tangled eyebrow twitched.

"Remember?" said Malcolm.

"To steal from a child," Angus began in a whisper. "To steal from the blind or a derelict, aye, for ye might call him that, but to steal from such a man? Tae plunder an act of pure charity?" He seized Frank's shoulder but continued to stare down at the crime scene, his voice filling with outrage. "And to steal *his* contribution? A man who can laugh at injury, his sweet voice mangled all the while? Who spends his last dollar to save the life of a dying woman he's never met?"

"But wasn't it us who decided to sell his buggy?" said Malcolm.

Frank made a face to halt Malcolm saying more. He told Angus, "It's a shame, but these things happen."

"No. Not on my watch they don't, Frankie." Angus added an incomprehensible curse, then left them abruptly to stride into the house.

"You really think someone stole it?" Frank asked Malcolm.

"I guess."

"Well, it's one less thing to put away," said Frank. "Whatever. Let's just get the rest of this junk back up to his room."

They went back to work, but a moment later Angus reappeared, armed with a Japanese sword. "Carry on about your business!" he ordered the astonished men. "I won't be long."

"Jesus, Angus!" said Frank. "What the hell are you doing?"

"The trail is fresh…"

"Put that back! You'll get thrown in jail."

But Angus was undeterred. As Frank went toward him, Angus ducked, a bunched mass of varied coat fabrics around the shining blade, then hurried off down into the yard. He pointed the sword at some invisible evidence by the flower bed and drew an imagined line of shopping cart departure. "Banzai!" he screamed.

"Come back!" cried Frank.

"Cool it, man," Malcolm warned the vanishing Angus. They watched him turn the corner of the street, brandishing his weapon, glancing left and right for his quarry.

"Oh," said Frank.

"Because of that primarily," the woman sighed, "we have to let you go."

Lida looked at her for a moment, then dug around in her purse and pulled out her cigarettes.

"No, please!" her recent employer protested. "That's just the kind of thing I'm talking about."

"You know how hard it will be to find another person prepared to work part-time without benefits?"

"All too easy in this economy, I'm afraid, Lida."

"You will go out of business," Lida prophesied. "Anyone can buy these same cheeses for less at the regular grocery store. And how often do people need great, stupid bottles of olive oil?"

"We're surviving, thank you."

Lida lit a cigarette. "I'm leaving," she said, waving aside the reaction. "Failing to lock your pathetic door for a night hardly seems justification for firing the best employee you will ever find. As though any thief in Asheville would want to raid this place? 'Quick, guys! There's enough fucking Brie in here to keep us for life.'"

"It's not just the door, Miss Barfield. Customers have been complaining. You seem to have zero interest in being here, zero interest in the company."

"A bunch of cheeses? The company stinks. I have a life to live."

"Then go and live it."

"You're aware I battle death each day, right?"

"So you keep telling us all."

Lida walked back to Carolina Court, crossing Pack Square and heading down Broadway. She made her way through town without glancing once at the closed storefronts to either side. A young man across the street eyed her appreciatively, then flinched when he noticed her cigarette.

As she turned into the little lane that led to the back of the house, she met Frank.

"Have you seen Angus?" he asked her.

"No."

"I'm looking for him. He's out here somewhere with a sword."

Lida made no response to this. A floppy, felt sun hat hid her eyes from view.

"You're right," said Frank. "Why should I bother? If he wants to get arrested, let him. One minute he's fine, the next…I don't know. You doing okay? I thought you were working this morning?"

"I have taken the day off for medical reasons. Do you need me to help you find him?"

"No, no. I'll be fine. You should rest."

"I can't rest, Frank. You say he has a sword?"

"Yeah, but I mean he's not dangerous. It's just Angus—"

"I'm not worried about Angus. I meant that I'm not ready to nap yet."

Frank apologized. His tenant still seemed to be waiting for something. "Oh right," he realized. "Look, I may not be able to get the furniture today for your room. Is that okay with you?"

"What kind of sword?"

Frank was caught off guard. "Japanese, I think. Somebody stole this shopping cart, and he went nuts. I don't know why.

It's worth nothing—the cart, I mean. He's out searching for whoever took it."

"So we are also looking for a shopping cart?"

Frank blinked again. "Uh, yeah. Yeah, I guess so."

Lida made a little scurrying gesture with her ringed fingers that suggested the pursuit should continue. Frank obeyed. She took her place unnervingly just behind him.

"What is he wearing?" she asked.

"Coats," Frank told her. "Overcoats. Kind of dark ones."

Looking over fences and down driveways, they retraced Lida's path back toward town. There was no sign of Angus.

At a street corner, Lida stopped. "What are you eating, Frank?"

"Sorry. That's just my stomach making noises. I'm pretty hungry."

"I meant for your meals. What do you eat?"

Frank thought about this. "Well, I know I should eat a better breakfast—" he started.

"The food last night concerned me. Potato chips, junk food."

"Those were just snacks. For the hootenanny."

"I passed through your kitchen," she told him. "No fruit. Not one piece. Well, an apple. Do you know what scurvy is?"

Frank nodded.

"It still happens," Lida shook her head. "Every day." She came at Frank with a sudden, electric smile and took his elbow, the orange brim of her hat bouncing emphatically between them. "I can cook," she told him. "You boys are not taking care of yourselves. Let me cook for you, Frank."

"Angus kind of does that already," said Frank. "It's kind of his thing."

"Angus? Have you seen his complexion? What does he feed you?"

"Um, stuff. Curry, squid…"

"Do you like moussaka?"

"Sure…"

"I need to speak to you about something, Frank."

"Okay."

"Something like this could help us both."

"You cooking?"

"Yes," Lida looked pained. "Frank, I lied. I lost my job."

"At the hospital?"

"At the cheese shop."

"Ah," said Frank. "Right." For the first time with Lida, he knew what was coming next.

"Of course, I'll get another. I always do. I always get jobs. But until I get back on my feet? Your very own chef? In lieu of a little rent?"

"Right."

"Besides," Lida smiled, "giving in this way is a pleasure."

Andy ran into Tansie at a popular coffee shop. Marveling over such a coincidence, they found a table. Andy told Tansie about her new life at Carolina Court. Tansie described ongoing changes at The Goddess Temple, biding her time, waiting for the right moment to startle Andy. Now that she was face to face with her dear friend, it was impossible to keep the promise coerced from her: Tansie ached to witness Andy's horror at the news about Emily.

"We went on this like, picnic," Andy continued. "He's nice and...super healthy. He writes poetry, even."

"Awesome."

"I don't know. What do you think? It seems like, kind of rebound thing."

"Totally."

"You think?"

"It's pretty normal," said Tansie.

Andy gazed down at Tansie with her troubled antelope expression. "It is? Am I a...rebounder? I mean, just bounding from person to person? From Dale to Emily to Corey?"

"Your crazy ex is still in town, by the way." Tansie told Andy.

Andy gasped. "She's still here? Oh no! But you said she was gone?"

"She told me to write that. She's nuts. She threatened me outside the temple. Then she like, totally broke my phone."

"She broke your phone?"

"She like, stamped it into like, a billion pieces. She's crazy. She's stalking you big time."

"Big time?" whispered Andy.

Beyond the white UFO mechanics of lights and X-ray cameras, Frank noticed a little bump in the wall close to the ceiling. A drywall screw had popped, and this little touch of humanity, like the snapshots of the dental hygienist's baby and the Jimmy Buffett piped over the sound system, put him in a contemplative mood.

After their search through the neighborhood, he and Lida had found Angus back on the porch chatting with Malcolm, the sword across his lap, his rage extinguished.

Lida had retired to her room, and they were left to listen to Angus's rumblings—first on crime and then returning to the idea of repeated yard sales. It took all day for them to clear the porch.

Frank's thoughts drifted. Poor Lida. Were you even allowed to fire a person for being sick? That didn't seem legal. Her promised dishes sounded good, but he couldn't trade those for rent for long.

"How are you doing there, Frank?" the hygienist asked.

Frank nodded, his mouth bared to her work. He liked Liljana. At their first appointment she had introduced herself as a Macedonian. Where was that exactly? Next to Greece, that whole bunch of little countries there. Interesting part of the world. He liked Liljana's accent. Lark's accent was kind of the same. Probably best not to mention his dance teacher, though. You never knew with the Balkans. Lark and Liljana might be obligated to deadly animosity because of some Ottoman thing that happened three hundred years ago.

"Are you a mouse breeder?" Liljana's face appeared above him. "A mouse breeder?" she asked again.

Frank shook his head. Jesus, what had she seen? Did his mouth show signs of some rodent-borne disease? "I have cats," he mumbled.

She lowered her mask. "When you sleep," she asked, "you breathe through your mouth, yes?"

"Oh," Frank was relieved. "I don't know. I guess. I'm kind of asleep."

"Try to not do this, okay?"

"Okay."

"Try to breathe through only the nose."

"Right. Say, do you guys eat moussaka in Macedonia?"

"Musaka? This is national dish. Like turli tava. Zelnik. You want I should make you musaka?"

"Nah. That's okay. Thanks. I was just wondering."

Liljana laughed at Frank's delightful ignorance of her homeland. Frank smiled with her. He opened his mouth wide and she went back to scraping his teeth.

What would it be like to breed mice? Easy, Frank guessed, but how would you do that, with the cats and everything? You wouldn't want to anyway. Just the sheer numbers. Those things cost nothing at the pet supermarket. Poor mice were just snake food, really. What if Lakeisha had puppies? How big is a Chihuahua puppy anyway? Little thing in the palm of your hand. Angus would need to name them, of course, and that would take forever, and they'd have to vote on each one, and the names would all sound kind of the same.

If Angus went to prison one day, Frank would take Lakeisha and Geezer to see him. They'd probably allow that, just not all the puppies. Angus would do well in prison, but he'd try to escape. He'd show up back at the house, of course, and Frank would have to hide him.

That's Cat Stevens playing now. Interesting, him converting to Islam like that. Ancient Egypt, now they knew how to treat cats. Was that just them? Odysseus had that great dog. That was sad. What if I went away for years, Frank wondered, and when I came back all the cats were waiting for me and smiling and wagging their tails... Perhaps Angus was right about cats after all.

The sheer numbers

Tansie's news had shaken Andy. She resisted a temptation to call her therapist's crisis line, however. Instead, with Senecan fortitude, she booked Dr. Pringle's first available opening. Her voice trembled as she left the message.

Although she doubted Dr. Pringle would approve, she found herself searching for Emily, rehearsing something between an apology and an accusation. Emily's house had new renters. Emily had moved out, a neighbor told her. At the restaurant where she used to work, the waitresses gathered around Andy and told her Emily was "super intense and needed major help." Andy told them they were right.

She looked a little further, stopping at places she knew Emily visited, but nobody had seen her. At last she headed home. She drove with her head held high, trying to look both brave and disdainful in case Emily was watching her through binoculars.

Her phone buzzed. It was a text from Corey about their planned visit to Eco Eatery. She stopped her car. Andy read the words again and saw past them to understand yet again, with renewed, piercing clarity, that everything was her fault. A path was chosen for her in life. It was a lonely one, she realized, because she must take it alone. Yet it must be taken. Take this path, Andy, she told herself. In case she was currently on view to her stalker, Andy signaled this decision with two, slow, meaningful nods. She could no longer be a bounder—or a rebounder. Her bounding days were over.

Twenty

Verus igitur amor ex sola cordis affectione procedit.
(True love comes only from the affection of the heart.)
—Andreas Capellanus, *On Love*

E<small>MILY HAD NOT</small> moved far. She'd found a little apartment north of town, above a shop that sold seeds and planters, and the owners had offered Emily a part-time job working downstairs. This suited her—the position allowing plenty of time to stalk Andy and the woman who had stolen Andy from her.

Emily had surveilled Carolina Court at different times of day and night and now knew everyone who lived there—the round man followed everywhere by his cats, the old drunk who carried clothes back and forth from town, the thin busker with his guitar, the jock student on his bike—but it was Andy's seducer who obsessed her.

If this woman worked at all, it was in a cheese shop downtown. Emily had followed her there. She went into the shop to learn more. From their brief exchange, over the purchase of some Amish cheddar, she learned only that the overdressed employee was in remission from cancer in her left breast.

This medical history had not softened Emily. Nor did it deter her. She hunted through Frank's mailbox to find a name for her elegant nemesis but found nothing.

Such mysteries only strengthened her suspicions. They were confirmed again by the strange party on the porch of the big house. Emily had parked her car out of sight, then walked back through the rain to watch the event from behind a screen of bamboo. At first there was no sign of the woman. Andy came in with the young guy and sat with some fat hookers. Then the beautiful slut arrived, wearing some fancy fur coat. They all did a stupid dance. Afterward, when everyone had left, Emily watched her move in on Andy. It was unbearable.

Near Carolina Court was a little secondhand bookshop. Emily hid here between missions. To do so was a pleasure. Emily loved to read. In their time together, she'd bought several books for Andy—mostly poetry—and it had challenged her that her partner, for all her scribe-like activity at her journal, seemed incapable of reading.

Emily was conscientious. On her first visit to the bookstore, she searched for something to buy as payment for providing her hideout. A volume beckoned from the poetry shelf, where Corey had last replaced it. She found a little footstool and sat down, close to the floor, to open Capellanus's *On Love*.

At once the medieval treatise, with its facing translation, stirred her. She bought it gladly. Emily kept it in her book bag from then on, and its pages were soon busy with folded corners and aphorisms underlined. Now and then, she would close her eyes and press the worn paperback to her heart. She found herself mouthing the Latin phrases, delighting in the lost language of knights and maidens, when people dedicated their whole lives to chaste adoration and didn't just freak out like total idiots to leave at the first true signs of love.

A History of Saints

A looping mountain road took Frank and Angus up out of one valley and down into another. Angus stopped reading a flyer from a Chinese restaurant and looked out at the fog. "The Barfly lost her job, eh?" he said.

"Everyone's losing their jobs," said Frank.

"It's a tough life," Angus agreed. "You do what you have to do. Take these people out here," he pointed at a flaking pink trailer where, unknown to them both, Lakeisha (then Angelica) had been born and raised among overpriced reptiles. "They know how to deal with a recession."

"How's that? Just don't have anything to lose in the first place?"

"Basically. Out here you live by a code of honor. You wouldnae find this lot stealing a man's shopping cart…"

"You think?"

"They know what would happen if they tried. Oh yes. Yes, indeedy."

Frank considered the sword incident. His tenant no longer took medication. Frank wanted to suggest Angus might try it again, but it was difficult. It wasn't his place, really, and he wasn't a doctor. Angus wasn't going to stop drinking. The pills might kill him. No, thought Frank, nothing could kill Angus.

"Are ye familiar with the term 'intentional community,' Frankie? That's the modern lingo, of course. These people need each other. Out here you look out for your neighbor, or else you'll end up with nothing. It's a different way of living. An older way and aye, perhaps nobler."

"Did we miss the turn?" asked Frank. "She said to look out for a goat on the left."

"What are your feelings about barter, Frankie?"

The homes of the Hicks family were scattered along a narrow creek that led into a steep cove. To spare his old truck from being jolted to pieces, Frank barely touched the gas, letting the vehicle pitch and heave along the pitted, rock-filled road. They saw Hessy up ahead, a large yellow dog at her heels.

"Hit's jest yonder," Hessy told them, pointing to a faded red barn. She and the dog followed the truck.

The sun broke through the clouds. To either side, pastures with a few cattle rose sharply to a burnished autumn tree line. Frank backed up the truck and let down the tailgate. Angus got out and strolled through a patch of cow manure.

"It's beautiful out here," Frank told Hessy as she walked up to them. Her dog ran to Frank.

"That's Fatback," she said.

Angus came around to pat the dog. Fatback sniffed his shoes.

"He does have a fat back," Angus noted. "Flat, too. You could set a wine bottle on that dog's back. Several, in fact."

"He wouldn't abide it."

"I wasn't planning to, madam," said Angus. "I was merely making an observation."

"He'll turn on ye, see if he don't."

"Take a look at this dog's back, Frankie."

"Can we just get this thing?" said Frank.

"Chifforobe's in there," Hessy told them.

The wardrobe had languished. Old boards and pieces of machinery were piled against it. A furry layer of dust, broken only by chicken prints and fresh guano, covered everything.

"Jesus," said Angus.

"Shit," whispered Frank.

A chicken appeared at the chifforobe's open door. It tilted its head and stared at them, then stepped out. Another followed. Generations of birds had used it as a home.

"We'll need to clean this," said Frank. "I guess we'll hose it down back at the house."

They took everything off the chifforobe and carried it outside. Frank checked the interior for further poultry. "No more chickens," he said.

"Chicken won't go in there," Hessy assured Frank. "Not for nothing. Not even if there's a racoon after him."

"Oh really?"

"There's a story goes with that ol' chifforobe. Harley won't keep it in the house. Not a one of us would."

"Do tell," said Frank without interest. He was already irritated by the state of the furniture.

"Folks say there's a haint in there."

"It's haunted?"

"Ol' Minyard could tell ye more. As I heard it, cousin of mine reached in there one time to fetch him a shirt, but what he took hold of was…a nose. Human nose."

"Just a nose?"

"Nope. There was a face attached to it. Human face."

Frank sighed. "Right."

"Midget of some kind, I guess. They say it was the ghost of some poor boy, hid from the Yankees—" Hessy stopped and turned to Angus. "Y'all need to quit foolin' with that dog."

Angus had taken an old mason jar from the barn and was balancing it on Fatback.

"I'm not sure it's that old," said Frank. "Chifforobes, I mean, they're pretty recent."

"It is," Hessy told him. "It's antique, alright, but ye can leave it if you want. I jest don't have but four dollars and a quarter right now."

"No, no," said Frank. "That's okay. We've paid for it, we'll take it. I'm just kind of surprised you didn't mention this nose before, when you were going on about the Indians and stuff."

"Must have forgot."

"Look at this, Frankie!"

As they headed home, Frank muttered about the potential Confederate in the furniture behind them. Had Hessy just tried to fleece him? Had others been duped into leaving the chifforobe behind with half their money? Possibly. Still, if this was some moneymaking ruse for the Hicks family, the dust that now covered both him and Angus suggested it was an infrequent one. He rolled down a window to counter the warming manure on Angus's shoes.

"I've got surgical spirit and Band-Aids back at the house," said Frank.

Angus took the injured ball of his thumb out of his mouth. "Soldiers back then were tiny, of course. On both sides. People back then were about five foot tall."

"Where d'you hear that?"

"It's common knowledge." Angus laughed. A new thought delighted him. "Christ! If we'd had the wee doggies with us—and a camera! What a picture that would have made."

Frank had learned to follow the lurching, lunar courses of Angus's mind. "You think he'd have preferred Chihuahuas to mason jars? You better just hope he didn't have rabies."

"What are the early warning signs of that anyway?"

"Good point."

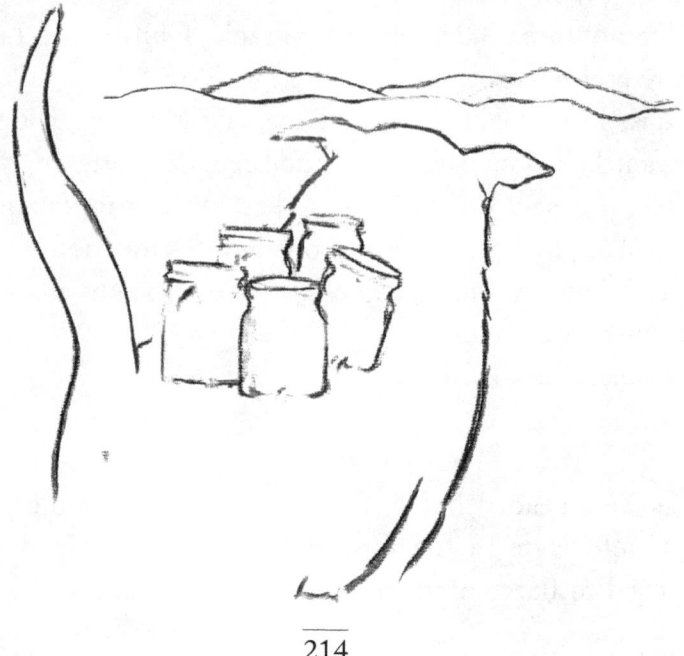

A History of Saints

Corey opened his door to find Angus busy at his desk across the hallway. His aged roommate was shoeless, gray with dust, scrawling notes as he stared at his computer.

"Hey, dude," said Corey as he headed downstairs.

Angus raised a hand bound with toilet paper. "Whoa, there," he said. "Not so fast."

"How's it going, Angus?"

"What news, laddie?"

"You mean with Andy?" Corey shrugged. "I don't know, man. She kind of called things off, said she wasn't ready."

"What?"

"Yeah. She said she had too much to process right now, that she was in a grieving pattern."

"A 'grieving pattern'? What is she, some kind of airplane?"

"Don't worry, man. Stuff happens." Corey put on a helmet and adjusted the straps.

"What happened to you?"

"How d'you mean?"

"One minute you're writing poetry and rolling around on the floor…"

"Yeah," said Corey. "It's weird, right? But then I was like, I get it." In his pointed headgear, Corey took a moment to frame his thoughts on the strange ennui that had seized him since that first, yet culminating, kiss of his courtship. "Have you ever had like, workout fatigue? Well, anyway, I figured out what happened. I was totally overtraining with like, poetry and chivalry stuff and then suddenly, when I got what I wanted, my energies just shut down, exactly like after a super intense workout."

Angus looked at him.

"Yeah, so her needing to process right now is actually pretty cool, because it gives me time to rebuild my own energy levels. I'm actually still feeling super tired. In my brain."

Angus seemed unimpressed by this theory. He changed the subject. "Look at this," he said.

Corey leaned over to take a look at Angus's computer. A number of circus acts filled the screen. The precarious animals pleased the tired knight. "Awesome," he said.

"You're the expert on those beasties," Angus pointed to one image. "Can they really do that?"

"Probably just trained bears. They don't have chairs in their natural habitat."

Lida sat at the bar of Randy's Steakhouse. She read McKuen while she waited. Across from her a man in a cap was trying to catch her attention. She glanced over an original pair of Schinasi cat-eye glasses at him, then texted his description to Melody. *Hey baby,* she wrote. *im @ the bar u can't miss me wearing a red hat n blue shirt c u soon.*

Melody texted back. *xo baby cant wait.* This was typical of her—she was the most forward of the babies—bold enough to suggest sharing her hotel room directly after a first encounter.

Lida's phone lit up again. It was a brief text from Chrystal to say she was running late.

Now the man in the cap was tapping his glass and smiling at her. Lida looked directly at him and shook her head. She texted Chrystal. *@ the bar, wearing a red hat c u soon.*

Lida sensed a petite figure standing close to her barstool. She swung around. Emily glared at her.

"Ah," said Lida. "The lesbian in the bushes."

Lida's composure took Emily aback. "You saw me?" It was all she could think to say.

"Of course. I miss very little. You also came into Olive to Eat Cheese, I believe?"

"What?"

"My former place of employment. Why are you following me? Who are you?"

Emily recalled her purpose for this confrontation. "She's mine," she stood with her fists clenched at her sides. "Keep away from her."

"Who?"

"Andy."

"Oh," Lida took off her spectacles. She looked Emily over. "I see."

"Stay away from her. I mean it."

"So you're her ex? I had no idea. I thought she was straight."

"How d'you know I'm gay, anyway?"

"For one thing, you dress like a young Montgomery Clift."

Emily sneered. "Yeah? Well, I could hardly dress like an old Monty Clift, could I?"

Lida took a sip of her drink. "I think I would enjoy talking to you," she said, "but I'm currently engaged." Beyond Emily, she saw Misti coming into the restaurant.

Emily followed her gaze. "Are you meeting her here?"

"Who? Andy? No. I'm here on my own."

"I don't believe you." Emily was trembling. "You're up to something. Are you cheating on her?"

"You seem very…put out," said Lida.

"My fucking heart's broken, okay?"

Emily was clearly not going to leave. Lida signaled the bartender and pointed at her drink. "I'll have another, and get one for her."

She led Emily over to a booth. "Let's sit here," she said.

Emily sat down, defeated. She put her cigarettes next to the ashtray, then took a napkin out of a dispenser and blew her nose. She looked at the tabletop between them, unable to face Lida's gaze. "Can you just leave her alone?" she said. "Please."

From where she sat, Lida could see Misti search the faces of the few single men in the room for some reaction to her arrival. The glass door opened behind her, and Melody came in. Melody immediately waved at the man in the cap.

"You're wrong about me and Andy," said Lida. "I barely know her. She's just moved on from you, that's all. She's dating Corey now."

"Who? Who's she?"

"He. He's a lunk. Nice enough."

"A lunk? A guy?"

"Yes."

Emily plowed her thin fingers through her black hair. "A fucking guy? She said she was over guys."

"You're ex is the needy type," Lida told her. "'The funeral baked meats' and all that."

Emily said nothing. Her head was still bowed. She looked like a child against the high polished back of the bench.

"Drink your drink," said Lida.

While she let Emily deal with the truth about Andy, Lida watched her arranged pantomime unfold. At the bar, the man in the cap was listening to Melody. He was grinning, but she looked vexed. Lida wished she could hear what Melody was saying.

Misti had not moved from the center of the room. She sent a text. Lida's phone buzzed in response and she put it away in her purse.

Chrystal came in wearing a small gold dress, looked around, then waved at the man in the cap.

Emily wiped a tear off the table. "Who are you anyway?"

"Lida Barfield."

"What is this fucking place?" Emily looked around. The room seemed full of young women in cocktail dresses, opening and closing their phones. "Is this a gay bar?"

"Hardly," said Lida. "I believe they specialize in steak dinners. I like it here because I can smoke."

Emily still wanted to be angry at Lida. She picked up the slim volume of McKuen's poetry Lida had been reading, then put it down. "What's your story?" she asked bitterly. "Wearing fur coats, having cancer and shit?"

"Who said I had cancer?"

"You did. At the cheese shop."

"Oh."

"Does she love him? The lunk?"

"I think they've been on one date."

"Fucking unbelievable."

"What's your name?"

"Emily," said Emily.

After a while Lida said, "Do you see that girl, Emily? Over there? That's Melody."

Emily looked at Melody. She and Chrystal were showing each other the messages on their phones.

The bar was noisier. As one expectant exotic after another filled the room, it was now understood by the locals that the "right" red cap possessed qualities somewhere between a powerful aphrodisiac and a winning lottery ticket. The hatless were assuring Melody and Chrystal that red hats were in their trucks. The man in the hat was disputing this. Misti was listening to this exchange as she watched the door. Heather came in.

"That's Chrystal," Lida told Emily, "and that one's Misti. The girl who just came in—that's Heather."

Emily stared.

"Don't stare," said Lida. She reached across the table. Emily let her light the cigarette she had been holding for a while.

"Who are they?"

"They're all sugar babies."

Emily looked at her.

"Their intent is to marry for money. Or merely trade sexual favors for the same."

"I know what it means," said Emily. "How d'you know they are?"

"Please don't stare. I invited them, through a website, yourtrophybride.com. They've all come here, driven a long way, to meet a man, men, who don't exist. I invented them."

"Why would you do that?"

Lida shrugged. "It's a hobby. I have my reasons. I don't like sugar babies."

"That's a weird fucking hobby."

"Not to me."

Emily looked at the disappointed harem again. She turned back to Lida, "*'Verus igitur amor ex sola cordis affectione procedit.'*"[2]

"Try telling them that," said Lida.

---

[2] "True love comes only from the affection of the heart."
Andreas Capellanus, *On Love*

Twenty-One

It is also a fact that men, in their turn, through clothes and ornaments, are not entirely devoid of certain stimulating influences upon impressionable females.
　　—Herman H. Rubin MD, *Eugenics and Sex Harmony*

As they wrestled Lida's long-delayed furniture into High Cotton, Angus told Frank he'd be late with November's rent.

Frank listened to his excuses. At last he understood why Angus had been pressing for a series of yard sales to continue through the winter. Frank was spared voicing his doubts again about that notion, however. Angus had lost interest in the scheme. He now agreed with Frank that the proceeds had been slight and the prospects dim. Despite this admission, the Scot was cheery. He assured Frank his financial situation was fleeting.

His landlord was less optimistic. Two of his tenants now had money troubles. Frank realized the additional rent from High Cotton, substantial and unexpected, had made him careless. He'd spent his time hosting hootenannies and attending dance classes. Elaine's addition was nearly finished, and there was no further work on the horizon for him—the little jobs he might have taken over the summer had all been canceled in response to the tumbling stock market. When the wardrobe was in place, Frank walked around his garden, picking up a few leaves, not quite sure what to do.

Malcolm wandered from rack to rack in search of a costume. The men's section was limited. There were pirate outfits, old military jackets, some rags for zombies. A selection of caps and sombreros were dominated by three large Easter rabbit heads. There was a space suit of sorts, but it was clear Malcolm would not be trick-or-treating with his family as an intergalactic stormtrooper. He settled on a ninja costume that came with a hood and plastic throwing stars.

He took his place behind another customer at the counter. The man ahead of him was saddened by the Spider-Man suit he'd reserved for an office party. The little stocking garment lay between him and the owner on the glass countertop.

"But this is like, a public event…," the man explained. "People will be there. All the people. Jeff will be there, and Leslie Pellman, she'll be there, too. I needed the Spider-Man suit."

"That is a Spider-Man suit."

"Not this one," He nudged the suit toward her. "The other kind. This one is just stretchy."

"You don't want stretchy?"

"Yeah, of course stretchy, but with muscles. This has no muscles."

"Oh," the lady understood. "You wanted the one with the six pack?"

"Yeah, and the chest bits, and the arms."

"Those are so awesome, aren't they? I'm sorry, but this is the only kind we have."

The man shook his head mournfully. He took a step toward the door. "But I have…this." He caressed the full curve of his belly with the downturned eyes of an expelled Madonna. He looked up at Malcolm.

"Sorry, man," Malcolm told him.

"I think we still have a Hulk somewhere," the owner offered, but the suggestion only fell as a final blow. She turned to Malcolm. "That's a shame. Poor guy. You want the ninja suit?"

"I guess. You don't have like, a stormtrooper suit? The *Star Wars* kind?"

"We used to, but it got a lot of wear and tear. Guys act like kids in that stuff. We have a Chewbacca head."

"Do you have a ninja suit with muscles?"

Andy brought water for herself and goji berries for Lida. She no longer carried her journal—it lay on her desk, unopened for days beside Angus's Viking ship. The tragic facts of her existence were too much to report. Visiting Lida in her unemployed, terminal condition was a good deed she could do—and a reminder that things could be even worse for Andromeda Megan Bell. She wore a fat, woolen Andean cap with woven braids to either side because it was cold and misty in the courtyard.

"Hey," she whispered. "I just wanted to see if you were okay?"

"Yeah," said Lida. "Come in."

"I brought you these."

"What are they?"

"Goji berries. For immunity."

Lida put the bowl to one side.

"Have you found a new job?" Andy asked.

"Not yet." Although the recipient of both Andy's concern and her berries, Lida seemed a little chilly.

Andy shuffled toward the bed and sat down, her movements somewhat restricted by a Nepalese meditation blanket. "I can't believe they did that. They should totally apologize and give you your job back."

"I wouldn't take it if they did."

Andy noted the chifforobe. "At least you have somewhere for your clothes now."

"What are you wearing exactly?"

Andy smiled. "I know," she admitted, "but it keeps me super warm. Just like you wearing your fur coat, right?"

"Hardly."

"I came to thank you for the food, too. I love that kind of food, especially lasagna, although I can't eat it right now because of my diet. It's so kind of you to cook for us, particularly with you dying and everything."

"I don't mind."

Despite Lida's strange mood, Andy persisted. She desperately needed someone to confide in, and her final visit to Leaf Pringle was some days away. "Lida," she said, bringing her hands together. "I'm leaving. I'm leaving Asheville."

Lida stood up. She went to her preferred spot at the window and looked out. "You are?"

"I have to. I have to go away and maybe never come back for at least a year."

"Where will you go?"

"Somewhere," said Andy. "Austin, probably. It has a super cool music scene."

"But why are you leaving?"

"I'm a cow person," Andy told her, "in a china shop."

"A what?" Lida came back to sit close beside Andy. Her demeanor had changed.

"A cow person. You were right. I break people's hearts, you see? I don't mean to, but I do! I don't know how—I guess it's just my natural beauty and stuff, even though I have this stupid—"

Gently, Lida took Andy's hands away from her nose. "Whose heart have you broken?"

"Well, I just broke up with Corey. So that's one!"

"You broke up? I thought you just went on a picnic?"

"He wrote me poetry, remember? He's been in love with me since the day we met. I'm so selfish I couldn't even see he felt that way."

"When did you break up?"

"A couple of days ago. He's hiding it, but I can tell, his heart is broken for sure. Men can hide stuff like that—not like us. But that's not even the main reason I'm leaving."

"What's that?"

Andy pulled her blanket around her. "My ex."

After a moment, Lida said, "What about him?"

"I didn't tell you everything. Like, first of all, she wasn't a guy."

"A girl?"

"Yes." Andy needed water now, but her bottle was across the room. She began her avowal with an ingrained church phrase from Graniteville. "At that time in my life I was a practicing lesbian. I didn't tell you—I wasn't sure how you felt about stuff like that. I was confused when I got here. I even thought about living in the Goddess Temple. You probably don't know what that means?"

"I know what that means."

"Now I don't even know what I am. It doesn't matter. Nothing matters anymore. I totally broke her heart. She said she was leaving to go back to Trenton, but she didn't. She stayed here—to stalk me. She broke my friend's phone, too."

"She sounds unstable."

Andy defended Emily. "She's super intense. And hyper-monogamous. She wrote *Love is it, dummy. Period.* on my windshield, with my Red Dahlia Burt's Bees lip balm. She was always writing poems. Everyone writes me poems, and I don't deserve them."

"She does sound intense."

"For sure. That's why I have to leave. With me gone, she can heal."

"That's good of you."

Andy placed a blanketed hand on *The Anatomy of Melancholy*. "Is there anything in here about stalking?"

"Kind of. Section I, Subsection II, under 'Suspicion.' Would you like to borrow it?"

"Thanks, but I don't know if I can lift that right now. I'm pretty weak. I'm going to ask Frank if I can stay here long enough to perform my dance, but then I must go. If Emily is still here, I have to."

"That's her name?"

"Yes. Emily Maria Ignazia Nazario. She's part Italian, and that's why she feels stuff like love super strongly."

"And you don't?"

"Oh no, of course I do! I'm actually too romantic. But I must walk through life alone, at least for now."

"That's probably best. It's a shame you have to go. I'll miss you."

"I'll miss you, too. Please try to stay alive. Please."

"I'll try."

"We'll meet again, I feel sure."

"Would you like a Xanax?"

"Thank you. You're so kind to me. You've taught me so much." Andy watched Lida find them both pills. "I think I should get a tattoo before I leave, although I could get one in Austin just as easily. It would help me learn from this experience. I was thinking a self-portrait—but of myself as an old woman. What do you think?"

"Or you could get one of yourself as you look now," Lida suggested, "then just let it wrinkle up with you over time."

Andy shuddered.

"Austin sounds quite enchanting," said Lida.

Andy made her way over to her water bottle. "Am I making a mistake?" she asked. "Am I just running from myself? Do you think I should stay?

"No," said Lida. "You should go."

A History of Saints

When Frank got a call about a small project to paint a bathroom, he was quick to respond, making an appointment for that same morning to price the job. The meeting went well, and the young couple seemed nice. He felt relieved.

On his way back, he stopped at a rundown shopping center to get a sandwich. There was a single café table outside in the sunlight, and Frank sat there to eat his lunch and read his paper.

A sidewalk ran the length of the stores. Frank noticed a strange shape heading his way. As it got closer, the great, brown wedge waved. It was a man in a foam suit, fashioned to resemble a happy slice of pizza, complete with mushrooms, pepperoni, and olives. With a smile, Frank understood what he was seeing. He waved back. As it reached him, the slice folded a placard it was carrying in two and stuffed it into a garbage can.

"'Morning, Frankie."

"'Morning, Angus. I was wondering where you hurried off to this morning. Congratulations. Looks like you found a job."

"For now."

"I just got a job, too. Small one, but it's something."

"Bravo, laddie."

"You look really cheerful in that suit."

"The mask of comedy, no more than that. Drivers wouldnae stop for a scowling pizza."

"I guess not."

"You probably think this kind of thing pays well? You'd be surprised. When I deduct bus fare, I'm barely breaking even." Angus was somehow able to sit down on the delicate metal chair opposite Frank. The employees inside the sandwich shop pointed at him. Angus waved back.

"I'm sorry to hear that," said Frank.

"The manager's a bloody tartar."

"Is he?"

"They start out well enough, these kids, but then they realize the power they have. If you wore this for one day, just one day, aye, you'd understand totalitarianism. For years I've been saying the foam suit workers of America—"

"Shouldn't you be out there, with your sign?"

Angus waved Frank's suggestion aside with a vast hand. "I cannae focus in all that traffic or hold a pencil to make notes. Anyway, I'm through for the day."

"Already?"

"Free as a bird." Angus leaned very slightly forward. "This is just to fund a new project. I think I've hit upon something, laddie. Something extraordinary, even for this town. That sandwich looks good."

Frank moved his sandwich away from Angus. "They're just five bucks. I'll treat you to one. We're celebrating."

Angus looked into the restaurant again. "Thanks, but I can wait. What I really need is a cigarette."

"There's moussaka in the fridge at home, and lasagna...," Frank stopped.

The huge, painted eyes surveyed him. Below, Angus's face was veiled by the black mesh of the smiling mouth. Frank could make out the glint of his sunglasses.

"We need to talk about that, Frankie."

For days, the preoccupied Scot, at his desk or pacing the landing, had said nothing about Lida's new role in the kitchen. Clearly that moment had come. From the pizza's grave tone, Frank guessed that Angus had also learned of his arranged barter with her. "I was going to explain that," Frank began. "I was hoping you wouldn't mind. It's just until she gets back on her feet—"

A mirthless laugh issued from the netted grin. "I've suffered worse. My cuisine offended you, I understand…"

"No, not at all…"

"You crave her heavy Mediterranean dishes over my light oriental fare? I get it. And I see that you would accept her cooking as a form of rent rather than offer me the same chance. Makes perfect sense. She's a beautiful young woman; I'm a broken old man who can still be put to work at the side of the highway, buffeted by—"

"It's not like that, Angus."

"Don't worry, lad! I'm playing with ye. I'm not offended. Besides, I'm too busy now to cook. I wasn't referring to the fact the Barfly's playing housekeeper, but rather *why*? Eh? Why? Always look to motive. The moussaka situation is serious, y'see? Mark my words—deadly serious."

"Huh?"

"We'll discuss it later." Angus changed the subject. "Listen, when you were a child at the circus, what was your favorite act?"

"What?"

"At the circus?"

"I don't know. Clowns? What do you mean about the moussaka?"

"Did ye ever see a dog pushing a pram? A stroller? A dog dressed as a young mother? With a dog in the pram, dressed as a wee baby?"

"What do you mean 'deadly serious'?"

"Dogs dressed up as people? Victorian gentry?"

Frank gave up. "No. I don't think so."

"Perhaps you will."

"Where?"

"Here! In Asheville, of course. What better place?"

"This is your new project? I thought you'd have learned to keep away from dogs."

"Flatback was an anomaly. Pure Madison County. His thyroid problem made him short-tempered, that's all."

"I don't think they allow those kind of acts anymore," said Frank. "You have to go someplace like Mexico for circus stuff like that."

Angus was undeterred. He gave Frank a spirited overview of his progress so far and then concluded with a revelation. "Ye'd think 'Keisha would be the fastest learner, right? Me, too. But it's wee Geezer who's the sponge."

"Right."

"Can I get a ride home with you, Frankie?"

Frank had been waiting for this. "You won't fit. You're about seven feet tall in that thing."

Angus looked at Frank's truck. "I can lie in the back."

"Shouldn't you leave the costume here? Where are your regular clothes?"

"They're under this."

"Okay," Frank finished his last bite and stood up. "I'm ready. I think the sandwich people want us to leave anyway, seeing as how you're not a sandwich."

Angus rose above him. "Expect tae witness miracles, Frankie."

Frank helped the great slice as it climbed into the back of the truck. Angus lay down among the tools and debris. The costume filled the truck bed.

"You're sure you want to lie on your face like that?"

Angus mumbled something.

"Have it your way." A large black ring of foam lay by the truck. Frank picked it up and threw it onto Angus's back. "You lost an olive slice. Keep still, alright? I don't want to get pulled over by the cops."

———

Frank tried not to think about dogs or circuses or motives for dangerous moussaka as he drove home—better to focus on the good news that he and Angus were both working. Now and then he looked back. Angus was still there, quiet behind him in the truck bed. The contentment Frank had felt earlier was gone, though. Against his will he started to wonder how Angus would return to work the next day. Would he fit on the bus? Would he be allowed on the bus? Would he ask Frank to ferry him back out there?

As they got close to Carolina Court, Frank sensed activity. The rear window was struck by the tip of the restless pizza. Angus was trying to rise to his feet. Frank slowed to a stop and rolled down his window. "What's going on?"

Angus was standing. He pointed at a small blue house, then suddenly dropped to his knees. "Drive on!" he said in a loud whisper. "Keep going, keep going!"

At the sight of Frank unloading Angus, the circus trainees sped out of the house, barking furiously.

"What was that about?" Frank asked Angus.

"Hush, babies, hush!" Angus told the dogs. "Did ye see it, Frankie?"

"What?"

"Trey's cart? The buggy? Evans has it! It's sitting beside his house, plain as day!" Angus laughed above the growling and snapping. "I'm a fool! It was him all along, of course."

Frank handed him the olive slice. "What are you going to do?"

"I don't know yet."

"If you try going out with that sword again, I'll call the police myself."

"Geezer! 'Keisha! *Silencio*! Don't worry, Frankie. I'll deal with this."

"How?"

"I don't know yet. My God, the Welsh!"

"I know the guy who owns that house. He's not Welsh." Frank watched Angus search his costume for the vacant spot where the topping belonged. "It's meant to go above your right eye," he told him. "What did you mean about the moussaka, anyway?"

Angus looked around. He led Frank away by the arm, far from Lida's window. The dogs followed, snarling at Angus's huge feet. He whispered, "I'll just say this for now. Munchausen's is one thing—tragic, aye, often suicidal—but now we may be dealing with far worse."

"Can you just get to the point? What are you talking about?"

"Munchausen by Proxy. That's what I'm talking about."

"What?"

"How can you know so little about mental illness, man? You live in Asheville, for God's sake."

"Munchausen's by what?"

"Have ye been eating her food?"

"Who? Lida's? Sure."

"Don't touch it. It's clear she's stepped up her little game."

"What are you saying?"

"It's not enough for her to be sick, y'see? Now it's our turn. She's slowly poisoning us all. Then she can turn around and play nurse. Slowly, slowly, like a spider, she'll win our affection. I've read of the condition, of course, but never encountered it before."

Frank groaned.

"Don't believe me, then."

"It tastes fine…"

"It would. The poison used by such people is always tasteless. It tastes fine to me too."

Geezer made a leap and snatched the foam slice from Angus's hand. "Crikey! Did you see that, Frankie? The sheer agility?"

"You're eating it?"

"In the smallest possible portions. In a day or two I'll run some tests. I may be wrong but, unfortunately, I seldom am." Angus crossed his yellow arms. They watched the dogs tear the foam apart. Angus's suit cast a strange shadow alongside his landlord's, as though Frank stood next to some great, tapering monolith.

"I know what you're thinking, laddie. Theft, lunacy, what next? I feel the same way, believe me. 'Things fall apart,' aye, the Bard was right. It's the economy, of course, but there's more to it. A Taffy steals a shopping cart from a charity event? A woman claiming she's a nurse poisons a household with baklava? Just because her mammy didnae kiss her goodnight? The world's changing, Frankie. People are different now…"

Frank felt sleepy. His sandwich was bringing on a nap. "I think that was Yeats," he said.

Twenty-Two

Then Hirose asked if I had ever heard of ninjutsu, the art of invisibility or camouflage. Indeed I had.
—John F. Gilbey, *Secret Fighting Arts of the World*

LATE ONE NIGHT, Andy received an unexpected email from Emily. Her ex-lover's words were terse and strange this time—quite different from her previous, slurred messages.

To: AndromedaB@yahoo.com
Subject: Personal items

Andromeda Megan Bell,
    Trenton tires me. I am not wanted here. As I have items that I need to return to you, I plan to head down to Graniteville. If I do not find you there, I will, of course, return to Asheville - for these are the only two places I can imagine you being. I have a lock of your hair which I cut from your head while you were sleeping. I also have a T-shirt of yours. May we meet one last time? I would like to say goodbye properly.
    I look forward to parting from you forever,
    Emily

If Andy had any doubts about leaving Asheville, they were dispelled at once by this request. Emily's continued deception that she was in New Jersey, along with the dogged itinerary she planned from a place she wasn't, sent Andy into a panic. From tiny, hidden clues within the email, and despite the promise within its valediction, Andy sensed that Emily had not yet fully completed her grieving process. She still sounded nuts.

Andy got up and walked around her room. She picked up her Georgia Bulldogs bear, then put it down. She got on her knees and pulled her suitcase out from under the bed, opened the suitcase, and put the bear inside it.

Angus lay on Malcolm's couch, briefly detailing the Code of Chivalry. He wore white silk pajama bottoms and a black turtleneck sweater. His feet were clothed in festive socks.

"I don't know, man," said Malcolm. "Are you sure about this?"

"The madness ends here, Sir Malcolm." Angus unfolded a piece of paper. "*Evans,*" he read aloud, "*your actions have brought this upon you. To mock a gentleman's dog is one thing. I cannot however turn my back upon this fresh crime. Within a single day of your receipt of this demand, I expect the buggy returned to Carolina Court. Otherwise, I must demand satisfaction. This is your chance to convince the world that Taffy can do better. Should you insist upon your country's predilection, however, we must meet in martial combat. Your crime does not warrant death...*"

"Yeah, that's right, man," said Malcolm. "Be cool."

"*And so I prescribe the use of fist and foot, in a place to be determined, and to take place at dawn. I have already chosen my second, a Malcolm Dziedzic of Carolina Court. I suggest you do the same...*"

"Me?"

"Of course, my friend. Let me finish. *My personal preferences for the field of combat are, weather permitting, the tennis courts at the park or the children's playground at the corner of Flint Street and Magnolia Avenue. Should you eschew my challenge entirely, know this—Guy Fawkes Day approaches, and your hovel is made of wood, Sir!* How does that sound to you? It's just a first draft, mind."

"Scary, man. Is that the guy from the movie?"

"Guy Fawkes? He tried to blow up parliament. We still burn him in effigy every year, for the kiddies."

"You'd blow Evans's house up?"

"I doubt it'll come to that."

"What does Trey think? Couldn't he get the buggy back? I mean, he's a big, scary-looking—"

"A gentle giant, Malcolm. Trey is a flower of the field. Anyway, it's my penance. I didn't watch the cart. Now it lies in Welsh hands."

"What's the deal with you and these Welsh guys?"

Angus rolled onto his side and smiled at Malcolm. "You're right, of course, it shouldn't be that way. We're all Celts together, I see that, and by God, it's fine country. Still, there was Bronwyn—" Angus picked up a plastic throwing star. "Hello? What's this?"

"It's a throwing star. They go with the ninja suit."

"A ninja suit?"

"I rented one for Halloween."

"Is it black?" Angus was curious. "Figure-hugging?"

"Kind of. It doesn't have any muscles, though."

"Muscles?"

"You know, like padding."

"You wish to appear...bigger?"

"It doesn't matter. There's no point. Mister Jacky makes Trey look small."

"Show me this suit."

Malcolm passed him the garment.

Angus unfolded the suit and rubbed its shiny fabric between his fingers. He put on the hood, then took it off. "Have you perchance seen the pizza slice in my room?" he asked.

"Thanks, man," said Malcolm. "I'm not hungry right now. How old is it, anyway?"

"It's a costume. Quite singular. Very large."

"A pizza costume?"

"I have an idea," said Angus. He crumpled up his challenge and tossed it into a corner. "Come with me."

"Apparently some girl is obsessed with her," Frank told Elaine. "She's leaving right after she does her dance thing."

"That's a shame. I liked her. What about that nurse of yours? Has she found a job?"

"Not yet. Not that I've heard. But Angus got some work as a pizza. That's something."

"Yes."

"It should get him out of the house, too. He's pretty wired, what with testing Lida's food and sewing new dog clothes."

"Is he taking any medication?"

"Not for a while. He said it made him fat."

Elaine looked at Frank carefully.

"You think I should say something?" said Frank.

Elaine was thinking. She handed Frank a roll of masking tape he'd overlooked. The apartment was painted and ready, although now her mother was saying she might not move in after all.

"He is getting pretty intense." Frank tucked the tape into his overalls.

"Where do you find these people, Frank?"

"Angus just showed up, remember? And he found Lida. That wasn't me."

"Well, I'm sorry to hear about Andy. Maybe you'll find someone more reliable next time."

"Yeah. I can't remember what Angus wrote in the ad anymore. Something about *Gone with the Wind*."

"Maybe you should write your own ad this time."

"Yeah," Frank looked around the little apartment. "I think, after I find someone for Andy's room, I think I might go on a little vacation. To the beach or something."

"You should."

"I think I will."

Corey found a note slipped under his door, written on fine cream paper. It was a poem from Andy. At the top of the page was a drawing of a complicated unicorn. For a moment, Corey mistook the moon above it for the creature's frisbee. A sticky note was attached to the page. *My first poem, too! I hope you can come to my dance next week. I'm sorry I broke your heart, A.M.B.*

> You will find love again, Corey!
> Don't give up
> and you will see
> A humanoid as rare as me
> Rearing its head in majesty,
> Galloping along
> Beside the
> Sea.
>
> Death ends life,
> or so they say,
> Day after day we slip
> Away
> Or just drop dead one awful day.

Did you ever see a unicorn play
In a china shop?
No! They can't stay.
They shed one tear, and run
Away,

Not knowing if they're straight
Or gay,
But for their damage they must pay.
I touch you lightly with my hoof, and say,
"Goodbye, Corey, I'm on my way."

    Corey put the note carefully on his bed stand. "Damn," he said aloud. This was her first poem? As it happened, his mother collected porcelain unicorns, so Corey was able to visualize such a retail environment for the mythic beasts. Their expulsion seemed unfair. It occurred to him that the path of this one gentle exile was not unlike Andy's own. Like Andy, it was sexually confused. Like her, it felt bad. Like her, it was saying goodbye. He loaded his book bag with heavy textbooks and put on his helmet. At the bathroom door, he paused in respect for the readying pilgrim beyond.

    Lida surprised Frank by joining him on the front porch to greet trick-or-treaters. She carried a tray, filled with homemade loukoumi. She was wearing sharply pointed boots and a vintage kilim carpet coat. Frank guessed correctly this wasn't a Halloween costume.

    "Do you have another silly hat I could wear?" she asked him. "to humor the urchins?"

    Frank was wearing an old leather fighter pilot's cap. "I'm not sure," he said. He went inside and came back some minutes later with a plastic headpiece that mimicked an arrow piercing the wearer's head.

    Lida put it on. "I abhor the western states," she told him.

Frank helped himself to a piece of loukoumi. "Where did you grow up?"

"Many places. My father was an actor. We followed the stage."

"Oh yeah? Professional theatre?"

"Amateur. In the end, of course, that level of good humor grinds one down. I had to leave. Now there is only mother."

"I'm sorry."

"Who is this?"

A huge, shuffling shape was feeling its way around the side of the porch, using the spindles to steer itself through the flower bed.

"Hey, Angus," said Frank.

"Hey, man. It's me," said Malcolm.

Frank laughed. "You okay in there?"

"It's kind of hard to see out here."

"I thought you were going as a ninja?"

"Yeah, well, Angus wanted to trade." The pizza came to rest against the steps. "This is pretty impressive though, right?"

"You look good enough to eat," said Lida.

"You need some help?" asked Frank.

"Maybe just down to the street? To the light?"

Malcolm's ninja suit was taut around Angus's chest, tight under his armpits, too long in the leg, but he, too, was pleased with his costume. He'd left the silk sash and the throwing stars behind. For now he wore the hood pulled up over his nose so he could smoke. He approached Evans's home with a jaunty step, a nursery rhyme on his lips and a cigarette in his mouth. "Angus went tae Taffy's house, Taffy wasn't in, Angus found a shopping cart, diddle diddle din…" Even here, at the quieter edge of Montford, he had to step around little groups of children and their parents. Angus congratulated each and every one on their costumes.

When he reached his objective, however, "Taffy" was in. Angus had expected this. He tossed his cigarette over his shoulder onto a passing family. Pulling down his hood, he strolled incognito past Evans's house.

Evans sat on his brightly illuminated stoop, waiting for the kiddies, a plastic pumpkin-shaped bucket full of candy in his lap. In the picture window, his many Pomeranians moved restlessly back and forth. The shopping cart was still in the driveway, leaning against the side of the house.

Angus noted all this. He went a little further up the street, where Evans could not see him, and stopped in the shadows. As black as his suit was, there was no way he could approach the house unseen without a distraction. He waited for an opportunity.

Malcolm found Desiree, Mister Jacky, and Maybelle Jolene at a busy intersection. All around them, families in costume trudged in long lines from one decorated home to the next, slowed to the pace of the smallest child. Mister Jacky wore a Batman costume with a short cape. Desiree was dressed as Catwoman. Maybelle Jolene stood between them, complaining about the public bafflement at her homemade disguise. When she saw her father approaching, however, she pointed with delight. "Pizza! Pizza!"

Mister Jacky fist-bumped Malcolm. "Awesome costume, dude," he said.

"Thanks, man."

"Dad's a happy pizza!"

"Where d'you find that?" asked Desiree, casting a dietician's eye over the suit.

"A friend lent it to me." Malcolm patted the white mushroom that surely contained Maybelle Jolene's head. "You look cool."

"I'm not a jellyfish!" she made very clear. "I'm an octopus squid."

A History of Saints

A group of children turned onto Evans's path. This was Angus's chance. He moved quickly, darting from bush to fence to avoid the streetlight, stealing onto Evans's property, reaching the cart at the side of the house in a matter of seconds. He bent double to catch his breath, taking hold of the side of the buggy. It made a surprising noise.

Angus cursed. The cart was full of empty, crushed beer cans. This discovery placed him in considerable danger. Every last can would have to be extracted before he could wheel the buggy away. Gingerly, he lifted one out of the cart, careful to avoid another noisy landslide. He placed it on the gravel driveway. Taking the next can, he set it a little distance from the first. He continued in this way, dotting the ground around him, making sure to leave a pathway for his escape.

There was a small window nearby. A flicker of movement caused Angus to look up. He froze. A Pomeranian with a savage crossbite stared out at him, having climbed an armchair to investigate the noise. One of its eyes was sealed shut and it wore a plastic cone like an Elizabethan collar. Perhaps this adornment had enhanced the tiny dog's hearing, for it alone had left the group at the picture window.

Angus kept still. Fortunately for him, inside the room a lamp by the chair illuminated the glass, and the dog was reflected back upon itself. The disfigured sentry squinted at its portrait. Very slowly, radar dish-like, it tilted its head back and forth. It was listening. Angus carefully raised a hand. The dog made no response. Angus waited until finally it left to join the others.

"Pomeranian bastard," he breathed. He went back to removing the beer cans. There were old leaves and twigs packed in among the rusted metal. To another, this might have suggested Evans's ownership of the cart for more than two weeks, but Angus brushed such sedimentary evidence aside. When the cart was quite empty, he braced himself, then lifted the buggy with a gasp to tiptoe to the corner of the house. There he paused, waiting for more children to occupy the Welshman and his dogs.

A sentry of Pomerania

As Angus neared Carolina Court he came to a sharp stop. The carnival lights of a police cruiser were slowly approaching the house from a side street.

Angus shoved the cart into some bushes and climbed in behind it. He threw his hood aside and struggled to remove the top of the ninja suit. "I have no idea, officer," he rehearsed in a whisper. "None at all. I was merely taking the night air."

He peered through the leaves. Ahead of the police car he saw an eerie parade of silent figures. The vehicle crept along behind them, its blinding flashes illuminating their disparate, uncanny forms. Angus could make out a superhero-sized superhero, a tiny jellyfish, a dominatrix, and a family of zombies. Leading the group was a tall slice of pizza. This had nothing to do with his visit to Evans.

Malcolm's evening had been less successful than Angus's. The pizza suit had not wandered far through the crowds before it met with calamity. Quite as singular as Angus claimed, it was recognized on sight by the pizza restaurant manager, out with his own family for the festivities.

Malcolm was confused by the loud accusations. He had tried to explain. When the young manager, unconvinced and fierce in zombie makeup, seized Malcolm's arm, Malcolm had tried to run. Neither Mister Jacky's bulk nor Catwoman's whip were enough to stop the ugly scene that ensued.

A crowd of enthralled onlookers had gathered, and many stayed long enough to enjoy watching the pizza suit prove too large for the back of a police cruiser. Now, under the car's flashing blue-and-red scrutiny, Malcolm led the parties involved back to where he could change and return the slice to its rightful owner. Angus had only to recognize the manager's face to piece together his roommate's bad luck. "Pity," he said. "Damn shame."

He lit a cigarette and watched Batman and an officer help Malcolm find the porch steps. Frank rose to meet them. A while later, Malcolm reappeared, barefoot, in shorts and T-shirt, to hand over the huge, folded suit and matching gloves. It saddened Angus to see how diminutive Malcolm looked beneath Mister Jacky.

From the street, the jellyfish waved a tentacle. Malcolm waved back and went inside. Frank shook his head, then turned to say something to Lida, who, as far as Angus could tell, was apparently lying under a rug with an arrow through her head.

Angus decided to wait before he stole into the house. He remained in the undergrowth for some time, watching Frank hand out candy—and Lida no doubt fatal confections—to the neighbors' kids. He lit another cigarette. Around his feet, the black earth was sprinkled with butts from one of Emily's long vigils.

Twenty-Three

There are valid reasons to dress your dog.
—USAF Colonel Rex Marigold, *Little Body, Big Spirit: Living with the Chihuahua*, 1984

"Bad luck," said Angus. "Plain and simple." He brought his coffee over and sat down across from Frank.

"He could have been arrested, Angus."

"For what?"

"For being you, I guess. You're lucky he thought fast. He told them he'd found the suit in a dumpster."

"Smart puppy."

"Where were you last night anyway?"

"Out and about."

"Wearing that?" Frank pointed at the ninja costume draped over Angus's shoulder.

"I'm not a child, Frankie. This is Malcolm's. By God, he deserves something for keeping mum about me, although, of course, I was always going to return the suit."

"Yeah," said Frank. "You owe him."

"Perhaps a wee basket of fruit? We're surrounded by saints. D'you know that?"

Frank had more temporal matters on his mind. "Lida's leaving," he said. He would have preferred to share this troubling news with Malcolm first, but that particular saint was still in bed. "She told me last night. She can't afford High Cotton. She's moving out, moving in with a friend."

Angus stroked a nose hair, then rubbed an eye. He sat back in his chair. "I'm not surprised. The deadly are often fickle. You're worried about money, aren't you? Let me ask you something. Is good cooking, aye, I'll admit it, fine cooking, really a substitute for ready cash? Especially when it's laden with rat poison?"

"It's not poisoned, Angus."

"I can tell you don't think so. Look at ye, man. You've put back every pound you lost in mastering Baladi. She's fattening you up—but for what?"

Frank ignored this digression. "She was going to start paying again when she got a job. Now she's leaving."

"You've grown fond of her, haven't you? You're happy in her web."

"What's this whole friendly spider thing with you? The point is we now have two rooms to fill. I need your rent, too, Angus."

"Two rooms?"

"Hers and Andy's—"

Angus lurched forward. "Andy's leaving?"

"You didn't hear? Yeah. After her dance thing."

"What in God's name is happening, Frankie? Is this because of Lida?"

"Of course not. She's got some stalker after her, apparently. She's moving to Texas."

Angus sat back. "Texas?" He scooped up Geezer as he trotted past and put the dog in his lap. "What kind of stalker?"

Frank looked at Geezer's new waistcoat and gold watch chain. "I need new tenants," he told Angus. "Guys. Just regular guys this time. No 'gentle hand' stuff."

"Working men?"

"Yes."

"Good Christian souls?"

"I guess."

"I can write an ad if you want."

Dr. Pringle felt Andy's flight was unnecessary. "Isn't it possible that Emily is just trying to say goodbye?" she asked. "In her own…particular way?"

Andy knelt beside her therapist's aquarium. She stroked the glass between her and the fish, watching them hurry back and forth. "Emily frightens me," she said. "Why would she drive all that way to give me back my hair, when she's not even there in the first place?" She checked her scalp again. "Do you see like, a bald spot anywhere?"

"No. Leave your head, Andy. Do you want your bear?" Andy's toy bear lay abandoned on the sisal rug between them.

"Do you think I'm just running from myself, Dr. Pringle? Leaf? That's what I thought. But Lida explained to me why I should go. She thinks it's a good idea."

"This is the nurse?"

"She's leaving, too. She says she can't find a job. She says Balkan food costs too much—the ingredients. This world is so unfair. Now she'll probably die in her car."

Dr. Pringle took a moment to respond. "Can't she eat something else? Something cheaper?"

"She doesn't eat it. And that's not because it's poisoned, either. Only Angus thinks it's poisoned. And Malcolm." Andy saw her bear now, the Georgia Bulldogs T-shirt pulled up over its face, one arm flung out. She retrieved it and climbed into a chair. "She's the real victim. Part of my performance is for her. It's about someone who is misunderstood their whole life, but at the end the Goddess lifts them by the hand into a new dimensional space where everybody totally gets them."

Her therapist nodded.

"I hope she can make it to the Happening. She says she might have a headache by then. The other reason I have to leave Asheville is because of another life I've destroyed. I didn't tell you about that."

"I don't think so. This is someone else? Not Emily?"

"The handsome man who was attacked by a bear. The one I looked after?"

"Oh yes."

"He's a poet. He fell in love with me, but I guess he was only seeing the outside of me, my 'exquisite bullshit patina'—that's what Emily called it—even when I told him about how I destroyed her."

"And now you've destroyed him, too?"

"Pretty much. I told him our love couldn't last. In a poem. Do you think I could be a poet?"

"I..."

"I'm going to do a dance to celebrate him, too."

"That's kind. Will you do a dance to celebrate yourself?"

Andy thought about this. "Maybe. One piece is kind of all about my journey, I guess. Coming to terms with stuff, learning as I canter along."

"'Canter'?"

"Learning from the people I meet to accept myself as I am." Andy touched her nose, then checked the back of her head.

Angus showed Malcolm the shopping cart. He'd retrieved it from the bushes and hidden it in Frank's shed.

"Cool," said Malcolm.

"I wanted you to see it, laddie, before I return it to its rightful owner. You're responsible for my success, you know that?" Angus pushed the cart into the light.

"Are you going to clean it?"

"I cleaned it yesterday. I'm in your debt."

"No problem, man. Did you happen to find that other throwing star?"

Angus rolled the cart back into the shadows. "I don't think Frankie needs to see this right now. The poor devil has a lot on his mind. What time is it?"

Malcolm looked at his watch.

"I'll leave at 1100 hours. If Frankie's around, could you distract him?" Angus leaned forward, "As far as he knows, Evans still has the cart; as far as Trey knows, it was never stolen, savvy?"

"Okay."

Angus looked at the sun, then grimaced. "Trey could be anywhere, but I'll find him."

Corey wandered the junk store, searching for a gift for Andy. Finding a unicorn was harder than he'd expected. Now he looked for something else, something small she could carry easily on her journey. It was hard to shop for a girl. He'd found a ceramic pig, but it had *BBQ* written on its side, which would be sad for a vegan. A tall wooden staff caught his attention. It was capped with a plastic, bearded head. As he examined the lined face, Corey saw Angus coming toward him, pushing the dogs in the cart.

"What have we here?" said Angus. "Greetings! Have ye seen Trey, by any chance?"

"Hey, Angus," said Corey.

"The big feller, from the hootenanny? With the eyelashes?"

Corey shook his head. He showed Angus the staff. "Do you think Andy would like this? To take with her?"

"She's nae walking to Texas. Is that a wizard up there?"

"I guess. I'm really looking for something small, like that little boat you gave her."

"A parting token? Aye, good lad. Put the stick down, we'll have a look over there. I can't stay long, though."

"Thanks, man. That dress looks awesome."

Angus stroked Lakeisha's gown. "She's handling it well. This is their first time out in public as their characters."

It was after dark when Angus finally found Trey. He called out to the huge form resting outside the bus station. Trey looked up.

"It's me!" Angus shouted.

"Anguth!" Reaching for a shopping cart beside him, Trey clattered across the empty street.

"You got a new cart," said Angus.

"Of courth! You too, I see," said Trey, "but then, you have room at Frank's for as many as you want."

If Angus was stymied by this, it was only for a moment. "They're invaluable, Trey. Quite invaluable."

"Liddle Victorian doggies!"

"I'm showing these two creatures the town."

"Are thoth fireworks under them?"

"Absolutely. Tomorrow is Guy Fawkes night, and we're celebrating Andy's dance when she gets home. You're welcome to join us. I'll be making a curry, too. The Barfly is baking a cake to kill us all."

"I would, but tomorrow is free yoda night."

"You're a yoga man? I'm not surprised. I saw how easily you rolled off that bench. What are you up to now?"

"Well, I was athleep, bud now that I'm awake, I want to see the eledshun results."

"Good God! The election! Is that today?"

A History of Saints

Angus and Trey parked their shopping carts outside a cinder-block bar and took the Chihuahuas inside. The place was full, lit by permanent Christmas lights hung from the ceiling. Two large television screens broadcasted the returns. The costumed dogs pleased the crowd, and Angus carried them from table to table, explaining how their appearance related to their imminent careers.

Trey was sitting at the bar. Angus set the dogs on the counter, then put them on the floor when the bartender asked him to take them off the counter.

"Obama's widding," said Trey.

"I never had a doubt." Angus scanned the room for people of color. He saw three in a booth. When they noticed him waving at them, he punched the air triumphantly.

"Do you have a car?" he asked Trey.

"Nod these days. I have a DUI."

"I need to get these dogs to Mexico somehow."

"To set theb free in the desert?"

"I hadn't thought of that. No. They need a few days' training. Lessons I can't provide."

"Eggspert lessons?"

"Precisely."

Trey sipped his beer. "In what?" he asked finally.

"Balancing, walking on their back legs, that kind of thing."

"Like the circuth?"

"It's where they belong, amigo. It's where I belong."

"I like the circuth."

"We all like the circus, Trey. After all, what do people look for? When the bombs are falling? What do they seek?"

"A bob shelter?"

"Well, yes, a bomb shelter, but I'm talking about the economy. People want distraction, entertainment. I'm broke. You seem to flourish outdoors, but I can't face being on the streets again. In Mexico these lovely creatures can learn a trade and save the day. Help Frankie out, too."

253

"How will you get them down there? You can't hidgehike with pets, and they're too small to jump a train. Eden then, they would probably just fall out."

Angus looked the dogs over. They seemed interested in the news from a Virginia polling station. Lakeisha's bonnet was askew. Angus straightened it. "It's a bag on a bus then," he said.

"They can breed through liddle straws…"

The room erupted in a cheer. Obama's victory was announced. Angus laughed triumphantly. His eyes shone. "Andy!" he cried. "God bless her! I just remembered! She's going to Austin. She can take us to Texas!"

They watched the TV for a while. Trey was moved. He wiped a tear away. "Now thigs will change, Anguth. I predict an ed, an ed to rachel discord across this grape land."

"Momentous times, Trey. Momentous times." Angus waved again at the group in the booth. "Let us take these dogs, dear friend, and join those stately Africans."

Lida's offer of a poultice amused Angus. "Keep your salves, Livia," he told her. "I'll be fine." He rolled his eyes at Frank and Malcolm. A vivid welt across his forehead marked where he'd fallen the night before.

"As you wish," said Lida. She went back to moving pots and pans with loud certainty around the kitchen.

"I don't think of it as a Black name either," agreed Frank. "Trey means 'the third,' right? Something like that?"

"Of course it bloody does!"

"Now, Lakeisha on the other hand, that's tricky."

"He was just searching for excuses, Frankie! He should have voted. His friends agreed with me. Ye cannae take it out on a Chihuahua that ye didn't vote. And for his own kind, mind you!"

"Sometimes," Frank began, "sometimes—"

"And to suggest I'd dressed poor wee Geezy as a slave? Jesus."

"I don't know, man," said Malcolm. "I mean, he's pretty dark in the face, and they do look historical, I mean, dressed like that."

They looked at Geezer. Geezer looked back. Lakeisha lay by the fire in her gown.

"They're Gilded Age, laddie! Anyone can see that. Trey tried to tell them as much."

"The white dog has something of Emily Dickinson," said Lida, "around the muzzle."

Angus's opinion of this was stopped short by Andy's entrance. "Yay!" she clapped. "Yay!" She was wearing her Obama T-shirt and all her buttons. "Isn't it awesome?"

Angus saluted her. "There she is! The fair Andromeda!

"Angus! What happened to your head?"

"He told off some Black guy for not voting," said Frank, pointing to the dogs, "after he'd introduced the cast of *Birth of a Nation*."

"Is it true you're leaving us, lassie?"

Andy made a sad face. "I have to, Angus." She looked across to Lida, severe at the stove in her furs. Lida gave a small brisk nod.

"You ready for tonight?" Frank asked Andy.

Andy perked up. "I was! But now I have to add something to my dance about the election!"

"Maybelle Jolene is pretty stoked," said Malcolm.

"I'm so glad she'll be there."

Lida interrupted. "You are vegan," she told Andy, "but there shall, of course, be milk and butter and eggs in your goodbye cake."

"Oh," said Andy. "Okay."

"Dinnae fas' thysen', Andee! Leave it tae Angus and the braw spices of the Raj. I'll fix ye something worthy of a Jain."

Andy went to the fridge and took out a tiny dish. She sprinkled this with a few chia seeds. Staying at the counter, she nibbled at her breakfast, looking down on the kitchen—the old men around the table, the costumed dogs, the undressed cats.

"Are you all packed?" asked Frank.

"Pretty much," she sighed. Her bowl was so small Frank might have guessed she was spooning her sustenance directly from her palm.

"We'll miss you," he said. "You too, Lida."

"*Farewell and adieu to you fair Spanish ladies,*" hummed Angus. "A wee diaspora of loveliness upon the world, innocent or otherwise…" He spilled his coffee as he rose to make a toast.

"Are you okay?" asked Frank.

"He's probably concussed," said Lida. "Although in his case you could never tell."

Something of Emily Dickinson

A History of Saints

Later that morning Angus tapped on Andy's door. He carried Lakeisha as proof of the Chihuahua's tiny presence as a car passenger, even when draped in silk.

Andy was crestfallen that she couldn't help. She gestured to the luggage behind her. "I wish I could, Angus, but I don't have room for you all—my car will be super full. Anyway, I'm stopping in Graniteville first."

Angus set Lakeisha on the ground. "No worries," he said. "Run along, 'Keisha, be brave now."

"Why are you going to Mexico?"

"It doesn't matter."

"I'm so sorry. Is this about Juan's mom?"

"Juan's mum," Angus said slowly, then resoundingly, "Juan's mum!"

"Oh no! Is she dead? Has she died?"

"Madam Perez? Nae, she's alive. Very much alive indeed!" He struck the doorframe with renewed purpose. "Thank you, lassie! Thank you!"

Corey drove Frank, Malcolm, and Maybelle Jolene to the Happening. Malcolm's daughter wore her squid suit, still defiant at the public confusion it prompted. Her pale tentacles flapped around the vehicle as she shouted about the performance ahead and her own bitter struggles in ballet class.

Marshall lay a few miles north in Madison County. Andy was performing at a studio space on Main Street, long ago a thriving length of hotels and department stores but now mostly empty storefronts, pressed tightly between a steep mountainside and the railroad tracks that followed the French Broad River. A handwritten sign on the sidewalk directed them to a door, framed by two dead houseplants.

"I love this town," said Frank.

They followed Maybelle Jolene's mushroom shape down a dimly lit corridor, between studios dotted with pottery and unframed artwork. An audience was already seated in the courtyard. As Maybelle Jolene entered, a murmur went through the expectant group. Every face turned. Somebody clapped.

Frank understood their mistake. "It's just a Halloween costume," he told them. "Sorry. This isn't part of the thing."

He saw Lark across the courtyard and waved. "Let's sit over there," he said to Malcolm.

Behind Lark sat Tansie, along with another girl from The Goddess Temple. Toby lay at their feet, breathing heavily. The rest of the audience was made up of weathered locals, drawn out of curiosity to the event. Ringed and wrinkled hands patted Maybelle Jolene's hump as she passed.

"Frank," said Lark, "you are here for Andromeda, yes?"

"We certainly are. Hey, I'm sorry I've been so busy."

"The girls are asking for their protector, Frank. Do not be shy."

"I'll come back. Promise." Frank turned to the stage—a small, raised deck with three trellised arches, decorated with lengths of bubble wrap. To one side was a shop mannequin, her head missing.

Directly beyond this, Frank could see the rails and weathered crossties of the railroad. A couple of loose spikes were visible, rusting on the gravel.

From somewhere, the interlaced murmuring of several female voices announced the start of the performance. The crowd stopped talking. They watched the empty stage. A flute played a few thoughtful, discordant notes.

"Let's do this thing, people!" bellowed Maybelle Jolene.

"Hush, baby," said Malcolm.

From behind the brick wall that doubled as a wing, the long figure of Andy emerged. She was wearing something like a toga, along with a cloche hat and a number of colored scarves around her neck. The scarves reminded Frank of the classes he'd missed.

Andy took some time crossing the stage. It was evident there were tricky, if invisible, obstacles in her path. Each time she felt her way around, over, or under these, it cost her a scarf. Every loss was marked by sharp notes on the flute, and these followed by the amplified sound of paper being scrunched up. Andy would cover her ears, collapse slowly, rise, and soldier on.

By the time she reached the mannequin her neck was bare. Exhausted, she offered the torso an imagined cup. When this was rejected, she drank its contents herself. This seemed to put her to sleep.

Corey looked to Malcolm and Frank for an answer.

Andy's arm shot up. Her feet twitched. She turned an ecstatic face to the night sky above her. Wherever the flautist was hidden, they now played with squeaking fury. Back on her feet and fully recovered, Andy retraced her steps in a series of huge arcs, gathering up each scarf, offering them to the stars. Her wardrobe thus restored, she made her exit.

"Awesome," said Corey.

"I could do that," said Maybelle Jolene.

"So could Frank," said Malcolm.

Corey was the first to understand Andy's next piece—putting together the small, circling arm movements, the flared nostrils, the thin paper cone on her head. As with her portrayal of Lida, Andy's unicorn also encountered a number of unseen events around the stage. These caused her to alternately rear, shy away or—crises abated—lower her head and drink from ethereal streams. Once she pawed the ground. There was a lot of applause when she galloped off.

Corey explained the performance to Maybelle Jolene. He showed her his gift for Andy. With Angus's help, he'd found a medallion of a bucking bronco above the word *Texas*.

Now Andy reappeared, followed by a scowling young man wielding a Confederate flag. Her shoulders were slumped. All her equine energy had vanished, along with the paper cone. The young man gave her a shove. A Delta work song played. When Andy stumbled, the young man laughed cruelly. He took a length of black plastic garden chain and bound her hands, then wrapped the rest around her throat. Andy lay captive at his feet, helpless while he gloated.

Malcolm nudged Corey in the ribs.

The flute returned, but not for long. Somebody fluttered "The Stars and Bars" at the edge of the stage. This had a vexing effect upon Andy's overseer. He shielded his face, cursed, then ran off. Andy rose, spreading her arms very slowly, the plastic chains tinkling to the ground around her.

"Whoa," whispered Corey.

This quiet vision of emancipation did not last. There was a growing rumble. A deafening train whistle, followed by the thundering train itself, flung the audience back into their seats. The courtyard shook. Andy stood frozen, her shoulders hunched against the clamor, her hands pressed to her ears. Everyone else stared at the roaring backdrop of the graffiti-covered freight cars, like some vast set piece, filling everything behind her.

Malcolm shouted something at Frank. Toby started barking. It was clear the locomotive would be passing for a while. When Andy finally abandoned the stage, her fans left their seats, retreating into the studios.

Inside, the noise of the train was still titanic, but bearable. A table waited for them, ready with paper plates and goldfish crackers. Frank poured a little wine into a plastic cup.

Andy came out. "I'm so sorry!" she shouted. "We'll just have the intermission now. It shouldn't happen again tonight!"

"Don't be silly!" Frank yelled back. "Stuff happens. You're doing great!"

"I thought maybe you planned it!" said Corey.

"There you go!" Frank raised his cup.

Maybelle Jolene rushed to Andy with the news of the train. As Andy gave her a hug, the cacophony fell away.

Andy hadn't planned to be present at the intermission, but now she stayed, receiving everyone's praise with her usual humility. Lark admired her unicorn. Tansie called her a genius. Toby licked her hand. Corey was stunned when Andy revealed the evening would conclude with a portrayal of him. Maybelle Jolene went from group to group, voicing her strong views on both the charm and folly of mime.

Frank's phone rang. He didn't recognize the number. He left the others to answer the call, walking a little farther back down the dark hallway toward the street. He stopped at a faded poster.

It was Lida. "You need to come home, Frank," she told him. "Your house is on fire."

Twenty-Four

Contemn the world and count that is in it vanity and toys; this only covet all thy life long; be not curious or over solicitous in anything, but with a well-composed and contented estate to enjoy thyself, and above all things, to be merry.
—Robert Burton, *The Anatomy of Melancholy*

L̲ida's presence in̲ the kitchen had given Angus an excuse to resort to old habits. Annoyed at her monopoly of the stove, he went upstairs to prepare Andy's curry in his fireplace. For a while, Lida could hear him laughing up in his room. Curious odors slowly filled the house. When she took a break to have a cigarette, she discovered the fumes were just as strong outside. She looked up. A white cloud billowed from Angus's window. "Dunce," she said aloud.

She strode back into the kitchen and picked up her phone. She called 911 and then Frank. Then she went to the sink and filled a large pan full of water.

The upstairs landing was all smoke—not white now but black. As Lida reached Angus's doorway there was a high-pitched whine. A firework whizzed past her right ear. "Angus?" she called out. "Angus?"

His desk blocked her path. She set the pan on the floor and hurled the desk to one side, computer and papers scattering everywhere. The far wall of the bedroom was burning. A fireworks display glittered and spat around the fireplace, partly muffled by the clothes racks and stacked boxes. Lida searched the whistling room for dogs and cats, then dragged a coverlet off the bed and went for the flames.

For the second time in a week, the clapboard exterior of Carolina Court was lit by flashing lights. Emergency vehicles filled the driveway. Frank and the others found Lida on the front porch, surrounded by admiring firefighters. Her face was smudged and her singed coat almost devoid of fur.

"What happened?" said Frank.

Lida told him. She added, "Where he is, I have no idea. He stole your truck. I've reported the theft."

"This lady pretty much saved your house," a fireman told Frank.

Speck appeared on the porch. She stopped and looked at Lida in her skin coat.

"Jesus," said another fireman. "Is that cat okay?"

"The cat is fine," said Lida. "It was recently shaved by a lunatic. All the cats are safe, Frank. Angus must have taken the dogs."

"Thank you," said Frank.

Lida lit a cigarette.

"You shouldn't smoke, ma'am," advised a third firefighter, attentive at her knee. "It's bad for you."

Lida looked him up and down. She turned to Frank. "Angus is a dangerous buffoon, Frank. Evict him, or suffer his tomfoolery at your peril."

"I'd better go upstairs," said Frank.

"What kind of coat is that?" Maybelle Jolene asked Lida.

Lida looked down at her hairless coat. "It's a Karamitsos, child. From Kastoria."

On their journey to collect the chifforobe from Hessy Hicks, Frank had pointed out a hillside to Angus. The great field, enclosed by tall oaks, was marred by an untidy trailer park. "Juan lives up the top there," he had told his tenant.

Now Angus was back at the foot of the hill. When he thought it was light enough, he turned the key to start Frank's truck. Securing the loose dogs beside him with a hand, he slowly climbed the steep road between the trailers.

Angus's decision to abandon Andy's Indian dish in the fireplace and instead drive to Mexico was sudden, as startling to him as it was to the dogs. Resting the pan in the flames, he had turned to Lakeisha. "No! We should go now. This moment."

Lakeisha had narrowed her eyes. Angus took this as a sign of Confucian approval. He scrawled a short list on an index card, then stuffed a suitcase with a few clothes and an old atlas. To this he added the bag of dog food and a water bowl he kept under the bed, along with a bottle of wine he found there. He pulled the list back out of his shirt pocket and put a fierce line through the word *pack*. He carried the Chihuahuas downstairs, tiptoeing past the kitchen and Lida. The keys to Frank's truck were on a nail by the front door. He put the dogs in the truck, then hurried to the shed.

Angus parked in Evans's driveway and unloaded the shopping cart. Careless of the noise it made, he rolled it back to its spot beside the house. At once there was barking. A light went on inside. Angus rubbed his hands with satisfaction and strolled to the truck without looking back. He crossed the word *Evans* off the list.

When he reached the trailer park it was still the middle of the night. He stopped at the foot of the hill and sang old songs to the dogs while he waited for the sun to arrive.

At the sight of Frank's truck Juan stepped outside.

Angus backed up. He rolled down the window to salute the Mexican. "*Amigo, votre problemos sont finis!*"

Two little girls, dressed neatly for school, paused on their way to catch the bus. They stared at the costumed dogs. Lakeisha and Geezer stood in Angus's lap, their paws on the window ledge as they looked around.

"*Si!*" Angus shouted at the children. "*Los perros Mexicanos!*" He beckoned them over. "They will not bite! Pet them, yes! Pet them." He whispered fiercely into Geezer's tickle-trembling ear, "Do not bloody bite these kids, y'hear?" But he could tell from the flattened head and the hunched shoulders that Geezer was a liability. He set the animal behind him. "*El perro blanco est bueno*," he assured the little girl. He turned to Juan. "*Nos vamanos Juarez, Juan!* To see your mum! *Por visitez votre madre!*"

Juan did not move. Angus got out of the truck to explain further. Lines of mountains, hung with the rising vapors of a little downpour in the night, surrounded them on all sides. Angus was stopped in his tracks by the sight. "Good God," he said.

A History of Saints

A young woman had approached from another trailer. To his relief, Angus discovered she could speak English. "Please tell him," he asked her, "Frank wants me to take him to Mexico, to see his mother. He lent me the truck. It's all good. We want him to see his mother. She's sick, you see? I pay for gas, food, yes? All I need is a little help to find a circus for the clever doggies."

The woman took this in with a stony face. When Angus was finished, however, she turned and spoke to Juan.

Angus nodded along at the words he recognized. "*Si?*" he asked Juan when she was done. "We go now?"

Juan said something to the girl. She nodded. He said something else, and she told Angus, "He cannot go with you."

"Ah," sighed Angus. "Juan, really?" There was no protest in his voice. Not a drop. He took Lakeisha from the arms of the little girl and put her back in the truck.

Juan came over to him. He patted Angus's shoulder. "*Gracias,*" he said, "You sleep, yes?"

Angus took out his index card. Juan watched him put a line through a word. Angus saluted Juan again, then the young woman. "Not quite yet, amigo."

Frank was upstairs when the police called him. Angus had been found beside the interstate, sleeping with the dogs in the truck. They were only forty miles away. The truck had run out of gas. Corey and Malcolm watched Frank as he listened.

"He's telling the truth," Frank lied to the officer. "He didn't steal it. That was a mistake. I just lent him the truck."

He put the phone in his pocket. "They've found him," he said. "He got as far as Sylva. He's got the dogs. He was going to Mexico."

"I don't know, man," Malcolm began.

"Mexico?" said Corey. "Like, the place? That was super cool of you to tell the cops you just lent him the truck, Frank."

They returned to clearing Angus's room of wet and black debris. The house smelled of burnt clothing and Indian food. The walls were stained with smoke. The fire hose had broken Frank's staircase, and gallons of water had poured down through the ceiling of his bedroom to soil his bed and fatten the books that lay there. Frank's phone sounded the arrival of a text. Again, Corey and Malcolm stopped to watch.

The message was from Frank's former tenant David.

Hey Frank hows it
going? I miss u guys!
was just wondering
if my room was still
free? Love is hard man
 lol! b back
in aville fri or sat cant wait
2 c u guys! Say hi 2 the cats
frm me peace dude
Received:
Nov 9, 10:34am

Frank reread the message. Another followed.

btw did u read that
book i left u? instant joy!
what a joke
csl
Received:
Nov 9, 10:35am

"It's David," Frank told them. "He wants to know if his room's free. He's on his way back."

"No way!" Corey punched the air. "Awesome! Talk about perfect timing. Right, Frank?"

"What does *csl* stand for?" Frank asked.

"That's like, 'can't stop laughing,'" said Corey.

"Oh." Frank started to tap out a reply but then stopped. "I'll be back in a while," he told them. He picked up a bucket of the sodden fireworks and headed downstairs.

"Frank's a lucky guy," Corey told Malcolm.

"I guess."

"What happened, Frankie?" Angus looked at the overturned furniture in the front hall. The police officer standing beside him put down the Chihuahuas.

"You nearly burned my house down," said Frank. "You set your room on fire."

"I did? How?"

"It's hard to imagine. Maybe just by stacking fireworks around a fire and then leaving for Mexico?"

"You say you lent this man your vehicle, Mr. Reed?" The officer had a keen look.

"Angus?" said Frank. "Yes, that's right."

"That's not his real name, sir. This man's name is John Leonard Beasley."

"What?"

"Aka 'Lenny' Beasley."

"Lenny Beasley?"

"Yes, sir. There's no record of an Angus Sex Pardee. He tried that one on us, but his driver's license says different."

"Saxe-Pardee," mumbled Angus.

"You might want to run a background check on your tenants, Mr. Reed. In the future?"

Frank didn't know what to say. "Beasley? Is that a Scottish name?" he asked.

"Mr. Beasley is a Bahamian, sir."

"A Bahamian?"

"He hails from the Bahamas." The young policeman chose

his words in a careful, precise way that contrasted with his soft Piedmont accent.

"Yeah, I know what that means. He said he was Scottish."

"That's still possible, sir. The Scots are pretty much known for their migratory disposition."

"Lenny Beasley?" said Frank again.

"You'll need to get your truck off the highway, Mr. Reed."

"I'll take you out there, Frank," said Corey.

The officer reached down to ruffle Geezer's costume. "These Gilded Age?" he asked.

Nobody had eaten breakfast yet. Malcolm cut four slices from Lida's untouched cake and brought them to the table.

"You were seriously going to Mexico?" Frank finally asked.

"I wanted to take Juan to see his mother."

"No, you didn't."

"I'm sorry, Frankie. I really am. I'll help you fix everything."

Frank stopped him. "I'm tired, Angus, Leonard, Lenny, whoever you are. I've had enough."

"I'll get a job, I promise. A real job."

Frank raised his hand once more. He spoke to them all. "I called J.J. this morning. I'm selling the house."

"I don't know, man…," began Malcolm.

"He says he'll buy it as is, burnt and everything."

"Don't do it, laddie," Angus protested. "Please."

"It's done, Angus." Frank struck the table in frustration. "God damn it, I can't be fooling with a new name on top of everything else. I'm sticking with 'Angus.'"

They were all quiet after this outburst. Then Malcolm said, "'Lenny' doesn't sound right, anyway."

"If you have to sell it," said Angus, "at least don't sell it to him."

"He's the only one buying."

"You're selling the house, Frank?" Corey was still in shock. "Really?"

"Yeah," said Frank. "I've had enough, Corey. I'm sorry."

"What can I do, Frankie?"

"You can get back on your medicine."

"Aye, fair enough. Anything else?"

"I don't know. J.J. wants to be in here quickly. I guess we'll need to find homes for all these cats."

Angus nodded. "Not a problem."

Frank made a sudden decision. The dogs were at his feet. He pulled them free from their garments and placed them, bare and squirming, in his lap. "I'm keeping the dogs," he told Angus.

"They do love you." Angus wiped his mouth. "This cake is exceptional."

"You're keeping the dogs, Frank?" said Corey.

"I might could take a cat," said Malcolm. "Maybe."

Frank pushed his untouched cake away. "Let's go get my truck," he said to Corey.

"Your gas gauge is broken, by the way, Frankie."

"Yeah," said Frank. "Thanks, Lenny. I know."

Frank watched the two Mexicans put up a large, temporary sign at the corner of his garden. The frost had made it hard for them to dig the holes for the signposts, and now they struggled to pack the cold dirt around the lumber.

"I appreciate this, Frank," said J.J.

"No problem," said Frank.

The sign read, *The Self Center*. Below this was a large green eye. Green lines radiated from its lids. Under the eye were the words, *Coming Soon!*

"This is one big fucking yard, Frank," said J.J. with both admiration and concern. "Nature is great and everything, but it's a pain in the ass. You recommend anyone around here for yardwork?"

Frank looked around. All the leaves had fallen. Winter always shrank his garden a little, as the rocks walls and paths of his landscaping stood clear through the naked trees. "I could do it," he said, "if you're hiring. At least through spring."

J.J. considered this for a moment, then shook Frank's hand. "There's going to be a lot of fucked-up people in this town, Frank, across this whole beautiful country. People wondering what just happened—to their savings, to their jobs. They're going to need nature."

"I guess," said Frank.

J.J. walked back toward the house. "Still, the more I look at it, this yard could be a total value-add," he said. He stopped and turned around. He was wearing an expensive cashmere coat and tweed cap. "Like this area right here, Frank, this little area has major Chi. Super cool bagua spot if we can clear out some of these bushes? Put in like, a wind chime?"

The kitchen floor shone. The fridge was no longer covered in notes. Frank guessed J.J. would keep this room intact—too much trouble to convert—and besides, his enterprise would likely need a kitchen. It would be the bedrooms, the drawing room, the dining room, that would become offices. There would be fire extinguishers and exit signs, and an ugly access ramp to the porch, not unlike the one he and Juan had built that summer.

To celebrate this last Thanksgiving in his house, Frank and his tenants ate pizza off paper plates. The china and glasses were packed, waiting to go to a storage unit. Frank and Angus drank red wine. Malcolm had an energy drink, and Corey a Coke.

Frank was glad they were all staying close by. Elaine had offered him the use of her little apartment for as long as her mother didn't need it. Malcolm and Angus had quickly found rooms a few streets away. Corey had found a place to share with David. It was an easy time to find places to rent. They raised their drinks and made a promise not to drift apart.

"Andy says hey," Corey told them. He'd received a text that morning. "She says Austin is awesome. She's taking guitar lessons again. She wants to be a singer."

"Any news from the Barfly?" asked Angus.

"Nope," said Frank. "She left a nice note, that's all. Kind of weird. She left the chifforobe, too. I guess J.J. can have that."

"It's crazy I actually dated a humanoid who will be like, super world famous one day," said Corey.

"I don't know, man," Malcolm looked doubtful. "The music industry…"

"I'll tell you this," said Angus. "High Cotton will make a fancy damn office for one of Antietam's shrinks."

Frank took another slice of pizza. "They'll change the name, most likely."

"I'll take the sign with me, in that case, Frankie." Angus shook his head in dismay. "Aye, but it's hard to think of this old place filled with nutters."

"This pizza is good, Frank," said Corey.

"Pizza is the perfect food," said Frank. "I think it's my favorite food."

"Sometimes I leave the edges, though," said Corey. "Those are bad for you because they're like, fatter."

"There's no part of a pizza that's bad for you, laddie."

"I thought about Austin a few times," said Malcolm. "The music scene is different down there, though. Different sound. I'll ask David what he thinks."

Angus stood up. He searched his pockets for the fortune cookie but it wasn't on him. Instead, he made a rambling toast to their respective futures, then twisted the cap off another bottle of wine. He filled his cup and then Frank's. "You can have the High Cotton sign if you want it, Frankie," he said.

"Nah," said Frank. "You made it. You have it."

The four of them stayed at the kitchen table for the rest of the evening, discussing pizza for a little longer, then moving on to hot dogs, circus dogs and circus bears, homeless saints, and other matters.

Epilogue

Frank sat on the bench in his old courtyard, waiting to be paid by the new owner. Carolina Court had recently changed hands again, at five times the price Frank once paid for it. Although The Self Center had survived the Great Recession comfortably, the soaring property prices that followed were more than J.J. could resist. He sold the house to a retired doctor and his wife, who at last converted the place back to the family home it was built to be. This final restoration made Frank happy, and the new owners had kept him on to tend the gardens.

Ten years had passed since Frank had accepted J.J's offer to hire him. The decision led to a new career. Frank left behind the drywall and the paint buckets to become a gardener—first for The Self Center, and gradually for several other homes around Asheville. Carolina Court, reclaimed from the kudzu and the rubble by his own hands, was naturally his favorite.

Every day Frank congratulated himself on this new life. Every day it seemed there were discoveries to be made among the flower beds and good news to impart to his employers. Juan still worked alongside him, and recently Juan's son had joined them.

Frank no longer lived in the neighborhood, although most of his work was there. When Elaine's mother was ready to move in with her daughter, Frank had left the little apartment and moved north to Marshall. There he rented rooms on Main Street, where he could enjoy the trains going by. He made friends quickly with the locals and found stray cats to feed along the railroad tracks.

Although he always meant to sell his furniture, in the end he kept it all. His landlord let him fill both floors above the empty storefront. Frank's new home looked like an antique shop. He left paths for himself between the dark sideboards and dressers, the bookcases and cabinets, and took pleasure in wandering from room to room—patting a chair or stroking the brass curve of a bedstead as he went in search of a particular book.

Sitting at the window each evening, encircled by empty armchairs, he would look around and tell himself that it was the objects we cherish that make a home—the paintings and keepsakes—not the walls around us or the roof above us.

Frank would not own a house again, but he never felt a martyr to the recession. Instead he told everyone how lucky he was to have left that world behind. For who would want every obligation of a landlord, merely to share the disordered life of one's tenants? And his friends, loving Frank dearly and not wanting to point out the hardships and expenses that surely lay ahead for him, assured him he had been right in his choice.

Each day he drove to Asheville with the dogs. His rusting truck boasted a new sign that read, *The Chi Gardener*. After lunch he would take the Chihuahuas for a walk. They were elderly now—Geezer's black face quite white, Lakeisha struggling to keep up as they followed the familiar streets. Sometimes they were joined by one of the old cats. Frank would pad ahead, pointing out a quick lizard on a rock wall or a squirrel nest high in a tree.

A History of Saints

After he sold Carolina Court, Frank would often run into Angus. The Bahamian had found a place only a couple of streets away from Elaine. Sometimes they shared a glass of wine on the porch of Angus's new home. There were no hard feelings.

Angus was still busy, still arranging yard sales and setting out strange, elaborate signs on street corners. Every time he saw Frank, he reached into a pocket and drew out some strange, useless gift for him.

Then one day he was gone, entirely gone. Frank went back to where he had lived but the house was empty, being renovated for new owners. Nobody knew the whereabouts of an Angus Saxe-Pardee, an Angus Sex Party, or even a John Leonard Beasley.

For a long time afterward—at the grocery store or walking downtown, Frank would catch a glimpse of someone who looked like his old tenant. Once he even followed a man wearing two coats through a crowd, but when he called out "Angus?" and the man turned around, it wasn't him.

Malcolm never changed his name. When he couldn't afford to live in town, he found a place in the country. Here he took up with an active hiker called Deidre. Together, they embarked on a fiercely healthy lifestyle that left him often asleep at his dinner plate. He still played in coffee houses and sometimes Maybelle Jolene would perform alongside him, having taken up both clogging and flatfooting in her teenage years. When Frank's gardening business needed extra hands, Malcolm was glad to be hired by his old friend.

Corey stayed in Asheville for a while after graduating. He found a job as the sports coach at the Leonardo Academy of Innovations, a charter school housed in the former shell of a Circuit City store. In the end, though, he moved back to Knoxville. The last Frank heard, he ran a gym of his own and had a family on the way. As he once promised Maybelle Jolene, Corey never wrote another word of poetry.

After several months in Austin, Andy came back to Asheville. Texas was too far away from her family. She did get a tattoo made there—from her drawing of herself as an old woman, but it was often mistaken for a beardless Abraham Lincoln and this disappointment marked a turn in her enthusiasm for body art.

For years she continued to wait tables. Under the guidance of Leaf Pringle, she stumbled through a series of relationships with alternating men and women until, at last, she met a farmer who raised bees and kept a stable. She fell in love and married him.

Frank was always glad to see her at the farmers market. He bought the honey she made and passed on the business cards she gave him that offered riding lessons. He was sure Andy would make a good horse whisperer.

None possessing a fortune sufficient to halt the sale of their temple, the goddesses disbanded. Tansie took Toby to West Virginia, where he ended his days in a large, fenced yard with unlimited bathroom access.

Trey's tongue never fully recovered. He remained joyous and inarticulate until, one January morning, he was found lying in a park, his body dusted with frost and his hands tucked under his white cheek. A fine mandolin was in a shopping cart nearby.

———

One day, a year after Frank sold Carolina Court, a letter had arrived there. J.J. passed it on to Frank.

> My Dear Frank,
>
> I am not sure if this will reach you, but I am sending it to the dear old home anyway. I still hope you changed your mind and decided not to sell? I think of Carolina Court often, and the carefree time we all enjoyed there, albeit interspersed with ghastly misfortune.
>
> After many months of traveling, we have found sanctuary. At first, Emily was unsure, but upon reflection, and after our difficult time in Palermo, she has fully embraced the ways of Lesbos.
>
> The island has welcomed us with open arms. We have a charming home, quite tiny, from which we serve coffee and sweetmeats to the tourists. Our little venture is flourishing. We have a few olive trees behind the café and a goat now, that we have named Andreas.
>
> Emily is a spirited young woman and we work daily on her hormones. She assures me she cannot even recall that hulking girl's face. This a lie, but a kind one.
>
> As we recently explored the winding streets of Mitilini together, searching for small pieces of furniture to complete our happiness, I thought

of how sweet you were to act on my behalf that evening- paying the crone for the chifforobe I was promised by your demented friend. That gesture was typical of you, Frank. You are a good man. (Do you still have the piece, perchance? I quite forgot to tell you that it was possessed, and therefore might be worth something to the especial collector of haunted furnishings.)

Over our final bottle of Ouzo, I told Emily I would write to thank you again for your many kindnesses. Although she still suffers from associations attached to her nightly vigils outside your home, and the humiliation she received at the hands of that vicious giant, Carolina Court remains for me a sacred place. After all, it was through my brief time there that I met the future companion of my days.

I hope this letter finds you well. I feel it will. Asheville might teem with stinky, tattooed types, but it has one distinct charm- it does not change.

Be Blessed,
Lida

Asheville had changed. To Frank's dismay, the speculation halted by the recession returned at its close with an intensity that quite altered the city. Ever more popular as a tourist destination, Asheville blundered toward a theme-park version of itself.

Over the next decade, a handful of breweries became dozens, while bars and restaurants opened every week. Tour buses and pubcycles circled the packed streets. Above the crowds the skyline was busy with cranes and new hotels. In every neighborhood pricey new eco homes perched over every available patch of wasteland.

For those desperate to remain in the neighborhoods they had worked so hard to restore, the answer to the climbing taxes was to share their homes with strangers. An internet company in California (created in the same week that Angus had once suggested "a room to be let by the night") made this considerable sacrifice seem easy—even profitable.

Frank saw how Elaine had flourished with Airbnb. She talked about quitting her day job all the time. With two bedrooms in her house always rented, she was making enough now to do all the traveling she wished, assuming she could ever find time to get away. When he stopped by to visit, Frank was amused at how often her phone disrupted their conversation.

Her device was not alone. Frank had resisted for as long as he could, but in the end, like everybody else, he put his old phone in a drawer. It was Elaine's idea and, as always, she was right—his new smart phone, and the Instagram account she helped him open, had helped his business.

Only this morning he had taken photos of the azaleas at Carolina Court. He was supposed to tweak such snaps and add important hashtags, but he didn't know how—or why that might matter. He much preferred to post pictures of the dogs and the cats for his friends, but Elaine advised fewer of these.

Now Frank saw the phone on the bench beside him light up. He had a new follower and several new likes. Then a comment arrived under his most recent post.

Way to go, Frankie!

Frank was curious. He went to the follower's page: Ornamentalhermit74, Oxfordshire, UK. There was a picture of a bearded ancient, smoking a cigarette at the mouth of a concrete grotto. A sign behind him read, *High Cotton*.

Frank laughed, "Oh my God." He told the dogs, "You won't believe this." The Chihuahuas blinked at him. He showed them the picture of Angus, holding the phone close to their weak eyes.

Another comment came in.

How are those doggies?

Frank tapped out a reply with a fat finger.

F: Hello Angus! How are you? You look well fed for a hermit.

A: They treat me well, laddie. Looks like you're as busy as ever. Was that a picture of the Court you just posted?

F: I'm sitting here now. I still look after the gardens.

A: Voltaire, eh? Good lad.

F: Kind of. The dogs are good. They're here next to me.

A: The aristos here keep Borzois. Sleek buggers. The dogs, I mean. I'll post a picture.

F: Are hermits allowed to have smart phones?

A: Good point. Technically, no, and I may have to sign off soon, chum. There are guests on the estate today. I think I see one now.

F: How did you end up there?

A: Long story. The family's barking mad, of course.

F: Of course. It's good to hear from you, Angus. Or is it Lenny?

A: Roger, actually. Good to find you, Frankie.

F: Good to find you, Roger, over and out.

The owner came outside with her checkbook. "Are you okay?" she asked Frank.

"Oh yeah, I'm good." Frank wiped his eyes. He took the check, folded it in half and put it beside his phone. "Just heard from an old friend, that's all. I pruned back the dogwoods like we talked about, repotted a few of the plants on the patio."

"Thanks, Frank. We'll see you next week?"

"Sure," Frank scratched his head, looking amazed and delighted all at once. "When I lived here it was a madhouse. A bunch of grown men, living like students. Nothing ever got done…"

"You told us. The fire and everything. Your crazy tenants."

"It was nuts. But I didn't know, not until just now, that I missed the mess."

About the Author

Julyan Davis is a British-American artist living in Asheville, North Carolina. For more than thirty years he has painted the vanishing architecture of the South. Collaborating with musicians, historians, and writers, his traveling museum exhibits chronicle the folklore and lost histories of the region. His work can be found online at julyandavis.com and on Instagram at @julyandavis. *A History of Saints* is his debut novel.